Books by Renee Hayes

Rim Walker Novel Series

The Girl Who Broke the World
The Girl Who Freed the Darkness

I0593513

Praise for The Girl Who Broke the World
Book One in the Rim Walker Series

'This masterfully told post-apocalyptic tale will captivate lovers of YA fantasy. In her debut, the first in a series, Hayes dazzles with a masterfully told tale of post-apocalypse survival and the ultimate triumph of good versus evil. The author's fanciful and intricately wrought world will spark readers' imaginations immediately, and her well-drawn characters will immediately draw their loyalty and attention. Hayes excels in proving that people aren't just black and white; instead, everyone is various shades of gray. Lyrical prose leaps off the page, ending in a gentle tease that will have readers eager for more. Readers who have a love of powerful world-building and multi-layered characters will be eager for more.' *BookLife Review for Publisher's Weekly - Editor's pick for book of outstanding quality*

In Renee Hayes' futuristic fiction odyssey, humans still walk the earth, though as penance for once decimating its resources they are contained by mystical forces and shapeshifting guardians within an area known as the Rim. Now as a new threat emerges, the fate of the world falls on one young girl who has just discovered she contains special magical powers, and must find the power within herself to make hard choices as well. THE GIRL WHO BROKE THE WORLD is a vivid and absorbing tale of uniqueness, devotion, and consequences. *IndieReader Reviewer*

This book was a breath of fresh YA air. It's a dystopian, YA coming-of-age fantasy that explores the world of a young woman named Zemira (affectionately named Zee) and her journey to save or destroy the world she knows. It's full of daring, adventure and characters that you can't help but fall in love with. It explores the theme of inner demons and the choices we make in our lives in such a clever way that you are left wondering if you would have done the same. I loved every second of this book with an ending had me in a choke hold. I can't wait to see where the story goes in the coming books! *Skye Gordon, ARC Reviewer*

The Girl Who Broke the World is a fantastic read that will leave you wanting more. Renee has built a stunning world full of magnificent detail and unforgettable characters to both love and hate. *Edith Twaddell, ARC Reviewer*

Mythical, enchanting and amazing! Every chapter gets you more and more intrigued. The way Renee describes things makes you feel like you are actually seeing everything with your own eyes and not just reading it! Can't wait to see where the Rim Walker's journey will take us next! *Kaitlynd Power, ARC Reviewer*

So captivating and enchanting! The way the author describes her characters and each Rim Territory is fascinating and magical. The storyline with each chapter makes you want to just keep reading and not put it down! It is wonderful to read something that is exciting, intriguing and original! I can't wait to see what happens next! *Myra Cumming, Verified Amazon Reviewer*

Fantastic Read. Really, really enjoyed this book. Colourful, relatable characters in a beautiful and dangerous, futuristic world that reminiscent of Avatar or Narnia. Looking forward to the next book in the series and will be purchasing a few extra copies for Christmas gifts! *Verified Amazon Reviewer*

Top-notch fresh take on a YA Fantasy. *The Girl Who Broke the World* explores the theme of inner demons and the choices we make in our lives in such a clever way that you are left wondering if you would have done the same. I loved every second of this book but that ending had me in a choke hold. I can't wait to see where the story goes in the coming books! *Skye, Verified Australian Reviewer*

RENEE HAYES

THE GIRL WHO FREED THE DARKNESS

A RIM WALKER NOVEL

Queensland, Australia

Cover design by Judith San Nicolas
Typeset in Goudy Old Style 9 & 11 pt/Harrington 24 pt
Printed and bound in Australia by IngramSpark
Prepared for publication by The Erudite Pen: theeruditepen.com

A catalogue record for this book is available from the National Library of Australia

The Girl Who Freed the Darkness ~ 1st ed.
ISBN 9780645587128
eISBN 9780645587135

Dedication

This book is for everyone who has gone through debilitating and life-changing pain, whether it be mental, physical or both. Never let it beat you, and never forget that you are not less... you are not broken... you are still you.

Contents

Map of the Dark Rim

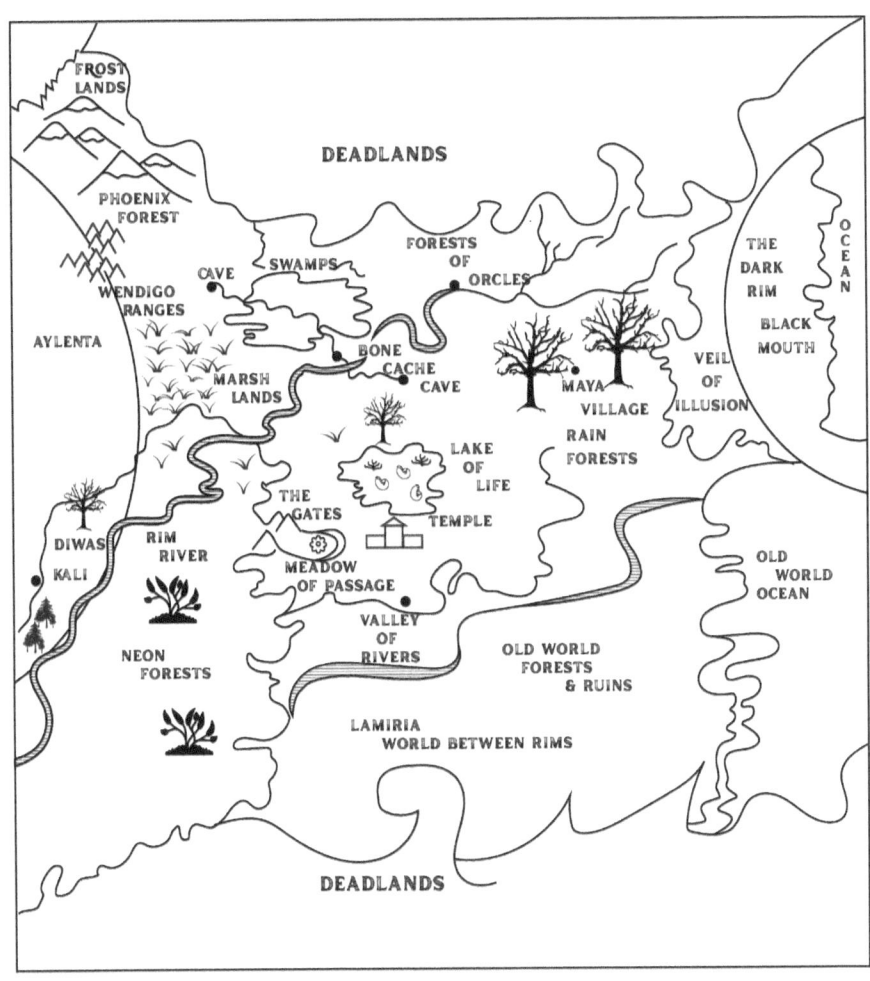

Part I

Prologue

The West Rim, Thorta, 2531

The rancid, boiling, almost-sentient sludge of the west radiation field of Thorta bubbled and released an acrid mist of thick gas that burned its way down Thaylon's ever-resilient throat. His black-stained hands gripped the shovel handle as he continued to transport the vile mess left behind by the ancient humans more than half a millennia ago. The sludge was still just as potent and dangerous. He didn't wonder why no one bothered to notice that he outlasted every other outcast, prisoner and unlucky soul who ended up here. Did they even notice? The vicious human bastards overseeing this hellhole certainly didn't care, that much he did know.

As his punishment centuries ago, he had been forced to live alongside these unfortunate humans. He had watched them, studied them and had seen how the radiation affected the weaklings. First the burns would start, then the weeping would take hold. Pus and blood seeped from every exposed area of their skin. Their teeth would follow next, loosening, the gums bleeding, until eventually their teeth fell out.

Then miraculously, as if their own bodies were toying with them, a spark of hope would bloom in their weary, hopeless eyes. The burns, as if alive from the radiation sludge, would appear to crust over, almost as if their immune systems maybe, just maybe, were winning the fight. This was his favourite part to watch: their feeble hope. It was entertaining, and besides, he had to find some enjoyment in everyday life. His sneer would show his straight white teeth as the sweat beaded down his dirt-encrusted face.

After this brief glimmer of hope, the sludge would attack. Thaylon always watched with satisfaction as the humans' skin blistered and burst, while the ulcers all around their eyes, nose, ears and under their fingernails would peel and flake away like decaying bark. And then the best part, he thought, the toxic waste would find its way into their throats and cause a thick mucus there that they all inevitably drowned in.

And none of them saw it coming.

A snide chuckle almost left Thaylon's mouth as he reminisced about the look of sheer panic and absolute defeat that crept over their features like a slow-moving morning mist on the blackened fields. *Yeah, that was the best part for sure.*

'Thaylon!'

A shout ricocheted through Thaylon's skull, echoing out across the burning black swamp ahead of him.

'You got that load finished? They're ready to start Incinerator 6. We need the last load now!'

Thaylon deliberately slowed his large hands and placed the shovel into the wheeled cart of thick, steaming gloop. He didn't rush, and he didn't bother himself with a reply to the guard. They all left him alone once they saw what he was capable of. Yes, that first one who had messed with him had looked much better with only one ear.

His hooded eyes narrowed on the guard addressing him as he came closer with his wheeled cart loaded high. Thaylon's stomach growled a little. This one's ears were the size of a battilux's. Oh, what a good snack they would be. As if somehow sensing what Thaylon was thinking, the guard gave him a wide berth as he passed, his nervous eyes darting all around, hands gripping tightly to the sword at his side.

'Don't keep 'em waiting, Thaylon.' The guard gripped his sword tighter as he commanded the huge man.

Thaylon towered over the guards, making him the hardest of their prisoners to control. Most of the souls who ended up here lost their fight within the first month or two, along with any physical strength from the radiation they handled daily. But not Thaylon. His dirty blond hair hung in straight clumps just past his hooded deep blue eyes that were always scanning his surroundings with a sharp intensity, like a predator watching his prey. If it weren't for the build-up of dirt, sweat and grime on his skin, he wouldn't look like any of the Thorta-born prisoners here. Their skin was a light, pale pallor, whereas his was a deep other-worldly bronze that still remained even though he hadn't seen the sun in over four hundred years.

A deep growl erupted from Thaylon's throat just at the moment he passed the panicked guard. The guard leaped backwards and almost tripped with fright. Thaylon's laughter barrelled out of his muscular chest, a snarl lighting up his face. He slowly kept wheeling, taking his time despite the orders. When he reached the incinerators, there were even more guards overseeing the weary humans carting their hauls up to the blasting fires to melt the miniscule amounts of sludge they carried away from the edge of the Rim.

Did these humans really think they were somehow righting their ancestors' wrongs? *Fools.*

Ahead of him, a thin husk of a woman collapsed in her rags. The chemical burns had probably reached her lungs. A guard walked forward, but there was no rush. They had all seen this before. The guard didn't dare touch the woman's skin with bare hands to check for a pulse, just scooped her frail frame up and tossed it on top of her own cart. More fuel for the fires. Burn away the sins. Thaylon watched them, these disgusting human beings. He would outlive them all. They were flies, barely alive on a fresh carcass and then dead the next, leaving behind writhing maggots of offspring.

But at least there was some mild entertainment to be had here with their over-heightened emotions. The fear, despair, pain. Oh, they suffered so much. So weak, the lot of them.

Just as Thaylon started to reach the mid-line, there was a rumble from within the sickened earth. The others swung their heads around, some dropping to the ground, and a few let out a cry of fear. Thaylon dropped his cart. Standing tall, he towered over all of them with his six-foot-five stature. He was a god dropped among the filthy peasants. He turned around with ease to eye the iridescent Rim wall shaking and shimmering where it cascaded over the blackened radiation fields. It stretched out far past the wall from Thorta. Out into the dead man's lands. The Rim wavered, light fracturing off and around it, wavering like something had impacted its strength.

Hmmm, interesting. The guards were all in a panic as the ground began to shake, jittering small stones around.

'Earthquake,' a guard yelled out in fear. To the other guards of course, not to the prisoners. The filth. The guards all fled away from the smelters, afraid the burning mass of molten rot and bodies might pour out of the giant wells if the earthquake were to topple them. But still there was a feeling. Something was coming. Thaylon felt it. He couldn't take his eyes from the Rim wall in the distance. Again it wavered, the rumbling coming in a wave. Carts were toppling, pouring the blackened radioactive mess all over the cleaned ground at the humans' feet. He backed away from the chaos and the line-up as everyone tried to dump their carts' contents.

'Where do you think you're going?' A deep voice and the sharp prick of a sword were suddenly at Thaylon's back.

He raised his hands. 'Nowhere, Sal. Just spectating.' The wall gave one last wavey shimmer as if impacted again, and then a huge boom shuddered the ground, making Sal fall and Thaylon's knees nearly buckle.

And then he felt it, as if *it* seethed in as the whole Rim wall dissolved. Just like a cloth ripped from a fine table, the wall cleared within a moment, and was then gone. The Rim wall was *gone*. A large smile truly crept onto Thaylon's harsh face now as his power returned and his cage opened. His dirty muck-caked hair flew past his forehead as a blast of air rushed past him upon the disappearance of the Rim wall, the cage he had been forced within. And where he had been forced to watch and work alongside these human vermin for *years*.

Thaylon spread his arms wide, this time not in submission but in praise to absorb the powerful sweep of energy. Sal got back on his feet as Thaylon started to wander away.

'And just where do you think you're going?' His voice was firm but his eyes widened as he realised what had just transpired with the Rim wall in the distance.

Thaylon took his chance and swung his fist hard. It connected and crunched as Sal's jaw cracked in two. More guards surged towards him as they saw the incident. Thaylon's smile grew. *Yes, more entertainment.* He had been waiting for this day. He grabbed a shovel from the ground as he sprinted towards the pack of guards. One wisely slowed and deferred, smarter than the rest. Thaylon swung the shovel and connected with not one but two guards. The first's face crushed in like a rotten fruit ready to implode. The disturbing sound only made Thaylon's heart race with excitement.

Both soldiers dropped to the ground. A third swung his sword high and barely connected with Thaylon's shoulder. His anger at the guard fuelled his pursuit. He used his shovel like a spear and drove the blunt end into the guard's stomach with such force it pierced skin and slipped between his ribs as blood poured from the blow. The guard's shocked face drained of colour as the ground still rumbled and a smelter was ripped from its supports. Thaylon glowed with death. The other soldiers wisely withdrew and ran as fast as they could away from him.

Thaylon turned from the chaos and left, elation shining on his blood-stained sinister face. *I am coming, my lord. I will find you and free you. And we will rule over these parasites together, taking this earth for our own, as it was supposed to be.* He dropped the shovel and replaced it with a sword from one of the fallen guards. The one with his ear missing from that time long ago.

Hmmm. Thaylon's eyes sparked. *Well, it would be unkind to leave him in such an unbalanced state, and I do need a snack for the road...*

A Curse of Her Own

Aylenta, one year later, 2532

Zemira Creedence lay with her head of stone sunken into the soft pillow, while her eyes begged to stay shut for a little while longer. Was it wrong to wish for it to end? Zee had been suffering in silence for a long while now. She had once wished for adventure, for a little excitement. She had wished for fun, for *a life*. But now the spoils of that adventure pulsed a dominant greeting to her, aching viciously inside her left arm. The constant pain was almost unbearable. *And I thought I was strong... I thought I was so tough.*

Inside, Zee felt herself crumbling piece by piece each day as the pain blasted on. It was like a vicious storm, just there. Brewing. Simmering away. She desperately wanted it gone. She wanted *her* gone. Zee no longer fantasised about adventure, hunting or exploring the new lands. All she could feel, could focus on, was the incessant ache thrumming through her body. It was worse when she was alone. *Especially* when she was alone.

She'd even started to *speak* to Zee. *Kyeitha.* She was in there, Zee knew it. Somehow, a piece of her was leeching off Zee, like a parasite. She could tell that the voice in her head was real. It was no illusion. Kyeitha, the former guardian of the Rim and all its inhabitants, was real. Torturing Zee, punishing her, haunting her, repaying Zee for destroying her.

Or trying to put her out of her misery, more like it.

What remained of Kyeitha was a nasty, twisted thing. Zee tried to ignore her, concentrating instead on regaining her control. The boom, boom, boom of perfect rhythmic pain was still steadily there though, never leaving her.

Great... it was time for another day.

She lifted up her heavy head like a rock from within a river bed. *Time to go away, pain. To the back of my mind, please, where I can block you out.*

'NO,' the voice whispered. 'Murderer, fake, mongrel!'

The words seethed inside her mind like a poisonous mist. Zee's arm burned fiercely in time with the foul words, as if it had been jammed in the fireplace. Her legs were dead heavy, as if filled with borenium and ice.

Ice. That would be nice right about now. Would that soothe the pain? Stop it! Don't think of him. Of Ravaryn. You don't need anyone's help. You certainly don't need his help.

She was strong. She was tough. She could deal with this. It was just pain.

Zee's throat tightened as her hand automatically tried to wipe away a tear. She doubted anyone else could help her anyway. Diwa had been exhausting herself daily trying the heal Kyeitha's mark with little to no success at all. The old woman had drained herself endlessly for Zee over the past year. For what? It wouldn't go away.

She was the curse breaker, and now it seemed she was cursed herself.

Stupid girl. Mongrel girl. The voice inside her head mocked her.

Her legs swung over the bed, and her long feet dropped onto the warm, woven mat floor. Soft fibres greeted and comforted her weary toes as her head began to spin. Zee stilled herself and concentrated on the morning light gently streaming its way into the bedroom window of her parents' small cottage home in the Black Forest of Aylenta.

I can do this. It's just another day. Stay busy, stay distracted, maybe it will miraculously go away. Tiny dust specks danced in the morning glow, as if cheering her on slightly.

'Useless girl. Broken girl,' the voice seethed.

'Shut up!' Zee snapped back out loud to Kyeitha's voice in her mind. She dropped her head down to stare at the ugly, marred mark on her left arm. A handprint. A brand. She forced the tears to stay in her eyes as her fists clenched, nails biting into her palms.

I am not broken. And I will not break. She opened her eyes, and their attention was caught by a shimmer. A sparkling glint of silver, like a little star catching the morning's light inside the ring on her finger. The mesmerising black swirls within were somehow comforting.

Ravaryn.

It felt like a lifetime ago, but also like yesterday since she had seen him that night at the Mother's Moon festival in Kali. The night he gave her this ring. Zee's stomach shifted uncomfortably. It had been so strange, and he had been so different that night. So free. Now it seemed she was the one who needed the freeing. The one who was trapped.

Would he come if she called? Or had he already forgotten all about her? Had he moved on with his life now he was free from the Rim and had his powers back? She'd broken the Rim wall, she'd broken the curse, and now she wasn't needed. Well, she didn't need him either. She didn't need anyone.

'Liar.'

Zee stood, leaving her bed, her oasis of comfort, warmth and safety. *To the Mother's moon and stars, I love you, bed.* She stood still for a moment and let her head adjust, rooting her feet to the floor to steady her body. It felt like a bucket of eels was swirling madly about inside her. Her arm sent her another boom of pain.

Come on, Zee. Just another day. You've got this. You are Zemira Creedence, after all. The girl who broke the world. You are powerful, more than just human.

She lifted her eyes to stare at the young woman frowning back at her in the large bedroom mirror adjacent to her bed. Dark hollows bloomed under her eyes. Her ebony hair was a wild mess, and her collarbones were jutting a hello.

A flash flickered in the mirror. A disturbing vision of another woman appeared briefly where her own image should be.

Or did she? Zee rubbed at her sleepy eyes, the lids still feeling too heavy. Today was going to be a good day, she decided. She ignored everything else and eyed her favourite leather boots across the room near a tower of potted vines, next to her two most treasured books – gifts from Warwick's stone house on the hill in Nerissa. He and Jill had gifted them to Zee for her nineteenth birthday last year at the Mother's Moon Festival, the first ever festival she had gotten to attend. It seemed like a lifetime ago.

Zee struggled to ignore the arm pain that tried to compete with her thoughts. She was an expert at ignoring things now. The vines twisted in and around her bedroom walls, exuding their calm aura. Zee breathed in deeply their fresh smell, loving the feel of their peaceful yet strong energy. They silently sang a good morning that only Zee could hear, lending her their energy, coaxing a small smile on her pale face that now lacked its usual sun-bronzed glow.

She sucked in a deep breath and slowly whistled it back out again. They were going to hunt raspor's honey today. The thought further dulled the pain to a quiet, manageable hum. Zee dressed quickly and slipped her hunting knife on her hip. The brand on her arm twitched. This was the same knife she had used to end Kyeitha with, the Rim guardian whose sole job it had been to care for and protect the Rim and the creatures inside and outside of it. And Kyeitha had failed.

Zee hadn't planned on killing her. She had gone there to warn her, to help her. She'd thought she was doing the right thing. By the Mother, she had been so sure of herself. But she'd been so wrong about Kyeitha... and she'd been so wrong about Ravaryn. Zee had thought he was the evil one, the one who needed to be stopped. How naïve of her. She cringed at herself for how foolish and stupid she had been. The feeling made her fall further into the tunnel of despair she was getting buried in day by day.

As she walked into the living room, the cottage's front door burst open and a bright, handsome face greeted her. Chestnut eyes were alight with excitement, breaking her self-loathing circle of thoughts for the moment.

'You ready or what?' Paxton's smile poured from him with more warmth, if that were even possible, from the day before. He'd been trying so hard lately to cheer her up. Trying too hard if you asked Zee.

'Geez, can't a girl get a sleep-in these days?' Zee feigned grumpiness, lips twitching up at the sides as her emerald eyes met his tallowpine ones.

'It's hours past first light!' Pax replied, exasperated, his hands raised slightly in the air as he spoke.

'Your mum and dad left for town to open the shop hours ago.'

Zee's mother Verena hadn't been the same since she'd lost the baby. She thought she'd seen the worst of her mother's depression all those years when her father had been absent, but somehow right by their sides as Wolf. She was glad her mother had him as the man, Orion, to lean on now though. Zee didn't think she would have been strong enough to be there for her mother this time. Her parents hadn't even realised what she'd been going through, but she couldn't tell them. She couldn't burden them with her pain as well as their own right now. There'd been so much heartache since the Rim wall fell, and somehow it seemed all her fault.

How was it that she sleeping longer and longer each day yet was still exhausted? Zee's body moved stiffly towards the front door where Paxton eagerly waiting for her. She felt ninety not nineteen.

'A girl needs her beauty rest.' She pulled at her shirt, comically looking for wrinkles, smoothing her hair with closed eyes and raised brows.

Paxton laughed, and Zee noticed that he couldn't show any more teeth if he tried when she opened her eyes.

'If you get any more beautiful, you'll start to glow. Now stomach some breakfast and let's get going.' His loving gaze never left hers.

Zee's insides warmed a little at the compliment, thawing her mood slightly. 'Alright, sweet talker,' Zee said. 'Let's go cheat death and find us some raspor's honey.'

11

Raspor's Honey

Wind blasted past Zee, tangling her dark hair and whistling alongside the grey cliff face that the pair were scaling. They looked like tiny black ants clinging to the side of a monstrous mountainside down in the forest below. Zee dared not to close her eyes, instead taking long, slow, steadying breaths in of the crisp morning air.

That's better. This is just what I needed. I feel so alive up here in the wind. The picturesque canopy of the forest below with the mountains stretching far into the horizon were laid out before her like banquet, one her soul could recharge from. Her legs were shaking, making her carefully check every foot placement that she made, ensuring it would be the best decision before she took it.

Pax climbed just metres above Zee's head, in the lead. She was careful to try and follow his footholds. Zee would usually be the one in front, and her heart dropped a little inside her chest knowing how weak she'd become. She had *always* physically bested Paxton. At everything. But now she felt second best... and she didn't like it. Not one bit.

'You okay down there, Miss Beauty Sleep?' Pax called out, his voice competing with the howl of the wind.

A competitive spark ignited within Zee, dragging some unknown source of hidden energy into her. His teasing always pushed her to try harder, to best him even though she was struggling just to cling to the rocky side of the cliff. She scaled up faster with shaking arms, the sweat beading on her brow in the morning sun.

'Maybe you should try it one day,' Zee yelled back, her voice also fighting against the wind. It was a weak retort, Zee knew, but it was all she could think of right now.

She finally scaled up to where he had stopped. Both of them were smiling, clinging to the cliff, shoulder to shoulder. The raspor's nest, a small hole about the size of a small fireplace in the side of the rocky grey cliff, was just above their heads.

'You want to be look-out? Or do you want to be the collector?' Paxton asked a little nervously, one of his eyebrows rising.

'I can't see any raspors near us or around the cliffs at the moment. They're either nesting inside their small dens or they are out collecting.'

A few zipped in and out on the far side of the cliff, looking small in the distance, like little insects. Zee's arms shuddered, and her legs burned more fiercely while her whole body shook. She could barely cling onto the rock, and her muscles would have screamed at her if they could. If she tried to climb up and dive into that small cave, holding her body steady while also trying to collect the honey, she would fall for sure.

'I'll watch your back.' Zee's smile was strained, but she tried not to show it.

'Okay, but if you let me get skewered, I'll never forgive you!' Pax laughed out loud as he scrambled closer to the opening before changing his mind. He crawled head first into it instead, his legs dangling out comically as Zee clung to the cliff just beneath him.

'Pass me the sack.' A muffled yell came out from the tight space his body was half hanging from, indicating that this nest must have been empty; otherwise, there would have been a very rapid back pedal from Pax to get out of there.

Zee carefully wriggled the cloth sack from her back so as not to lose her tight grip on the sharp rocks she was holding. Her fingers protested, her palms sweaty and her knuckles white. She slid the top of the sack up and shoved it into the hole alongside Paxton's body.

'What does it look like in there?' She tried to angle her head around in the gap between his hip and the rock to get a better look.

'It's awesome, Zee! All sparkly, and the honey is like crystals growing out of the sides. It's really cool,' Pax explained, his voice filled with child-like awe.

Mother, he made her smile sometimes as he oozed happiness and light. All. The. Bloody. Time. Next to him, she felt like a miserable, worn-out old shoe. She squeezed her head in just a bit between Pax and the rocks and waited for her eyes to adjust to the darkness. Little yellow and pink crystal-like growths were hanging from the edges of the nest's walls. Paxton struggled to snap them away and scrape them into the jars they had brought with them inside the sack. As he scraped carefully with his hunting knife, the honey poured out from inside the crystal structures. In his awkward position, he collected as much as he possibly could into the jars.

'Oi, you're supposed to be watching my back!' he pointed out to Zee, as she tried to watch him collect all the best-looking honey deposits within the hole in the cliff.

'Oh, fine!' She rolled her eyes and twisted her head out of its difficult position, and her exhausted body thanked her. She was glad all the same though that she had looked inside the raspor's nest. Inside, it was truly beautiful, and she almost felt a little guilty about taking some of the hard-earned honey from the raspor that owned this nest. Almost. Her mouth watered just thinking of the honey drizzled over one of Diwa's warm cinnamon cakes, and her distracted mind let her foot slip.

Zee's heart skipped a beat as she scrambled to hold onto the cliff's edge. Her heart racing, she dragged in a deep breath while the wind continued to roar past her, not noticing her mistake. The slip reminded her that what they were doing was actually pretty dangerous, and she should not let herself be so distracted by such daydreams right now. As she righted her footing and found a better foothold on the cliff face, she rested her achy limbs again for a second. Zee tried to keep ignoring her burning arm and pretend that the pain wasn't making her mood fouler today than it usually did. But suddenly a loud buzzing noise rang in her ears in the air right behind her.

'Nearly done!' Paxton yelled out, completely unaware of the visitor hovering in the air just behind him. Not visitor, the owner of the nest. This was clearly the raspor whose nest they were raiding of its treasured honey... *shit.*

Zee swung out a shaky hand away from the rock and the hold that she had it clamped around and hurled a blast of air towards the raspor, stopping it from ramming its sharp beak straight into Paxton's behind. Rocks shifted as her body pushed back against the cliff's edge, and Pax slid rapidly out of the hole.

'What was that?' he yelled, his pupils wide.

'Time's up! Let's go!' Zee shouted.

The raspor was clearly much more annoyed now than it was initially upon finding them both raiding its nest of its hard-earned bounty. It reared back from Zee's blast of air and rapidly dived again with much more speed and ferocity.

Zee's arms shook. Her skin felt cold despite the heat her body was radiating. Sweat beaded all over her now while the wind still blasted past, trying to sweep it away into the breeze as if it wanted to help. Zee tried to swipe at the raspor again with a powerful gust of air. With the second attempt, she was barely able to use any of her powers. It hardly threw the raspor off its course at all, and the creature's steel knife-like beak smashed into the rock just centimetres from Paxton's right thigh. Pax slid fully out of the hole now, looked down at the falling rock and clung on tightly right next to Zee.

'Hell, Zee!' The realisation of what just caused the impact and the cascade of rocks to his right dawned on his face. His amber eyes shot wide open as he spotted the angry raspor in the rock unnervingly close to him.

'Let's get outta here. I don't want to be a kebab! How in the hell does Diwa do this?'

Diwa Mumasumi, the clever old lady who always had an abundance of raspor's honey, only the Mother knew how in the world she did it. And she never shared her secrets as to where or how she had procured it from either.

'Come on, I'll try to hold it off as we climb down! Don't you dare drop that honey or we'll never hear the end of it from Diwa!' Zee commanded.

The raspor buzzed loudly near the rock near Paxton's side, pieces of rock blasting into both of them. It pulsed its iridescent wings trying to back its beak out of the mountainous wall they clung to. Pax and Zee started to scuttle as fast as they could down the cliffside, like crabs evading a predator, searching for the safety of the waves. But the raspor freed itself all too soon, even though they were well on their way away from its nest, nearly halfway down. Zee's body was absolutely screaming at her, and her hands were torn open on the sharp rocks as she carelessly half-climbed, half-slid down the exposed craggy rock. Exhaustion rattled through her veins. Paxton was now further below her. Faster, stronger and quicker, his body surer, he was healthy, strong and free of the darkness that was poisoning Zee. How she envied him.

'Hurry, Zee! It's circling back, and I think it's angry!'

The raspor spiralled towards Pax again, this time not with its metallic metal beak but the sharp, poisonous barbed stinger on its tail. The creature tucked the stinger under its body and aimed, like a wasp.

Shit, shit, shit! Zee could barely summon a sneeze let alone another blast of air. She felt completely spent.

'Pax, look out!' Her voice trembled.

The raspor slammed into Paxton, crushing him into the cliff just as he twisted sideways.

'NO! 'PAX!'

She could see the raspor retract, then it shot backwards away from him. Paxton's hold on the side of the cliff slipped, his footings were gone... and he fell right before Zee's wide eyes. She sucked in a sharp breath, her heart faltering as though it had missed a beat. It constricted violently inside her chest as she watched, as if in slow motion, her friend fall before her from the safety of the cliff's edge.

Zee outstretched a useless hand in the air towards him. She felt the blood drain from her face. A cold sweat was rippling through her whole body now. She tried to cry out for him, but her voice was crippled. Zee couldn't even conjure a squeak as she watched her best friend fall to certain death towards the forest below.

Let him go... the voice slithered in her head. *Add him to your collection of kills... Murderer...*

'No!' Zee's mind screamed back at the voice.

Her body was shaking for another reason now: fury. She forced every thought of Paxton to the forefront of her mind; she saw the trees below and felt the vines within, their strength. They were survivors always searching for the light. Always fighting to take over, growing rapidly, faster than any other plant in the forest. A sharp pain ripped into the centre of her outstretched palm and a vine shot forth at marvelling speed from within her, straight towards her free-falling friend.

Sharp barbed thorns ripped into Paxton's ankle, and she braced against the cliffside for the impact of his body, his weight against the vine's strength. The pack of honey flew from his grip into the forest below, and his body connected with hard rock. It was luckily nowhere near as bad as Zee was prepared for, the vines slowing his fall as he slammed into the side of the cliff. Not gently, but also not as catastrophically damaging as her worst fears had initially told her.

Kyietha's voice was gone again. *I'll show you, you monster,* Zee fumed back at her inside her head as Pax dangled dangerously below. The realisation hit Zee that she was again talking with voices in her head, and that it was most definitely not okay. Kyeitha's thoughts budded like small flowers in her brain and also instantly made her excruciatingly tired.

I can deal with that later. Zee looked down as her heart beat furiously in her weary chest. Paxton was dangling like a fly caught in a spider's web. Dangling, but thankfully still conscious.

'You alright down there?' Zee asked, her voice returning to her.

'Just,' Paxton scraped out a reply, breathless.

The raspor was nowhere to be seen. It was probably fuming inside its empty nest, or it had left to try and replenish its lost treasures. Paxton grabbed hold of the rock, and Zee's vine, as if sensing he was now safer, loosened enough for him to right himself and tighten his grip on the cliff face. They climbed agonisingly down, Zee's dark vine still imbedded in Paxton's poor leg. Then they both dropped and slid awkwardly the last few metres off the rocks and onto the spongy leaf litter of the forest floor. Panting, arms and legs trembling, bloody, bruised and covered in cold sweat, they lay side by side sucking in unsteady breaths of cool forest-drenched air.

Zee was unable to move her shivering body and was trying to slow her pounding heart, which was slamming into her chest like an axe into wood.

'You gave me a scare,' she wheezed out.

'I gave myself a scare,' Paxton panted back.

After a moment of slight recuperation, he lifted himself up onto his elbows and looked down at his ankle.

'Um... I'm super glad you decided to save me from pancaking into the ground, but do you reckon you could retract your vine thingy from my leg now?' He grimaced. 'It kinda hurts.'

Zee still lay on her back, her breath steadying, staring up at the leaves swaying in the canopy above them. She heaved her leaden body up onto her elbows, her open palm facing the sky with a thick rope of vine exiting from it.

'Um, I don't know how to.' She looked wearily at him then twitched her fingers, curling them in one by one while relaxing her muscles. Calming her mind, she tried to withdraw the vine with her powers, taking comfort in the forest around her and thanking it for its help.

'It's okay,' she told herself. 'We did our job, now it's time to rest.'

Nothing happened.

Zee felt a sudden pain deep in her gut. It roiled around like a snake snared in a trap, and she knew within an instant that she was going to be sick.

19

'Pax, I think I'm going to be sick,' she forced out, turning pale like the crumbling rocks of the cliff they had just escaped from.

'What's happening, Zee? Zee! Are you okay?'

Zee rolled on to her side towards him, her head angled close to the ground, while she sucked in rapid, uneven breaths. She was fighting the nausea.

Pax grabbed her shoulders in panic and forced her to look at him. His face contorted with shock. 'Your eyes, Zee,' he stuttered.

Zee saw a bright blue glow envelop his face. *My necklace.* It was a warning of some kind, like an alarm system for danger, and it was at that moment Zee felt herself fall away from him, far away, sliding somewhere. She couldn't see or feel or hear a thing. It was like she was travelling down a silent dark tunnel, and she ended up somewhere dark and empty. *I know this place. I've been here before,* were her last thoughts.

Zemira was shaking in Paxton's grip. She looked even paler than usual, and he thought she was going to be sick.

Panic gripped him. His ribs felt like they were being constricted, just like the vine that was puncturing his skin, squeezing his ankle like a boa constrictor.

Zee's necklace was glowing that bright blue, like the night they were attacked on Warwick's boat, the night the vipen attacked. Oh no. *It's a warning.* Zee looked up at him, pale as the moon, and her eyes, her eyes weren't her own. They were now a bright blue and speckled with silver stars.

'Zee!' Pax yelled straight into her face, shaking her shoulders a little.

She just stared back at him with no expression in her strange face, then a terrifying grin spread across her features, features that were not her own. Pax had *never* seen Zee look that way. His fingers started to tingle, and his pulse raced. He tried to swallow down his rising panic. She didn't say a thing, just stared at him, and the grin on her face grew wider into a terrifying sneer. Zee flipped around like lightning and straddled Pax, and *not* like they we're wrestling or mucking around. Her thighs squeezed into his sides with such force his breath was knocked out of him.

'Zee,' he wheezed. 'You're hurting me.'

A laugh poured from her mouth, and the green vine retracted its thorns and released Paxton's ankle. It slid back into her hand a little, then swirled around at him like a snake. She aimed it at his throat, and the vine turned black like the mark on Zee's arm. Pax could see that her whole hand was now turning black, and the vine's thorns elongated into sharp needles as it snaked its way around his neck. He didn't know what to do. Tears pricked at his eyes as he tried to push her away with his hands. He didn't want to hurt her, but there was something terribly wrong. This wasn't his Zee at all.

Pax saw the flash of a redheaded figure then a strong freckled hand. The hand slipped to Zee's hip, grabbing the knife out of her belt and slashing it upwards through the black vine-like growth sprouting from her palm. Pax sucked in a breath, like he'd just been swimming under water and had barely been able to resurface. Zee's body was forcefully thrown from him. He could feel the warm blood trickling from his neck, and his head felt light as he sat up to see Zee strewn across from him on the forest floor. The vine was gone from her palm and tears were streaming from her eyes... her emerald eyes.

A strong hand slid behind his head, holding it up, and cradled him into a lap that supported him in a sitting position. Bright friendly eyes of a different shade of blue, a summer's day sky framed by flames, stared down at Paxton. The dark red locks of hair accompanied a worried look on the face he'd seen before... a face that had saved him before...

'Pax! Pax, talk to me. Are you hurt? Zee, what did you do!' The deeper version of the voice he remembered urgently questioned them both.

Paxton's eyes were still full of shock as he took in the face above him. 'Tye?'

Kyeitha's Vine

Zee sat up and stared back at Pax on the ground from a completely different viewpoint. Someone else was there too. Someone whose fiery red hair
and large ocean eyes she would recognise anywhere. *Tye.* But a larger,
much more handsome version of the boy she had saved from the Borztan
mines and from the clutches of the twisted blacksmith's cruel punishment a year ago.

It was amazing what a year could do to a person. Tye had blossomed
like a beautiful forest lily, while Zee had withered away like a river weed.
It was then she registered the looks on their faces. The fear. *Oh stars...
what have I done?* There was blood on Paxton's neck. His face was ashen.
There was a very protective stance to Tye cradling Pax's head. His long
arms circled around him, protecting him. From *her.*

Tears pricked at the edges of Zee's eyes, and she felt so disorientated,
so confused. She looked down and there was blood on her hands. Paxton's blood was on her hands. She couldn't breathe. Her chest was
closing in on itself. Their faces... they were just staring back at her, riddled with shock.

What did you do?

Her whole body reverberated with panic. She couldn't bear their looks of worry, of shock and of distrust a second longer. The utter desolation of not being in control of her body and spirit consumed her. Her mind seethed at Kyeitha as her body twisted around to drag itself up from the forest floor. Then she ran.

Zee ran like she was being chased by a creature of the damned. She ran as the tears poured, blurring her vision and chilling her face in the wind. Faster and faster her pace grew as she tried to leave the panic of her complete lack of control behind. Her own voice slithered in her mind mingling with that of another. *Murderer.*

'No!' The scream ripped from her throat into the empty forest. Leaves, branches and barbed vines all tried to slow her pace, and as she ran, they tore little slithers off her skin. But she didn't feel a thing through the icy chill that had descended over her body. Her legs were wobbly and her muscles ached, so she could barely hold herself up. Zee's pace slowed just as she came to the edge of the forest's tangled interior. It thinned, and she stopped just in time to look out from above, over the northern part of the Rim river. Its cool dark waters meandered for many metres below.

Her breath rattled from her chest, and Zee's throat felt as though it were on fire from sucking in the cool air too rapidly. She dropped to the edge of the cliff as the sobs racked her body. Pent up since Kyeitha had stained her with the curse of her presence and pain. A punishment Kyeitha had somehow managed in her last dying breaths.

She had tainted Zemira and was like a painful parasite living off Zee's energy reserves and happiness. Her left arm boomed through her nervous system.

Stop! she pleaded with the pain. *Please.* Zee saw the dark waters swirling and moving about beneath her and trailing away behind the next bend in the mountain's forested cliffs. She slid closer to the edge. *Would it hurt? Would the water swallow me up? Would Kyeitha take over my body and let it end me for her revenge?* It would all stop though... the pain... it would all go away.

Pebbles fell from the edge of the cliff and tumbled down, making tiny unseeable splashes into the water as her boots slid even closer. *I'm falling apart... I can't think straight... I can never think straight these days.* Her mind was always clouded with the overbearing shadow of agony swirling all around the edges of her brain, fogging over everything.

Just as she drew a rattled breath in, wind gushed past her face, and a pleasant whisper of calm settled over her. Her ebony hair was brushed out of her face and some of the tears dried a little on her pale skin. A whole flock of sunravens swept past the edge of the cliff and dove down to the river's dark waters below.

Zee scuttled back a little from the edge, her heart jumping a fraction as if only now realising how close she'd been to the edge of the cliff. She watched the sunravens' magnificent wings glide through the air, silver feathers shimmering iridescently in the sun's rays. Vibrant blues and greens, and some brighter shades of green with a sunny yellow shine. Others were a stunning white with feathers that furrowed out from the crowns of their heads to spin wildly in the wind. The ends were tipped with a bright yellow, making them even more mesmerising. She watched them glide majestically in rhythm with each other. Each in tune with its neighbour. The group flanked each other, turning perfectly in unison with the smallest of inflections from the one beside it.

It was like watching water flow smoothly around a rock or bend in the river. A beautiful flock, a family. All together they flew away into the distance and out of Zee's view. And all of a sudden, she felt lonelier than she had ever felt before. Why had she run away? Why did she just leave Paxton there? Injured. She couldn't do this anymore. She knew she wasn't safe to be around, not now. She couldn't risk hurting her family. They didn't understand. They didn't understand what it had been like to live like this every... single... day since ending Kyeitha.

Even though Zee had always been different as she'd always had something more - powers and a connection to the land, to her environment - she'd never felt so different as she did now. Never like she was a danger to those around her. She needed help. Zee looked down at the ring on her finger, the ring that Ravaryn had given her. She hadn't seen him for so long. Would he come if she called? Would he understand? He had mysterious powers of his own. Maybe there was something he could do to help her? Something more than what Diwa could offer her?

Diwa Mumasumi had been trying for months to remove the blackened hand print on Zee's arm to help ease the pain. In the beginning, her efforts had worked well. But the mark had grown stronger and stronger. All Diwa could offer her now with her healing powers was a slight reprieve.

Zemira stared at the tiny swirling clouds of sparkling liquid inside the ring on her finger. Swirls of silvery grey and onyx intertwined together in a soft, sweet dance inside the gem, chasing each other gently around inside the sphere. Another tear, uninvited this time, slipped down Zee's cheek. *What's the worst that could happen?*

She sent a spark of her power into the metal encasing her finger, into the ring's mysterious swirls of magic. A tiny spark, a small burst of her power, was all that she expelled. Nothing happened. What did she really expect? That he would materialise out of thin air and solve all her problems? No. No one was going to sail in on a sunraven's back and save her.

Twisting around, she pushed herself up, lifting her body from the earth with both hands. Her body felt so heavy. She needed to face what she had done. But first she needed Diwa. Diwa would help. Even if it was only a hug to keep the sadness away for the moment. She took one last look at the river below her, and a deep roiling in her stomach slid unpleasantly like a serpent: fear. Fear of herself, of who she was becoming. Of how her control was wavering.

Zemira pushed past leaves and branches and started the journey back through the forest, her heavy feet leading her to Diwa's. On the ground, where Zee's hands had pressed into it to help herself up, shimmering in the sunlight was a sprouted patch of small dark shoots. They spun around and reached up to the light, rapidly unfurling and opening, blossoming into large velvety patch of petals. Petals of the darkest black blooms, like that of a raven.

*

Zee dragged her body through the tangled forest. Her palms were still crusted with the blackened blood from where the vine had sprouted forth to save Paxton from falling to his death, and she guessed later from trying to choke the life out of him when Kyeitha's lingering spirit had taken her over. Great. She was a walking, talking curse. Was this how Ravaryn had felt when he was cursed? Not likely. He would have swaggered on in without a care in the world and planned how he would have saved himself. Unlike Zee, who seemed to rely on everyone these days. She felt she was incapable of even being alone now, it seemed. Her face was contorted in self-loathing and covered in dirt. Tears stained her cheeks and crusted blood from scratches littered her bare skin. She couldn't believe she had just run away from Paxton like that. How could she? The look he had given her though... and Tye...

Zee's heart squeezed in on itself. Like someone had their hands inserted inside her chest and they were wringing it out for all it was worth, which Zee felt wasn't much these days. Sure, she had saved the Rim world from a war. From Kyeitha and the creatures she had created to end all human life that got in her way. But Zee had also destroyed the Rim wall and the safety it seemed everyone had so desperately needed. They wanted their happy little cage back. The people lived in fear now, for no reason. It was her fault and she felt they all blamed her. She knew it, even though she didn't bother to go into the village much to watch the vision screen in town, despite being free to do as she pleased now. Zee knew it would be plastered all around anyway, on the news feeds. The girl who broke the world. Great. Just great.

She reached the top of Diwa's glen as the afternoon sun sprinkled through the huge tallowpines. The scents of her garden, jasmine, dewfruit flowers, mistflowers and more, were in full force and comforted her more than she felt she deserved. Zee wished she could curl up in a patch of juneberries or nasturtiums and just let the earth swallow her whole. She wandered through the garden patches, feeling as though her body absolutely hated her. Her entire being was singing out at her in a foul song, aching. Her boots scraped the earth as she finally reached Diwa's crooked wooden door. *Strange...* Diwa always seemed to know when Zee was coming to see her, when she needed her. Zee never had to actually open Diwa's door as the old woman was always standing there ready to greet her.

A realisation hit her, as funny as that sounded. She could feel the strangeness of the air, feel something was different – a current, an energy that didn't fit with the serenity of Diwa's cottage, or her gardens. She lifted her arm to open the cottage door and saw that the black mark was creeping further up her arm. Her face twisted into a snarl, but it disappeared quickly as panic tugged at her still-foggy brain. *Oh Stars, what if something's happened to Diwa?* She quickly forced the door open with her leftover bit of energy and called out in a sharp tone. 'Diwa? DIWA!'

Her old friend was not in her colourful kitchen, nor seated at the old wooden table. Zee's eyes raced to the small sitting room opposite her, and there she spotted the two figures in Diwa's large armchairs before the fireplace. Diwa's small body was nearly swallowed in her huge chair, and a large Cheshire-cat grin was on her sweet old face.

'There you are, my dear.'

Zee looked over at the armchair beside Diwa at the other form taking up the entire chair, knees crossed over each other, a charming smile on his face. Raven hair curled down slightly over his forehead, and he held a dainty teacup in his large hands.

'Zemirahhh,' he rolled his tongue as her name purred out of his full mouth. 'So good to see you again.'

His smile looked genuine, warm even.

Ravaryn.

Ferns & Feathers

Black Forest, Aylenta

The black wolf's coat shone in the morning sun glittering through the forest canopy, where he sat hidden behind a huge tallowbark trunk in the thick patch of floxel ferns. His large yellow eyes were trained on her – the young woman.

The Rim Walker.

The Queen Slayer.

Zemira Creedence.

She was with the young man again, this time scaling the craggy raspor cliffs in the northern part of the Black Forest. He had been tracking her over the months, this lithe mysterious one. The young woman had defeated the most powerful being that the outer Rim lands, and Lamiria, had ever known. She had ended Kyeitha's reign along with her torturous command over him.

Aytac's midnight coat shimmered as he ruffled his fur at just the thought of Kyeitha, a foul sensation accompanying her image in his mind and making his gut roil. The excruciating deal that he'd had to strike with her to keep his sister safe. To keep Kyeitha from ending her had cost him his freedom. He had obeyed her till her last day. But this young woman had defeated the forest queen and broken his deal with her, his curse. Aytac had served Kyeitha for what seemed like a thousand torturous years, but in reality it had been far less. The threat of his sister's life had always been dangled out in front of him, like bait on a fisherman's hook, if he even let himself glimpse the idea of mutiny or betrayal. So he had been constantly reined back in by the threat of his sister being harmed.

The wind tickled gently past through the swaying ferns, and the pair, it seemed, were being intercepted by an angry raspor upon finding them raiding her nest. Aytac watched motionlessly, taking in their latest adventure. The young man was slammed into the hard cliff face by the angry raspor, and he fell. Aytac felt a slight jolt in his chest, but no real worry. The young man wasn't his concern, only the woman. Zemira.

Just as he thought the man was surely doomed, what looked like a rope, no it was a vine, a lifeline was sent spiralling from Zemira's outstretched palm towards her companion. It caught him mid-air and slowed his trajectory towards the ground and certain death below on the sharp rocks at the bottom of the mountainside. Instead, he collided with the hard cliff face.

Amazing, she had done it again, shown mercy and saved her fellow hunter. He watched as they scurried down the cliff and disappeared into the forest brush, the raspor losing interest and leaving them. Abandoning its attack, it zoomed around rapidly to investigate its now-empty cache inside the rocky nest, the sun shining off its iridescent rainbow feathers.

Aytac stood still in the ferns, taking in a large breath of the forest air around him. The refreshing smell of leaf litter and tallowpine needles mixed with the scents of rich earth and fragrant wild flowers soothed his mind and eased his racing heart. He mulled over the thoughts that sped around in his mind, trying to muster them all into a plan, into some kind of order. He still marvelled at what it felt like to be free of her. Kyeitha. Free of her command. But he still didn't have his sister back, and he still didn't know if she was safe. Was she injured? Was she still alive? Where had Kyeitha taken them all? The 'betrayers' as she had called them.

The forest queen had wisely never trusted him, her right-hand, with the whereabouts of the prisoners she'd deemed disloyal. She knew that if he had found out where his sister was being held, there would be nothing to stop him from getting her back. His sibling, his twin, the other half of himself. The pain forced into and around his heart, like a viper strangling its catch. His anger at Kyeitha taking her away spiralled around the organ, still leeching the pain of his sister's absence, even after all this time.

Aytac took in another deep breath of the forest air, and a floxel skittered past him out of its hole in the fern patch he was standing in. The floxel need not fear him. Even though his heart had hardened over time as Kyeitha's right hand, his compassion was somehow miraculously still intact. He didn't need to eat, so he wouldn't hunt or harm the small creature for fun. No, he was well and truly done with seeing harm come to the innocent. And once he found out exactly where the prisoners had been stashed away, hidden from him, he would act.

His plan would be sound first, and then he would come for her. The Rim Walker, Zemira. Then he would find his sister with her help and free her from a punishment she didn't deserve. His huge wolf head hung down between his shoulders. No, it had been his fault, his mistake. He would get his twin back and maybe just free himself of the guilt that had weighed down his heart and crushed his spirit for years.

Zenya, Kymera

The duellerat's soft white coat and thick, strong feathers of its large wings rustled with anticipation. Mazda sat a stride the giant beast, its eagle-like head twitching as it waited for the command. Its taloned feet scratched impatiently one a time through the powdered snow.

'That's it. Well done. Now remember, no matter what – Do. Not. Let. Go,' King Ravaryn calmly reminded the young girl with bright blue eyes staring back at him on top of the icy cliff. She nodded her head swiftly in reply, not daring to look down at the drop of the icy chasm ahead as she perched up on top of the duellerat's back.

'You've got this.' Ravaryn squeezed her arm, standing reassuringly beside her on the icy mountain, his tall build making the duellerat not seem so large.

'I've got this.' Her eyes connected with his, and she nervously smiled back. The wind swept her fiery tangles of long curls out far behind her, past her thick, hooded blue moscow coat. Her hands were shaking the reins around the beast's long neck.

'You ready?' Ravaryn prompted.

'No...' it came out as a squeak.

'I'll be right behind you. Now, mush!' he commanded the duellerat.

Finally, it seemed to say as it took two steps and leaped powerfully from the edge of the icy cliff. Large, shimmery wings spread out impressively from its furry body, blending perfectly into the brilliant white surrounds of the snowy mountainous terrain. The small blur of blue coat and auburn locks attached to its back let out a piercing scream. First of pure terror as they plummeted down the chasm, then the duellerat levelled out and swept through the air horizontally, righting itself with ferocious speed. After a while gliding more stably, Mazda's adrenaline replaced her fear with pure exhilaration.

'Yeeha!' A yell of pure joy ripped from her throat. A war cry of elation.

Ravaryn's dark wings pounded through the air as he watched her. Her happiness was contagious, and he pushed his large dark wings harder to catch up, coming to glide beside her and the snow creature.

'You okay?' His smile was magnetic, the proud shine in his ebony eyes unmistakable.

'That was awessssome!' Mazda exploded. 'Blaze, you're amazing,' she praised the handsome creature. Blaze replied with a loud caw, confirming he approved of the praise.

'I can't believe how fun this is,' she yelled through the icy wind to Ravaryn gliding through the air beside her.

'You think that's amazing, just wait for what's next. Hang on!' Ravaryn replied, full of vigour. 'Blaze, up!' The two sped forth together, shooting up to the heavens.

Large, powerful wings beat together, one a set of darkest night and the other a set of shimmering snow, up through the thickly clouded sky to break through the misty grey veil. The sun glittered over the smooth expanse of clouds that billowed out for miles, like farmed fields of glowing cotton. Mazda felt tears prick her eyes and couldn't compare this moment, this beauty, to anything else she had ever experienced in her entire life.

'What do you think, Maz?' Ravaryn took in the view, the crisp morning light illuminating the expanse of smooth clouds around them that glimmered in the day's first rays.

'I think...' Mazda bravely removed a white-knuckled hand from the thick, woven reins attached to Blaze, and wiped at her eyes. 'I think this is the best day of my life.' Her smile was luminescent, her freckled cheeks glowing. 'I'm glad I made the jump,'

'I knew you would. You're a survivor, a tough little gem carved out from the troubles that life has thrown your way. And you're braver than you know,' said Ravaryn gently.

The two hovered in the field of misty clouds, the frozen air cascading around them as the sun rose and lit the sky in front of them. Ravaryn's heart felt fuller than it had in a very long time. He was so proud of his young protégé. She was smart, caring and brave. Mazda would be his successor. She would rule over Kymera one day, and she would be *magnificent*.

The icy air rippled along his dark wings, a sensation he had not felt in nearly fifty years or so. How he had missed this. He had missed the utter freedom of this gift. Just then, a warm spark spiralled into his hand through the onyx ring on his finger, distracting him from the elation of the flight. The swirling black mist within rippled silver and then turned *green*, spinning around into little vines in the tiny sphere. The black ring was a twin to another that he had given away, gifted to a miraculous young woman.

His heart leaped inside his muscled chest as a tingle spread from the spark, warming a trail up his arm and through his body. She needed him... she wanted to *see* him. This time a bellow of triumph exploded from his own throat. Mazda just smiled, assuming his exhilaration was also from the flight into the sparkling clouds.

'Hang on tight, Maz!' Ravaryn boomed, the handsome features of his face lighting up with warmth.

Mazda tucked her body into Blaze as Ravaryn had shown her and held on tightly, wanting to force her eyes shut but holding her composure. She wasn't as afraid as she had first been, and she definitely didn't want to shut her eyes. She wasn't going to miss a thing. 'Blaze, down!'

The pair tucked in their magnificent wings in unison and dropped, spiralling down, the air blasting past them, bodies spinning through the clouds and breaking through into the icy air below.

Ravaryn and Mazda glided back over the top of the glittering sky pines with their small sapphire blooms; these were the large trees that held up the towering city of Zenya. Mazda's cheeks were flushed and the smile never left her young, bright face.

'That was seriously *the best*.' She squeezed Ravaryn hard after dismounting from Blaze atop the ice castle on the edge of the Alvion Sea.

'You're most welcome. You did so well.' He embraced her back, his own face glowing, his immaculate smile widening.

'Maz, I have to go away for a few days. You will be in charge while I'm gone.'

The sixteen-year-old girl raised a quizzical brow. 'Okay, but where are you going?' she asked curiously.

'Never you mind. Just hold the fort and don't let Ilga boss you around while I'm gone.' He winked. 'And don't forget to feed Chester.'

'Fine, don't tell me. I'll find out on my own anyway.' She tossed her glossy fiery curls over her shoulder and glided off with her head raised high, mocking him.

Ravaryn laughed behind her but wasted no time. He strode off after Mazda to gather a few things for his flight. He would get to Zemira as quickly as he could. But he had to make a quick stop first. It was finally time to visit his mother.

A Long-awaited Reunion

In the Black Forest of Aylenta, Diwa Mumasumi shuffled about her cosy little cottage amidst the towering tallowbark pines in the small grove of her gardens. Humming a joyful tune to herself, she dusted and cleaned and plaited the long, spindly roots of the fig tree overtaking her dwelling.

'Just to keep them from dangling in front of the windows, my love,' she said gently to the tree. She plaited and tucked them up and around the window, framing it beautifully.

Diwa then felt a rush of energy course through her body and steadied her hands on the wide sill of the wooden window. Her eyes misted over and she stood still in concentration as the vision overtook her for a moment.

'Ravaryn,' she whispered, after a moment.

'My son. He's coming.' Her wrinkled old hands sweated, and her heart fluttered a little in her chest. She took a breath in and quickly proceeded to her bright kitchen to pick two teacups. Her hands swept forth in front of the old painted shelves containing small mountains of unusual and unique cups.

She settled on a dainty cup with purple mists of flowers and bees, and another lined with faded and chipped gold that had twisting patterns of swirling flying lizards on it. Her hands shook as she tried to steady them. Diwa placed the cups down on the bench and proceeded to sift through her cupboards of strange jarred ingredients, searching for the right ones.

Ravaryn's favourite: raspberry and thistlehorn tea. At least it used to be his favourite, years ago before Kyeitha had banished them both. Cursed them to forever live inside of the old Rim world that no longer was. Before she had murdered his family and—

A hard, sharp knock rattled her front door. Nothing hardly ever fazed Diwa Mumasumi, but she took in a deep, steadying breath. Had he forgiven her? She blinked away a threatening tear and made her way to the misshapen door, her mouth dry and her knobbly old hands sweaty and shaking.

She opened the heavy door with a creak, and there he stood tall as ever, dressed in fine black clothing, his black hair a curly mess as it always was, dangling just above his shining onyx eyes. He didn't look a day over twenty-five.

His gaze shifted down to look at her, his dark eyes unreadable. Mother and son stood unmoving for a long, tense moment. Then Ravaryn's face shifted as if deciding on something.

'Ravaryn...' It came out as a whisper. 'R-Ravrayn I—,' Diwa stuttered.

He bent down and swooped her into a hard, warm hug, squeezing her gently but firmly in his strong arms, nearly disappearing her in his embrace. She smelled of cinnamon, rosemary and of home.

'Mum. I've missed you.' The words floated out gently, with no hate, no resentment, just warmth. Diwa was a very old soul and had honed her composure down to a fine art over the many years of her life. But in that moment, she broke. She squeezed him back fiercely with all her might as the tears brimmed and fell from her ancient, sparkling grey eyes.

'My son.' Her heart ached. 'I've missed you too.'

*

After talking for hours and reconnecting in the cottage's lounge room by the fireplace, Ravaryn and Diwa both felt a small piece of each of them was set right. Diwa apologised and admitted to her guilt about choosing Kyeitha as her apprentice. Ravaryn comforted her and profusely reassured her it was most definitely not her fault. He had never blamed her in any way for what had happened all those years ago.

'She'll be here soon,' said Diwa, staring into her now-empty teacup. The leaves had conjoined and rested on the bottom in a swirling vine laced with large, sharp thorns. 'Hmm.' Diwa's brows furrowed together in worry. 'She is not well, Ravaryn. The mark. I've tried to heal it for so long and all I've been able to do is minimally stop the spread each time. I cannot heal it. I cannot heal her, and I fear that there is a piece of Kyeitha still in there, attached to her. It threatens to destroy her from within. You have to help her. I don't know how much longer she can live like this.'

Diwa's lost look was foreign to her face, which was usually always so sure. So knowing. So confident. The creak of the cottage's door broke the moment and the uncertainty in the air between the them.

Zemira stepped through Diwa's door. Dirty, tear-soaked, dishevelled and an utter mess. Ravaryn's heart leaped in his chest. She was just as beautiful as she had been over a year ago when he'd made her help him destroy the Rim wall. But he hid his elation when he saw her eyes. They were filled with despair. Her collar bones protruded just around the collar of her shirt that hung from her thin frame, and there were dark circles encompassing her deep emerald eyes.

'Zemira. So good to see you again,' he said softly, as if to a frightened animal. His heart fluttered into his throat, and he forced his expression to stay calm, strong, unreadable. But inside there was a twist of worry in his chest, and his fingers begged to thrum.

Diwa left her armchair and quickly shuffled over to the young woman, embracing her in a strong hug. 'My dear, what has happened? Come in, come in and tell me all about it.'

The Sunravens

Diwa Mumasumi crushed Zemira into a warm, fierce hug. It should have comforted Zee but she felt the tension in the air and the slight tremor in Diwa's embrace. Zee's arm zinged with sharp pains. Tears threatened again, but she kept them in. Diwa was clearly worried, and Zee wasn't sure how to deal with this. She couldn't recall a time she'd ever seen Diwa like this as the old woman was always so sure of everything. And as for Ravaryn being *here...* her heart raced at his penetrating gaze over Diwa's shoulder, and their eyes locked. It was so strange to see him here. In Diwa's tiny cottage. In Diwa's and *her* cottage. Well, it *felt* like it was hers as well, after growing up for most of her life in the Black Forest and spending a part of nearly every day here. And he didn't fit. Yet he was Diwa's son after all, so he had every right to be here. So why did she suddenly feel angry? Isn't this what she wanted? Him to come for her? And here he was. *Hell.* Maybe this was a mistake.

Zee's legs nearly buckled as if she was just remembering her body's absolute exhaustion. Ravaryn saw the slight inflection and moved swiftly from his chair, placing the dainty cup upon the kitchen table and coming to stand very closely near the pair. His head brushed the roof, vines ruf-fling his onyx curls.

'Zemira, please sit down before you fall down.' He motioned to a chair and pulled it out for her. The once aqua-painted chair, a heart carved in the centre of the back, looked inviting. Zee didn't protest, she could barely stand. Diwa released her and she just made it to the seat. Ravaryn gripped her thin arms and gently guided her, catching her just as she was about to drop. A warm, tingling sensation shot through Zee's arm. It wasn't painful... it felt warm and strange. The second Ravaryn's large hands released her body, she once again felt sore, tired and empty. How much longer could she handle this?

Zee stared down vacantly at the notches in the ancient wooden table.

'You need tea, dear, and food. And to tell us what has happened,' prompted Diwa.

Ravaryn gracefully moved away and pulled out an opposite chair at the table to seat himself, directly across from her, while Diwa busied her-self in the kitchen.

'Zee, I know you're tired,' Ravaryn very gently coaxed. 'But please, what has happened?'

Where was this kindness, this patience, coming from? She didn't feel like she deserved it. Zee lifted her eyes from the twisted knot in the wood she was focused on and looked into Ravaryn's steady gaze. His ebony eyes were deep and inviting, as they had been that night of the festival the last time she'd seen him, sparkling with their own light through his gold and black jewelled mask. He was too damn handsome, she realised. And she must look a right mess.

Her shoulders suddenly felt even heavier, and a long breath expelled from her hollow chest. 'Kyeitha.'

Ravaryn's posture changed ever so slightly, but Zee caught it. He tensed, his jaw tightening.

'She's still here, somehow inside me. I can hear her speak, in my head.' Zee placed her left hand on the table and looked down at her blackened arm. Her hand rubbed it gently, the beautiful tattoos that matched her opposite wrist of woven swirls and snowflakes were now engulfed in black.

'She somehow she took me over,' Zee choked out. 'And I think she tried to killed Pax.'

A teacup slipped from Diwa's grip and clanged down on the bench, nearly breaking, but only a slight edge of the delicate base cracked away.

'Oh, my dear, how long? How long has this been going on?' Diwa asked, her concern making her silvery eyes huge.

'I-I've heard her for a while.' Zee looked back down at her arm. 'But she's never taken over, not like this. We were collecting raspor's honey this morning, and Paxton fell. I managed to save him. I don't know how I did it but I channelled a strong vine and actually created it from my own hand. It shot forth, and I caught Pax as he was falling. When he got to the bottom, I tried to retract the vine, to withdraw the magic. But the vine wouldn't listen. I then felt horribly sick like I was going to throw up. Then I can't remember. I went to the dark place... the one I've been to before, and I was staring back from metres away on the ground at Pax. His neck was—'

Zee took a steadying breath. 'It was covered in blood, and a black-thorned vine was wrapped around his throat. It was coming from my hand. Tye was there, holding him, protectively, from *me*, and he had my knife. The looks on their faces.' Zee cupped her forehead in her hands as a few tears leaked down her dirty face.

Ravaryn watched her, his expression steady, unreadable, but inside his heart was heavy for her. Diwa came to place a small hand on her back and set down a cup of dark orange tea in front of her.

'Drink, love. It will help with the pain, and your nerves, temporarily.' Her small hand slid from Zee's back and glided down her left arm.

'No, Diwa. Please don't exhaust yourself. I'm okay.'

Diwa ignored her. 'You're most definitely not okay.' She gripped the black mark forcefully with her gnarled but very strong old hand.

Zee grimaced in pain and then felt it leave her. She relaxed and took a deep breath.

Diwa's healing light extracted the pain. A black mist poured out from Zee's skin, revealing her hidden tattooed scars. The mist spun and twisted viciously around itself in the air, a voice accompanying it. 'Withered old hag.' The malevolent hiss filled the air, and Diwa swiftly swiped her other hand through the mist away from Zee and towards the kitchen.

'Oh, shut up, you vain little prude!' Diwa whipped back as the mist spun then sped out the cottage door. 'Miserable moscow!' Diwa scowled.

Zee felt the pain disperse and said, 'Diwa, I don't want you to exhaust yourself anymore. This isn't working. It takes too much from you, and it just comes back.'

'Drink your tea, love. I think you must go with Ravaryn as you don't have much time. He can help, he can guide you and keep you safe through the old outer Rim lands. You need to go to the lake of life at the guardian's temple in Lamiria and immerse yourself in the life-giving waters. The Mother's water. I've seen the two of you there in a vision, and the water will heal you. I'm sorry, but you must return to where you ended Kyeitha. She still hangs on, clinging to your light, draining you, cursing you.'

Ravaryn stayed silent, his jaw clenched. What was he thinking of all this? Did he even want to help? Zemira hated being the one who needed to be 'helped'. But would he drag her across the land and help her drown Kyeitha out for good? Zee couldn't help it as a scowl crept over her face.

'We need to leave as soon as possible.' Ravaryn's serious tone was calm but authoritative. 'It is much worse than you have been letting on, isn't it, Zemira?'

She just eyed him emerald daggers. 'I'm fine,' she snapped back. Realising her harsh tone, she paused and collected herself again, taking a sip of the comforting, warm tea. Zee allowed her mind to try and wrangle the turbulent mess inside of her that Kyeitha was feeding every minute of every day, like a malicious garden of poisonous weeds.

She answered this time, feeling a little more herself. 'I'm just in need of an exorcism, that's all.' Zee even managed a very small twist of her lip, a slight smile and a raised brow. She tried to be light, nonchalant, unaffected. Tried to cover herself in fake bravado, hide behind it.

'Indeed.' The word slid from Ravaryn's mouth like a velvet caress. He crossed his arms in front of his broad chest and leaned back in his chair, and she knew he saw straight through her.

*

Strong arms wrapped around her legs and back, encasing her in a safe yet much too intimate hold. Ravaryn's large wings glided them through the air high above the clouds, and the patchwork of humseed fields below indicated they were nearing Zenya and the ice castle. The wind was frigid and whipped a few stray ebony hairs around her face, but she didn't care. She loved this. Flying. It was like no other feeling she'd ever experienced, except when she flew that time with Orion in his eagle form. And Ravaryn's wings, *actual wings* that were gliding them gently through the streams of air, were unreal.

Flying was lifting her spirits higher than they had been in months. She could barely feel her arm. Diwa's tea and healing powers had given her a little more temporary relief. For how long she didn't know, but she would enjoy this moment before it was taken away from her again.

They had left a teary Diwa at her cottage taking with them a supply of salve and tea. Zee took in a steady breath of the fresh, chilly air as they glided into Kymera's territory. She couldn't believe she'd just left Aylenta like that, in the blink of an eye. What were her parents going to think? And about *who* she'd left with. What would Pax think when he found out? *Shit.* But somehow even coated with guilt, she felt *light.* She felt *free.* Like a beautiful ripened fruit, inside sweet and perfectly fresh, but the outside was covered in spines that buried into skin, stinging and burning.

A shudder shook through Zee's body and not just from the encroaching cold. She was inwardly cringing, imagining her parent's reactions. Would they be distraught? Of course they would be. She knew her mother would be furious as she hated Ravaryn with a vengeance. Her father Orion was going to lose it for sure. But they didn't understand. They thought that she'd been fine, that she'd been managing okay this whole time. It was so very far from the truth. They didn't know. It felt like they didn't even know *her* at all anymore.

I'm not their little girl, their little wolf anymore. And Paxton. She couldn't even let herself picture his face. He would be so cut up, it would damage her more than the look on his face the last time she'd seen him, after Kyeitha. Zee tried to shake the images from her mind. She had to do this. There was no other way. She wouldn't survive much longer if she didn't. Zee knew it deep down in her heart, like something entombed in the warm, damp earth. A lost seed, a feeling. *I have to do this.* But she still felt like a traitor, like she'd run away, and her stomach swirled, unsettled.

Don't fester on it, Zee. Diwa will explain everything to them. Diwa will make them understand, she promised. She'd said that they had to leave straight away, and Zee believed her. She'd been ignoring the situation for too long. Way too long, she'd realised all too late. She couldn't do this alone anymore. She needed help. That feeling didn't sit well, and she felt resentful. But why? Ravaryn's strong jaw and handsome face was stoic as she looked up at him, stealing a glance at his sharp-angled face. He looked ahead, expression calm, steady. They didn't speak. The air pouring over and past them at his powerful speed wouldn't allow words to be heard, not at the moment anyway. He must have been concentrating on getting them there as fast as he could. Or maybe just as far away from Aylenta as quickly as he could before Diwa enlightened everyone to the fact that Zee had left with him.

Zee couldn't believe it. Ravaryn's *speed*. They were nearly there. His arms didn't tremor, his large wings powerfully propelling them forward, not missing a single beat. He hadn't even broken a sweat. And Zee could barely hold her weary head up any longer. Ignoring every instinct that she had telling her not to, she let her head gently drop and rest against his warm chest. She was already cradled in his arms, so how was this any worse? She felt the muscles in his arms and chest tense a little as she leaned into him, softly at first, then when she felt him relax again, she let her weight rest against him fully. She couldn't see it, but it almost *felt* like there must be a smug smile creeping onto his face. Her cheeks heated and her chest felt a little tight around the quickened beat of her misbehaving heart. She was so glad he couldn't see her face from the position they were in. Her head felt heavier and heavier. Moments later she fell asleep. Mental and physical exhaustion finally gripped her entirely in a sharp-taloned grasp. As she slept, she dreamed.

Wisps of light lit the way before her in the form of tiny glowing orbs. They looked like glow beetles luring her into the darkened woods, but as she got closer, their colours blurred and changed into pinks, blues and greens, morphing into mischievous little millowisps. Zee followed them through the darkness around her, the black mist ebbing at the edge of the forest, spinning and twisting as though it were watching her every move.

She heard a sound like the whisper of a stream behind her, and she spun around to see black flowers trailing behind her on the ground in her wake. They grew rapidly and started to reach out for her. One twisted its little dark tendril around her ankle, suddenly digging its thorns into her bare skin there. She kicked away the offending vines but as she looked closer, they grew rapidly. Hundreds of black-thorned vines spread out, shooting towards her, towering more than thrice her height. She turned around on the mossy wet ground and ran, the millowisps now far ahead of her. Her heart ricocheted in her ribcage as she tried to keep up with their light, the darkness getting closer and closer.

Dark mists still spun like smoke on the edge, watching her. She reached the edge of the forest where she had been that morning, and a small patch of the same black blooms now glowed in the moonlight, shining like velvet and overlooking the river below. Zee could hear the crunching of crushed leaves and branches encroaching on her from the forest, and crawling up her arm crept black squid-like ink, soaking into her skin.

The vines were nearly there, and her throat felt tight with tears. Then she took short, sharp breaths and jumped. Instead of the cool, rapid waters racing towards her, she opened her eyes to find she was on the back of a sunraven, its large silken wings shimmering silver in the moonlight. As its powerful wings swept her away through the air, the black seeped from her arm onto the bird's back, staining its feathers like tar.

The feathers fell away like leaves in the autumn breeze, and the creature spun around and snapped at her with sharp silvery teeth. Glowing eyes rimmed with gold locked on hers, and the bird grew and transformed. Zee avoided the beast's maw, and its long wings now looked black, with a thin membrane connecting structured bones. She jumped from the creature's back as her poisoned magic disintegrated it before her eyes. Like ash in the wind after a wildfire, it was lost to the air, and Zee fell... and fell...

Kymera's New Queen

Zenya, Kymera

Zemira had never felt so tired in her entire life. Not even after she'd exhausted every ounce of energy she could muster once she'd slain Kyeitha and saved Orion, her father, from the queen's cruel grasp. Her body ached all over, but it wasn't with the recent endless drum of pain, it was a sore, gentle ache, if there were such a thing. Like she'd run too far through the forest, or hunted for too long without reprieve.

Her eyes opened to stars, a ceiling full of them. Small glowing sparks of light. She blinked once, twice, and then it dawned on her. *I'm in the ice castle. I've been here before.* Zee's hands slid through the silky satin sheets, which felt like petals from the deep violet evernight blooms in Diwa's garden. Zee used to make figurines from all sorts of petals, sticks, flowers, seeds and nuts when she was a child, and the evernight petals where always the best for the little people's deep purple silk dresses and shirts.

Her head compressed further into the cloud-like pillow. *Do I even want to get up? To leave this semi at-ease state?*

She decided she had to. Zemira had to keep on moving, keep on going. What other option was there? To her surprise, she realised she was in the exact same room as last time. There was a plush deep burgundy chair with a small pile of folded black clothes on it. *Mazda*. Recognition burst through her sleepy state. A real smile actually spread over her face, not the 'pleasing' grimace she had learned how to produce over the last year. She felt a tiny trickle of excitement as the last time she was here the young girl had made her the most fabulous outfit she'd ever worn. Zee knew her excitement wasn't just for the clothes though. It was the prospect of seeing Mazda. How much had the girl grown? Now she had something good enough to drag herself out of bed and into a bath for.

Zee's feet hit the soft woven fluff of a luxurious floor mat. She was still in the same clothes, still covered in the same muck, dried blood, tears, dirt. *Blood. Paxton.* An ache blossomed in her chest. Would he ever forgive her? Tears threatened her eyes for she'd done... for just leaving... or for running away, more like it. She couldn't think of him right now. It was time to focus on herself and get this curse out of her. Then maybe she could return and ask him to forgive her.

Realising her boots had been removed and were nowhere to be seen, she walked past the chair in front of the glowing fireplace and over to the colossal window that overlooked the sky-pine city out before her like a masterpiece. The twinkling lights of houses and buildings all clung around the sides of the massive tree trunks, and the pillars of the city glistened. Tiny cable carts glowed from inside like little insects slowly and carefully travelling to other parts of the city on silver wires that intertwined through the expanse of the mecca, like a shimmering spider's web.

After taking in the city and processing the fact that she'd left her home behind her, this time by choice, she craved the warmth and comfort of a bath. It was time to wash away the grime and the guilt. Heading into the bathroom, it was just as she remembered it. Thinking about it now, her last time in the castle felt like a dream, and a lifetime ago. Upon seeing the glistening green and blue metallic mosaic tiles, her heart swelled a little, even more so as she noticed that the bath was full. There were herbs and flowers floating in the water. For her. Diwa's herbs and nasturtiums. Totally uncrushed or broken, the fragile orange and yellow petals floated in the water, petals as perfect as if they were just picked. How on earth did Ravaryn get them into the bath? And how dead tired must she have been to not have heard him? An odd warmth entered her core. For just a moment, her whole body felt more at ease. With a small sigh of relief, she let her shoulders relax.

The bath was heavenly, and the clothes were just as amazing as last time. They fit perfectly and were so comfortable. *How did Mazda do it?* Everything was black except the shirt, which was a soothing grey tone. There was a black jacket with silver metal buttons. Zee was just guessing, no, *hoping* that it must have been Mazda who'd tailored them. She was eager to see her again, with an almost giddy-like excitement. It pushed past the sour tang of pain that had coated her everyday existence for the past year.

Zemira had never had a friend who was a girl. Only Pax. She wondered what she could have possibly missed out on. Hair braiding? Talking about boys? All the things she had no clue about. An uneasy sensation hit her: What if Mazda had changed? What if she wasn't the bright, admiring young girl that she had been last time? Zee shook it off. Her stomach rumbled in protest at being empty, and her long, wet hair dripped down her back as her toes curled and started to feel icy. She zipped up the new boots that accompanied the clothes and the smile spread across her face again. Having never grown up with luxury, she had also never wished or longed for anything material but still appreciated the luxurious outfit for what it was.

Her hands basked in the warmth as she stretched them towards the fireplace paved with smooth black stones, also drying her ebony hair a little more. Her stomach rumbled again. *Okay.* She drew in a settling breath and prepared to leave the room that felt a little too familiar to her now. Her finger found the rough spot on her thumb that she'd scratched away at subconsciously until she realised what a mess she'd made of her skin there.

A slight pinch of panic tingled down her arm as she reached for the door handle. What if it was locked? What if she was still some naïve girl and this all was another trick? Zee gripped the handle and forcefully swung it open, expecting to see someone there. Caden? A guard... anyone? But there was no one, and her chest flooded with relief like a dam pouring its soothing contents through a forest of worry. The whole situation had her out of her comfort zone and on edge. Actually, she'd been on edge ever since she'd realised she shared her body with a parasitic entity that she thought she'd destroyed.

Composing herself best she could, Zee ventured to look for Mazda and Ravaryn. At least she wouldn't be alone in the forests of Lamiria on the trip to the temple. What was the worst that could happen? She headed off into the ice and stone maze in search of them, and in search of some food, her stomach groaning loudly at her like a woverbine.

The halls twisted and turned; some of the pathways led to rooms she thought she remembered and others she didn't. Zee entered another cavernous room with crystal star-lit ceilings and a large window overlooking the black sea. The king was seated, and a wild-haired young woman sped towards her with arms outstretched and a beaming smile that made her bright summer eyes squint and her freckled cheeks bloom. Mazda collided with Zee, squeezing her into a fierce hug. Zee felt a sweeping wave of relief and was instantly happy. She returned the hug gingerly and produced a smile, the effort not evading Ravaryn from the sitting area metres away. But Mazda was definitely something to be joyful about as her glow, her aura, had quadrupled since the first time they had met.

'Mazda, you've grown so much! You're gorgeous.'

Mazda's cheeks bloomed further, giving her a fairy-tale look.

'Zee, how I've missed you. I heard all about everything! What you did! You're so brave, you're... also much too thin!' Her smile dropped as she really took in Zee at arm's length, giving her a quick up-and-down appraisal. 'Woman, don't they have food in Aylenta?'

'Maz,' a deep voice rumbled from the sitting area in front of the window that looked out to the dark sea.

'She's right. I know. I look like shit. You don't have to sugar-coat it,' Zee stated flatly, taking Mazda's side.

Mazda frowned and led Zee to a plush velvety lounge chair, this one a deep midnight-blue.

The sitting area was situated around an ornate wooden table, a stump of a large tree polished to a shine with small claw-like roots holding it up. Its bleached timber looked as though it could have washed upon the shore all the way from Aylenta. There were numerous plates of delicate, delicious-looking morsels of food. Mazda grabbed something from every plate, loaded it high and handed it to Zee.

'Eat!' she commanded, her sharp sky-blue eyes pinpointed on Zee, exaggerating the order.

Ravaryn chuckled from behind her on the adjacent lounge. 'You don't have to be so forceful. You're not a ruler yet, Maz.'

'Practice makes perfect,' Mazda whipped back.

Zee crossed her legs on the luxurious chair and started to down all the little swirls and configurations of different foods. Sweet and savoury mixed together in strange arrangements, not like the food of home, but still comforting.

'Ruler?' Zee questioned, finally looking away from her food and letting her eyes rest on Ravaryn. He sat there at ease – serene, almost happy-looking, in his finery. His loosely buttoned shirt and dark clothing were similar to hers, but he wore simple brown boots. His onyx hair shone under the bright star-lit ceiling and looked almost metallic. Her heart skipped a beat. *Zee, get it together.* She shoved more parcels of food in her mouth and waited for an answer.

'Mazda is my protégé. She is going to take over Kymera's rule when she is of age, and will be queen.' Ravaryn looked at his protégé, his adopted daughter, with such pride. It overflowed, making his silver-speckled black eyes glitter in the light. They were luminous, but not as much as his smile with its straight white teeth, canines slightly elongated when his lip curled into that ravishing, uneven grin. The contrast with his dark eyes made him a sight to behold.

'Queen? Oh, stars. Maz, that's huge!'

Mazda's smile beamed back.

'She's worked hard and will be just what Kymera needs coming into this new era. The Rim has had quite a shakeup in the last year, Zee, and people are afraid. And fear breeds chaos. They need to know there is no danger out there. When you are... better,' his eyes lingered on her arm for just a second, 'the people of the Rim need to hear from you. Some think you're a hero; others think you're a myth. But what you are is a saviour, and they need to know the truth. Some even believe you're a demon that escaped the Mother's grasp. The people need to know that there is nothing to fear. I have reassured them over and over, but my time is coming to an end. I have tread too much of a mistrustful line with rulers of the other territories, and with the people. But what I did to make you break the Rim... I don't regret it at all.' His face was a mask, an unreadable shield, the shield of a ruler, of a king.

A little doubt curdled in Zee's stomach, and she replaced the empty plate back on the polished wooden table.

'I did what I had to do, but I am the bad guy. I am the king who took people.' Ravaryn stared at the plush charcoal carpet. 'I enslaved, I kidnapped, I–'

Zee mulled over his explanation, feeling her own mistrust and roiling clouds of betrayal simmer deep and far away, and then collide somewhere inside her with her own storms of guilt and regret.

'It doesn't matter,' she cut in.

'It matters to the people, and I can no longer be trusted to rule in their eyes. I knew this would come. I anticipated that you may actually be the one to break the curse, to change the world. So I have trained Mazda for years to take over, knowing full well what my actions would do to the image of the king.'

Mazda was quiet. She rubbed intensely away at a silver ring adorned with small vines on her thumb.

'Well, I think you'll make a great queen, Maz.' Zee leaned over and touched Mazda's hand, restricting it from further polishing the ring. 'Trust me,' she said with a wicked smile, 'I've met one before, and you're already loads better than she was.' Zee smiled a little and waited for what she'd just said to register. She got the reaction she wanted. Zee always had a way to tell if people were in need of a small joke, a smile, a distracting comment away from some heavy conversation or feeling.

Mazda's eyes locked on Zemira's, sparkling with laughter and disbelief. 'You're wicked!'

Zee laughed too.

Ravaryn watched her with Mazda, an unreadable expression on his face again, but his king persona was gone for the moment. Good. Zee wasn't so sure about the other part of him that he wielded like a weapon, almost like a shield from his real self. Who was his real self? What was he really like behind all the finery? Behind the charade of being the ruler of the ice territory? And now he had his powers back, was his old self back too? Zee was curious, and even more curious still as to why he had agreed to help her. Why had he come to get her? Why had he answered her miserable call for help on that cliff overlooking the deep water of the Rim river?

The catch-up in the lavish lounge went on for a while until Chester the duellerat busted in through a door, knocking nearly all the plates from the table and sniffing Zee incessantly for a few minutes. 'Chester, anyone would think I'm a long-lost friend.' Zee laughed, pushing him away. He reminded her of Wolf, and she felt a pang of sadness inside her, a deep ache of guilt and homesickness.

'Zemira,' Ravaryn interrupted, 'I know this tea party and catch-up is all very pleasant.' He rolled a large hand in the air. 'And I am thoroughly enjoying it. I wish we could all spend more time together, but I feel like we must leave as soon as you feel up to it.' He eyed the black hand print already creeping out again from her left forearm.

Zee ruffled Chester's white-feathered and furry head in her lap. Her eyes scanned her arm, then locked with the king's dark wells of the unknown. She took in a deep breath, her shoulders slumping a little on her gaunt frame. 'I'm ready whenever you are.'

Thippleberry Salve

Black Forest, Aylenta, one day ago

Tye's strong, freckled hands still gripped Paxton protectively, his large ocean eyes wide with shock. They were made even brighter against the flash of deep red hair hanging just above his smooth brow. What the hell had just happened? Warm blood trickled slowly onto Tye's pant leg, seeping from Pax's neck. His neck was now riddled with strange strangle marks and puncture holes, all leaking the deep red liquid out of his body.

The blade Tye had grabbed from Zee moments ago that had severed the vine, that dark *thing* coming out from her, was dropped next to him while his strong arms found something more important to do: protectively encase Paxton. It was over a year ago now that Tye had seen her, but that was *not* the Zee he remembered. Her eyes – that look on her face – it was like she was possessed. Her entire left arm was black, like a deadened, burned tree branch after a summer wildfire. Black, dark and angry. And she was as scary as all hell. What had been going on since he'd last seen her?

Paxton was panting heavily, sweat now beaded all over his brow. He looked the same as he had when Tye had met him all that time ago in the Borztan mines, just a hell of a lot paler at the moment. Tye had come here to Aylenta on a whim to see his two friends from when Zee had been drawn down into that dark cave of lost souls and found him, *saved* him. But she was not the same person he'd met in what seemed like a short lifetime ago.

There was a momentary flicker in her face and then her whole persona morphed right in front of him. As if she somehow changed back, back to herself, after an internal struggle had been won. Dark rings were clinging underneath her glazed emerald eyes that matched the mid-morning forest around them. Her skin was drained of its usual bronzed colour, and she looked pale, skinny, drawn and almost empty-looking. Tye's heart squeezed a little for her. She looked *sick*.

Zee stared back at both of them in horror, as if she couldn't quite believe what she was seeing. Tye didn't think the look was for the surprise of seeing him there either. His arms instinctively tightened around Paxton's head and upper body to make a safe barrier against whatever that thing was. Just in case Zee changed again. Tye wasn't the same small, scared boy he was years ago when he was first dragged and dumped into the Borztan mines. He wouldn't be the one to let someone get hurt for him, to protect him, ever again. His heart was racing like a raging ice storm, like the blizzards that within a moment's notice could rip through the lower sky-pine villages at the base of Zenya city where he had grown up.

Then like a spooked deer, Zee took off. She leaped up, turned and ran, taking off into the forest behind her. She left them both panting but at least safe from whatever the thing was that had taken her over.

'Pax, talk to me. Are you okay?'

'Tye?' His name rasped from Paxton's coarse, strangled throat, relief flooding into him to hear Pax's voice. He couldn't be too badly injured if he was lucid and could still talk.

'Holy shit...' Tye breathed out. 'What was that thing? What's happened to Zee?' Tye helped Pax to sit up.

How long has that *thing* been Zee for? He had come here to repay a debt he owed to the two most amazing people he'd ever met. But he hadn't thought it was going to be like this. Tye had organised the surprise visit via vision-screen messages to Orion. He'd planned everything, and his parents' proud faces still loomed in his mind from the day he'd departed Zenya city. He had left to travel solo to Aylenta, to surprise Pax and Zee with a visit. But this was most definitely not what he'd had in mind.

'Pax, can you tell me what the hell is going on?' He slid around on the ground to face opposite Pax, giving him a moment to adjust to sitting up. 'But first, I've got to stop your throat from bleeding.' He now had a good look at Paxton's injuries from the blackened vine that had tried to choke the life out of him. Tye dove into his pack for something to stop the rivulets of blood seeping down his friend's neck and darkening the material on his collar. He retrieved a small cloth and some thippleberry salve from his pack, mentally patting himself on the back for always being prepared – the healer coming out in him.

'Take a deep breath,' he warned, and smeared the thick ointment hastily around Pax's throat. The thick, acrid-smelling paste immediately formed a barrier and stifled the bleeding.

Paxton hissed a small breath in. 'Tye, what are doing here?' he croaked.

'I came to visit, to surprise you both. I've been organising it for months, talking to Orion about the whole thing. He said you've been trying to cheer Zee up and thought my visit was a great idea. Now I'm thinking I'm lucky I wasn't a few minutes later. What on Mother's earth just happened?'

'I-I,' Paxton stuttered out a reply, trying to quell the shock, not of what had just happened but the crushed look of utter defeat Zee had given him before she'd bolted away.

She ran.

Pax's heart constricted painfully inside his chest, aching so hard and sharp his breathing was hindered for a second. 'She ran from *me...*'

'Hey.' Tye clicked a finger in front of Pax's face. 'Snap out of it. Take a deep breath and tell me what you remember.'

Pax's confused amber eyes locked on Tye's ocean-blue ones.

'That's it, Pax, just breathe.' *Gods, he's more handsome than I remember, even in this injured state,* Tye thought, patiently waiting for his friend's breathing to steady. The thippleberry salve having done its job, Tye returned it to his pack. He wished he had some more supplies with him, something to take the edge off the pain for Pax.

Paxton started to recall the morning's events to Tye, the raspor's honey story, but he faltered when he started to retell the events that had occurred just moments ago.

'Hey, don't worry, let's get you back to the cottage and treat your neck. I'm sure Zee will be okay. We'll find her. I promise it's going to be alright. We'll find out what's going on, what's wrong with her,' Tye comforted Pax, snapping him out of his morose.

'Hey, all things considered, it's good to see you by the way.' Pax's face lit up for real now, and Tye leaned in to give him a tight hug. 'Good to see you grew into those teeth,' he laughed, even though it hurt his throat.

Pax sat back and took a good look at him, as if just now able to concentrate on Tye, on something real and solid after what had just transpired. 'What do they feed you in Zenya? You've filled out everywhere.'

Tye grinned and helped Paxton to his feet. They realised they were nearly the same height now. Pax's eyes wandered up overhead, and Tye followed his gaze to see what he'd spotted. There was a cloth sack bulging with something and hanging from a few tangled branches high in the boughs of a twisted tallowpine.

'Is that what I think it is?' Tye asked.

'It sure is!' Pax said, rubbing a hand through his dishevelled dark chestnut hair. 'Now, how the hell do we get it down?' Another smile.

He's okay. Relief flooded through Tye's veins like an icy glacial river. He was glad that in some small way he may have gotten to repay a tiny portion of what he owed Pax for taking those beatings for him in the Borztan mines.

The Storm Dome

Phoenix Forest, outskirts of Kymera

The metallic pyre, the metal tower that Zee had been attached to in order to blast a hole through the protection of the Rim wall, was nowhere to be seen. But the shining Borztan bricks remained in an arch, providing an entrance to the outer Rim world now known as 'Phoenix Forest'. The words were written with beautiful sparkling swirls embossed on the top centre of the arch.

Beyond the arch were acres of trees, most just taller than a small dwelling. The blackened earth they were growing from was covered sparsely with some ferns and small vines. It was a new forest, rising up and growing from the once-desolate field where unthinkable and unnecessary pain and death had occurred. Darker vines wove everywhere, twisting and clinging to the small trunks of the new trees, with velvety black blooms shining in the dappled light. These velvety petals shimmered black, looking iridescent with an unearthly beauty.

'What is all this?' Zee's face crinkled in confusion, the sting of what had transpired here, what she had been forced to do, leaving a sour taste on her tongue. Her teeth found that familiar spot on the inside of her cheek to bite down on. More like what had been forcefully taken from her by that slimy scientist, Greymouth. The vision of him in her mind made her mood sour further and her anger flare.

'Phoenix Forest is named after you, Zee. In honour of you destroying the curse and ending Kyeitha's rule, and also for your heroism in saving your father, Orion. Wolf. I thought you would like the name Phoenix. I know what happened the night that you saved your father from *her*. You are brave, you are a true leader, and your power is the green flame of life, of change, of rebirth. You created a new start for everything.' Ravaryn's demeanour was stoic, but his eyes softened as he spoke.

'There have even been a few millowisps spotted, and small tree spirits have moved into the new forest, making it home already, blessing it with their presence. You should be proud of what you did.'

Zee stared curiously at the black blooms on the small vines, ignoring his praise. She didn't know how to feel. His words sat uncomfortably against the walls she had put up around herself, so she changed the conversation. 'What are these? I've never seen them before but they feel... familiar.'

'They are black bloods, or blood blossoms. They grow where there has been a great loss of some sort, great bloodshed. In this case, a loss of lives from both sides. Many of my soldiers fell here. Caden rests here.' Ravaryn's eyes glazed over a little as he tried to keep his composure, his eyes staring out into the sky above the newly emerging forest.

'I'm sorry. I didn't know.'

Ravaryn took a deep breath. 'Yes, he was killed in that battle. Along with many of those tortured creatures that Kyeitha sculpted before you broke her hold on them and they were released from her mind control. They all rest here in the earth, bodies mingling with the soil, their souls finally at peace. But not every soul was so lucky. Many of them retreated and ran, confused and frightened, after you broke her control. The moment they were released, I *felt* it. I knew. I knew that you had somehow ended her. Why did you seek her out? How did you know to slay her? How did you do it?' he pressed, unable to keep the questions from leaving his mouth.

'I didn't mean to,' Zee admitted, her right hand finding its way to rub at her left forearm. The sting was lingering there, steadily humming away. 'I-I went to warn her, to tell her about you, but... she was crazy, she was *terrifying*, and her hate for me was so real I could feel it seeping from her very bones. It coated the air, the whole atmosphere, and it told me to *run*. Then she attacked Orion, furious at him for bringing me to *her* temple. She was suffocating him; she was going to kill him. I couldn't lose him, not again. Then she forced her magic up into my mind, dredging up images, thoughts, feelings and false horrors. Things I'd tried to repress, hide away. Mistakes I'd made, things and people that I had broken by accident.

'Kyeitha was insane, but I somehow was able to imitate her. I mirrored her own magic, used her own powers on herself. And it broke her. She couldn't handle what she had done, who she had destroyed. But *I* could. Because I knew that those things weren't really my fault. But hers *drowned* her. She faltered for a second as she was shocked, dumbstruck by my power and how it could manipulate hers. By what I could actually do. *I* was shocked by what I could do, but rage overtook me and I saw all her fears, everything that had consumed her, and I used it all. All my power ended her from within. I drove my knife right up into her shrivelled heart and burned her alive from the inside.' Zee's pupils were huge, barely containing her rage at reliving the event. Her eyes locked with Ravaryn's, and she saw admiration reflected in them.

'Does that help soothe some of your need for revenge? Some of your anger towards me for taking her demise away from you? Robbing you of the revenge that had driven you on for all that time?' Zee's arms trembled at her side.

'Zemira, I'm not angry at you, or with you. What will be, will be. I was fully prepared to give my life to end Kyeitha. I hadn't even let myself think about living past that. About even having a life after I killed her. I think I'm actually grateful to you. You gave me back my will to live. You gave me a light I haven't seen for a very long time. You're like a torch in the night. A phoenix burning bright in the storm. You didn't just save your father from her that day. You saved me, saved me from giving my life to end hers. Now I'm just happy to be here with you, happy to finally be alive again.' Ravaryn's gaze held hers.

'I will repay you. I will heal you of her, I promise. I know you are strong and can fight this. Don't let her consume you with her poison; this isn't your doing.' Ravaryn's voice was soft as silk as he took Zee's cold hands in his, encasing them in the warmth he exuded.

'Please try to let it go.' A deep breath expelled from Zee's chest. The anger that had seethed there a moment before dissipated. 'There you are, the phoenix of the forest.' Ravaryn's shinning black eyes crinkled at the sides, making his smile even more irresistible.

Zee's heart flickered at his closeness. As his hands encased hers, sparks of energy began to pulse where his skin met hers. She thought he was an odd soul indeed.

They zigzagged their way through the fresh emerging forest, named in honour of Zee. And also in a way of Ravaryn, to honour what he had given up, without really having to admit to it. For he too played a massive part in breaking the curse on himself and Diwa. Maybe some of his old hatred towards her father Orion simmered instead of boiled now. She couldn't be sure, but she felt calmer walking through this place. How did he know just what to say? To ease her own guilt. She wasn't really angry with him – she was just *angry*. Pain could do that to you, making your control on everything looser, blurrier, harder to grasp onto. Things were changing. Her small world was indeed growing, morphing, emerging.

A deep rumble rolled in the sky around them as they left the edge of Phoenix Forest. It connected with the luminescent night forest that Zee had encountered her first time leaving the Rim world.

A loud crack snapped overhead as they travelled on foot, heading deeper into the ancient forest outside the now-destroyed Rim wall. 'We're about to get soaked, I'm going to say, in about five minutes,' Zee predicted, shivering.

'There's an old-world building hidden underground that I had planned on camping in for the night, but I feel we are going to have to change plans,' Ravaryn said as the sky thundered, the light dimming when the dark clouds glided in overhead.

The forest, as if sensing the oncoming cleansing rains, was coming alive and dancing in anticipation around them. The wind swept through the leaves and fallen flowers of every colour, whirling them up in the air like tiny tornados. Zee spread her hands wide, filtering the leaves and petals through her fingers. How she loved the forest. She took in a deep breath of fresh leaf litter and that amazing smell you get just before a storm breaks.

'Zee, we have to keep moving. We've got to make camp before the downpour.'

A gentle smile lit up Zee's face. She hadn't felt so calm and at peace for quite a while but knew it wouldn't last long. Closing her eyes, she took another deep breath and stilled as the air spun and whipped the colours all around her. She was enjoying the slight reprieve from Kyeitha's damning presence and the incessant hum of pain in her arm.

'This way,' she said, after a moment. Zee had sensed a small opening in front of an enormous tree, its roots so ancient and thick that they anchored it deeply into the earth. This tree felt strong, old and safe.

'Here.'

Another giant snap boomed in the sky above them, making her jump. Ravaryn dropped his pack just as large splotches of frigid rain started to pummel down.

'There's no time for the tent,' Zee pointed out. 'I can feel the storm, it's right upon us.'

Crouching down in, she saw that a small grove in front of the old tree was free. As if no other plants dared grow near the giant, dared to invade the forest ruler's space. Large splotches of rain hit the earth around her splayed palms. The smell was heavenly. She closed her eyes, stilled her mind and started her creation. Two perfect rows of willows sprouted from the ground either side of each other and rapidly intertwined, twisting and plaiting into their partners.

A dome of thick interlocking branches weaved around them. Fleshy vines with abundant leaves grew rapidly to cover over the top of the structure: a small cave, alive with the spirit of the forest. The raindrops were speeding up their descent. Sensing that in moments they were going to be drenched, Zee conjured plants on either side of the dome to sprout from the earth and produce large elephant ear-shaped leaves. These were layered over the top of the branches and fleshy-leaved vines. She smiled at the makeshift, hopefully waterproof, den. Zee scrambled in just as the sky opened up with another thunderous boom.

'Get in unless you want to get soaked through,' she yelled out behind her.

Ravaryn crouched his tall frame and almost crawled into the dome. The floor sprouted soft nasturtiums, and their flowers quickly bloomed all around them as Ravaryn seated himself. Then the sky opened up. The rain pounded the dry earth just outside, a metre or so away from them. It sounded heavenly on the leaves above their heads. The roof of the makeshift dome was incredibly watertight.

Zee closed her eyes, making a few final adjustments. A small swarm of glow beetles flew into the dome and roosted themselves in the interwoven roof, like perfect little lights, seeking refuge from the rain. Zee tucked herself up against the back of the dome against the old tree trunk, feeling its calming force behind her. She settled in to enjoy the sound, the smell and the feeling of the storm starting to rage all around them.

Lightning flickered in the darkening forest outside while the storm sang its song, loudly and heavily, but it was also cleansing for the earth, the forest and the air. Ravaryn manoeuvred his huge form into a somewhat comfortable-looking position with a look of awe on his usually stoic face as he took in what Zee had created in literally seconds.

'This is a surprise.' He turned his raised brow and handsome smile towards Zee.

'I'm surprised myself,' she admitted, hands squeezed together in her lap, legs crossed as she stared up at the glow beetles resting in the woven ceiling. 'I wish I had been braver, tried to call on my magic more. Before... before this happened.' She swiped up her sleeve to reveal the menacing-looking black mark from the forest queen. 'I'm so weak and tired all the time now.'

Why was she admitting this to *him*? She must already look like a weak, damaged mess. As if he needed to actually hear it. He probably didn't even care, was just doing this out of guilt and obligation. Gods, she must be akin to the company of an old, withered lake viper.

'Zemira.' Large warm hands slid over her clasped pair, and Zee looked up to see Ravaryn move closer to her. Not so close as to make her feel uncomfortable, but close enough that she could see the small lines that crinkled up around the edges of his dark eyes when he smiled *that* smile. The one that made her stomach flip without her consent.

'It's okay to feel, to feel angry, to feel unjust. You're in an immense amount of pain, you're exhausted and you've been battling on your own for far too long. I *will* help you. I owe you that much. You don't have to do this alone anymore.'

And just like something that had been hanging on by the barest thread, like a sunbird's nest held by a single string, she broke open. Her hard, crusted stone shell fractured a little, cracking her insides open like a geode. Her eyes blurred over with the ever-present threatening tears, and she tore her verdant gaze from his concerned face to stare out at the pouring deluge pounding just metres away from them.

'I hate this. I hate her and I hate what she's making me become,' Zee forced out through gritted teeth. 'I want it to stop and I want her to finally fucking die already.'

'She will,' he soothed, his look turning intense, turning unreadable again. His hands tightened around hers so firmly it almost hurt a little.

'I can't repay you for what you did for me, for the Rim, but I can help you finish her for good this time. Just hang in there, Zee. I know you can do this. I know you can win.'

Another zap of warmth sparked inside her hands as he held them. And she let him, she actually let him hold them there as a dam of emotion trickled out, tears slipping from her emerald eyes and down her pale face.

Ravaryn took one hand and brushed away the tears, his slightly cal-
loused fingers feeling rough and warm against the skin of her cheek. She
looked out to the forest again, not brave enough to meet his gaze this
time. He let go of her hands and face, taking his warmth with him. The
swirling mass of butterflies in her stomach died down to just a flutter, not
a swarm. He slid around to sit quietly and closely up against Zee, their
shoulders touching. Ravaryn leaned a little into her with his arm and
backed up against the tree trunk to look out and watch the storm.

In her peripheral vision she could see his long legs, knees up in front
of him. His arms now rested on them with his hands gently clasped. They
sat together silently after that, breathing in the rain and its energy, the
cooling smell of the forest mingling with the fresh drops. Sitting side by
side, Zee didn't feel as hopeless as she had been these last few months,
hiding from everyone back home. Somehow, she didn't feel as lonely, as
if she'd found the one person who would perhaps understand her pain.
Her curse. Having surrendered to her tears like the storm outside was
cleansing the sky of its own grey clouds, now she felt so damned drained.

Her heart racing, she moved closer towards him. Before she lost her
nerve, Zee let her head rest against his broad shoulder. She didn't see a
reaction, but she did feel his hard muscle tense for a second, just like
when he had flown her all the way nonstop to Zenya, and she'd rested
her head against his chest.

Zee felt the cool swirl of his aura relax against her. His energy was dark
and strong, and there was something else lingering there that she
couldn't quite put her finger on... the same ominous feeling she had
picked up on the first time she'd met him. When she had first seen him
face to face in the castle while she'd rescued her mother. If she reached
out just a tiny bit more, she could have put her finger right on it and
connected with it. But Zee didn't really have the energy or the curiosity to
explore his energy further right now. Ravaryn's shoulder a warm pillow
that her heavy head was nodding off on.

He didn't say a word, and after a while the tears stopped and her heart
calmed down to a respectable pace. She closed her eyes and breathed in,
not the storm's scent but one of her favourites: Ravaryn's earthy pine and

bark scent mingling with the fresh rain outside. And for the moment, the pain in her arm was quiet, and her body and mind were fleetingly peaceful, at rest, and she felt *safe*.

Wolf

Furious had not been enough to describe how he felt. Orion powered rapidly through the undergrowth in his white wolf form, flashes of brown and green blurring together past him as he sprinted. He wanted to expel as much angry energy as possible before returning home to his wife, as he then had to try and somehow placate her when he told her where Zemira had gone. When he told Verena what was truly plaguing and changing her from the bright energy-filled soul they had been gifted with, and *who* she had gone with.

Diwa had gently and calmly explained the situation to Orion when he had come in search of Zee. A few days going by without a word from Zee or Paxton was unlike them. He knew that she and Paxton had gone in search of raspor's honey, but he also knew that it wouldn't have taken more than a day or two for them to return. Diwa had confirmed the fears that he had stubbornly been ignoring: Zemira was sick, she was fading away, and she was *suffering*. She had been suffering right in front of his eyes.

He could sense it now, through their invisible bond. She hadn't been able to hide it from him completely that she was losing the battle. Orion now knew that it was a battle against a curse Kyietha had left her with, and not some other kind of sickness that could easily be cured with herbs or simple magic. Kyeitha's venomous, dying energy had somehow been inflicted upon their daughter, *her* own granddaughter. Her own flesh and blood. How had he been dealt such a hand? He'd had no father present for his entire life, and a mother who had slowly but surely descended into madness. Life was a spinning vortex of unknowns, and there were no explanations for these things, so Orion as always had tried not to think about them. It wouldn't have helped him anyway.

He panted rapidly, his heart hammering inside his large wolf's chest. Orion had run nonstop for hours, expelling his frustration and fury, but he still simmered with anger even now. *Ravaryn*. Why was it that he was always the one right in the middle of it when there was something bad happening? Why had she gone with *him*? *His* little wolf! He had been so preoccupied dealing with his own emotions and grief at losing the baby and caring for Verena that he hadn't seen what was happening to his daughter right in front of his face.

Wolf slowed to a walk, his large snow-white paws a stark contrast to the deep earthen browns of the path, the fresh smell of ferns and leaf litter calming him a little. Their soothing scents caressed his snout as he took in steadying cool breaths of the Black Forest around him. He realised that he'd taken himself subconsciously to their favourite spot: Zee's fishing spot and hidey-hole at the edge of the old Rim river. It was strange not to see the shimmery iridescence of the translucent wall spearing up through the middle of the dark blue and green waters. She was truly a powerful being, his daughter, and his heart swelled at the thought of what power she must truly contain, buried deep within her after being repressed for so long.

Wolf huffed then plonked his muscled body down on top of the steep bank of the ancient river, staring down at the dark swirling waters. When was the last time he had been here with her? Just been present? Enjoyed her company? When was the last time they had just spent time together here? Spent *any* time together? He missed her fiercely and realised how much their life had changed. Orion knew that when he had been cursed by his own mother and stuck in his shifter form that he had actually been truly blessed. He had gotten what not many fathers had the chance to have. He had gotten something that he knew Ravaryn had never gotten the chance to have, thanks to Kyeitha.

A chill ran through him at just how lucky he had been compared to Ravaryn. The strange watcher who could only partially shift, who was shrouded with dark energy and had become the king of a human territory inside the Rim. The king had still fought on after losing his family, his powers, and by Orion's hand, his future queen, Verena.

Yes, things could have been much worse for him, Orion considered. He was indeed fortunate. Orion had not just been able to have a child but one who had turned out to be his best friend, his hunting buddy, his daughter, and so much more. As Wolf, he'd still been able to watch her grow, to learn how to hunt and to secretly experiment a little with her gifts when she thought she was alone. Orion had still had the chance to watch over her, to protect her. His heart ached at the memories, even though he knew she was a grown woman and could do as she wanted now. But to leave with *Ravaryn?* A sharp growl left his maw.

This was truly some kind of sick joke that the Mother was playing on him. Some karma that had been in the background, stalking him and waiting for the perfect time to emerge its ugly head. And *Verena?* Gods, she hated Ravaryn fiercely, but it wasn't for any real reason in particular. She had been chosen, had volunteered for the position of queen all those years ago after meeting the King of Kymera. She had agreed to become his queen when she came of age as she had no parents, both had passed at a young age, no siblings or blood relatives of any kind.

Verena had grown up in share homes and had taken the chance will-ingly to have a different life from what she had been dealt. It wasn't that the king had been *truly* been cruel to her, at least not in the beginning, as she had explained in those early years when they'd first met. After Orion had collided into her balcony in the middle of the most vicious snow storm that he had ever seen in eagle form.

Verena and Ravaryn just had not been a match in any form of the word. They had disagreed on and had opposing opinions about *everything*. Like they had been like trying to get water and oil to mix into one, they just rubbed each other the wrong way. Ravaryn had actually tried hard to make a connection with her. To make it work. At the beginning, before Orion had come along, she admitted that she had tried too, tried but failed miserably.

Then Orion came barrelling into her life, and he had changed everything. He had ignited something inside of her that only he could have. We don't choose the ones we fall in love with. We don't choose our balance. Ravaryn had known then that the only way to eventually break his and Diwa's curse was for a Rim Walker child to be born. And that the child would somehow be the one to break the curse by destroying the Rim wall itself.

Ravaryn had just been under the impression that *he* was the only one who could have made this happen, the only one who could have possibly sired a Rim Walker child. Sure, he'd been pissed when Orion had swooped in and stolen Verena's heart, and literally stolen *her* away. No man in his right mind wouldn't have felt the burn from that rejection and betrayal. But love was love, you couldn't force it, you couldn't coerce it and you couldn't take it. It was what it was.

Orion's heart finally returned to a respectable pace as he realised that the world was the way it was, and what will be will be. He would not take out his anger on his beautiful, strong-willed daughter. If she had just chosen to go with him... to trust in *him*, her father, but she hadn't. So there was nothing in this world that Orion could do to change her mind. She was her mother's daughter. Yet if Ravaryn hurt her again or mistreated her in any way while they were gone, he had already thought of every single way Wolf would rip his throat from his neck and watch the blood pour from within.

Wolf took in a deep, mournful breath. It filled his chest and forced his large emerald eyes to shut tight for a moment. *Gods,* Verena was going to lose it. There was no power in this world that could stop the impending explosion that was going to be Verena when she found out her daughter had left Aylenta with Ravaryn to venture into Lamiria to heal her curse. If *he* felt this much anger, Orion knew it was going to be triple in his wife.

Taking one last look at the mysterious waters of the old Rim river, Wolf stood still. A bright light flashed as he shifted back into his human form, his tattooed scars glowing blue momentarily upon the transition. The wind gentle glided through his silver hair and pushed it back from his face. It was as if the Mother was trying to cool his rage with the smooth caress of a cool breeze. Orion's sharp emerald eyes focused on the river a second longer as he relished all the memories in this place, their special place – Zemira's and Wolf's. He then spun on his heel to return to the cottage on the hill he had built almost twenty years ago for a stolen queen and their Rim Walker child-to-be. Orion just hoped that he could be calm enough for the both of them when he told his wife where Zemira was. A deep rumble left his throat. *Gods, why did I fall for such a fiery woman?* This was not going to be a pleasant day, not in the slightest.

The Grotto

Lamiria

To her embarrassment, Zemira had awakened curled up against Ravaryn's large form, his warm back pressed against her sleep-ridden face. They were both still inside the dome, sleeping inside the nest of soft and edible nasturtiums she had managed to conjure right before the storm. She quietly and carefully pulled herself away from the warmth of Ravaryn's back.

The rain had stopped and the storm had passed. She slipped outside as quietly as she could and headed off into the woods to relieve herself. The woods were still and fresh, and the smell of rain still lingered from the storm. The rain itself had now been absorbed by the thirsty forest floor. Morning sun filtered in through the canopy of trees and sparkled through small illuminated wisps floating gently in the air. This forest was unknown to her but it somehow felt completely familiar. She loved its energy. It calmed her and fed her depleted soul.

Upon returning to the makeshift camp, Ravaryn was awake, packed and ready to move on. 'Good morning, Zemira. I take it you slept well?'

The light in his eyes and the smirk on his face told her he had not been fast asleep. Zee forced herself not to show any sign of discomfort.

'I slept great. What about you, Wings?' As she said it, she realised that she had actually slept well. Maybe the first real sleep her body had had in months. *Interesting.*

'Slept like a baby floxel, and so nice and warm,' he teased.

What a shit. She just smiled back, nonchalant. 'Lucky for me, or you would have been soaked and camping in the rain.'

'Indeed.' His eyebrows raised slightly, looking back at the living tent of foliage she'd created.

His dark eyes with that piercing gaze bored straight into her. How did he look so good after literally just waking up? It was like his hair had a life of its own, and its only job was to stay perfect and make him look damn irresistible. She bet she looked like three-day old carrion.

'Let's get moving. I don't want to waste any time as my arm seems unusually painless for some reason. Well, there's still an un ignorable hum of pain, but it's a lot quieter.'

'As you wish. I'll lead the way.'

And with that, they were moving, leaving the storm den behind and heading further into the forests of Lamiria.

'Why are we taking a different path to the temple? Why not through the gates?' Zee asked.

The gates were a thin mountain pass, like walking through a narrow valley lined with soft moss and walls of rock and ferns, where rock guardians resided in the towering mountains. They watched over and decided whether or not you were worthy to enter into the Mother's lands.

'Because I would prefer not to have a run-in with anyone who may or may not find out that I am taking you into Lamiria to the lake of life. If we travel the way I have planned, we will avoid any... altercations that I would much rather avoid. Wouldn't you agree?'

Ravaryn was talking about Orion for sure. Zee's heart squeezed with guilt inside her chest.

'I also don't want to risk the judgement of the rock guardians. I don't know how they will react to us both now. Seeing that I was banished and cursed, and you... well, you destroyed the last Rim guardian who was their queen.'

'Good point. So what does *your* way entail?'

'You'll love it,' Ravaryn explained, forcing his way through a particularly thick portion of brush. 'It's a lovely stroll through an ancient lava tube, a cave system that will lead us right to the northern fields near the lake. Or if you like, a relaxing boat ride across a misty swamp-like lake.' His voice was sarcastically light.

'Why do I have the feeling that that sounds like a sugar-coated load of shit.'

Ravaryn's laugh boomed in front of her, making her heart race a little. It was such a deep, joyful baritone sound. She hadn't laughed, really laughed, for a long while now.

'How is it, Zemira, that you can read me like a book without even sighting my face?'

'Because I know a bullshitter when I hear one.' A smile crept onto her face. And again, her arm stayed stable with just a steady thrum. How very strange.

As they walked through thicker terrain, they passed old structures and machinery that looked like skeletons in a forest of rusted metal and steel.

'What are these things?' Zee stared at the brown and orange rust-coated remnants.

'Relics from the ancients, old technology long gone with them. They used up all the earth's resources thinking it was making their lives easier. They had transport machines, machines to harvest their food, machines for literally everything you could think of. And they all used the earth's resources as fuel to power their machines and their greed. Oil, trees, wind, even the very water that they needed to drink to survive. In the end, it all ran out and they were left with weapons, fear and finally their own destruction.'

Zee swept her hand over the top of an old metal carcass full of ferns and interwoven with vines. It was barely visible amidst the new growth. The metal was corroded, rough to her touch, and had a sombre energy. A low, distant thrum pulsed from it. The energy felt strange, morphed as if two strange energies were wrapped in a constant battle of who would win. It was like nothing like Zee had ever felt or encountered before.

'There's none of this inside the Rim,' she stated.

'No, there isn't. Not anymore,' Ravaryn trailed off.

As the forest started to thin a little, they reached a bubbling black expanse of boggy marsh, stretching out for what seemed like kilometres in front of them. It was complete with dead trees sparsely clawing upwards through the swampy land, with a swirling grey mist hovering just above the top layer of the opaque molasses-like water.

'So, option A.' A light tone, as if he were actually enjoying considering crossing *that*.

What in the Mother's name would live in there? *Hell, no.* 'Definitely not.'

'What? But you haven't even seen the best part.' Ravaryn bent down to retrieve an orange-sized stone from the ground. Arching his muscular arm, he threw it far out into the swampy depths. A second later, large – no not large, bloody *huge* - eel-like creatures with mouths that resembled leeches sprang from the water, driving viciously up out of the bog with ruffled fins at their sides, just like a water waif's. A shudder rushed through Zee's spine, and a tingle of pain, as she remembered the water waif's claws sinking into her calf muscle.

'*Absolutely* not. Where is option B?' Zee replied, crossing her arms in front of her, her face scrunching with annoyance.

'But you haven't even seen the boa—'

'Nope. Not happening.'

'Alright then.' Ravaryn spun on his heal, theatrically clapping his hands together as if closing off that whole conversation for good.

Good.

The sun hid from them behind a shroud of fast-moving grey clouds as they made their way alongside the blackened boglands. The clouds didn't look ominous, like a storm would break, but as they traipsed on, the wind picked up, whipping long strands of loose hair around her. Zee's arm was starting to pulse as if waking up from a stunned slumber. Diwa's healing and tea must finally have finally worn away.

Great.

They reached a gaping maw of an entrance that trailed down into a cavernous dark hole, as if a huge larkaden had just swallowed the trail all the way into the earth's depths. Zee's stomach lurched. She thought this would look more appealing than the swamp full of hungry eel creatures.

'So, option B,' Ravaryn said, as if almost cheery, slowing to a halt in front of her and staring into the mouth of the ancient landscape.

Great, they had to traverse a dank, musty cave, and she would probably be worse company than those giant lake leeches now that the pain in her arm was returning.

'Oh, come on, it's not as bad as it looks. Trust me.' He winked at her.

'Ha!' Now Zee did truly laugh. 'Trust you! That's a request for a fool!'

'Well, Zemira, you're no fool and are tougher than you look. How is your arm? I can see it's starting to get worse. You look... worn out.'

'It's fine,' she snapped, her laugh disappearing. 'How long till we reach the temple, Wings?'

That smile again. 'A day or two at the most. If we get moving, we can reach the middle of the cave system, rest there and be out and into the meadows to stand before the temple by tomorrow night.'

'Then what are we waiting for? Please, lead the way. That way any other nice creatures that you're not telling me about living in *there* can eat you first. How long has it been since you travelled through here?' she asked the question, not wanting to drag up Ravaryn's painful past, but just to bring to the surface that in the last fifty or so years, a lot can change.

'It'll be fine, Zee, I promise.'

The silence of the cave became oppressive as they reached a narrower passage, and the atmosphere around them darkened rapidly. Ravaryn had a sky-pine seed that he ignited inside a metal wand-like torch. The metal reached up and encircled the ignited seed like a dragon's clawed hand.

Zee used her own green flames of light in her right palm, held out in front of her to light the way. Small creatures scuttled away, their little translucent bodies zigzagging, some with more legs than she cared to count. They came to a particularly tight section and had to squeeze their bodies through, after pushing their packs along in front of them first. More than once, Ravaryn's deep velvety voice spiralled back to check on her, Zee's heart doing that stupid glow beetle flutter every single time she heard her name roll from his lips.

'We're nearly there, Zemirahh. Just a bit further and we'll have reached the middle of the cave system.'

Zee was panting heavily and was now coated in thick dust. It stuck to her exposed damp skin anywhere it could as she squeezed her body through narrow crevices, scraping along every surface of smooth rock. How on the earth was Ravaryn fitting through ahead of her? His impressive form must have been made of liquid!

At last, a dust-caked strong hand reached into the last of the tunnels she was commando-crawling through. Zee grabbed for it, letting his powerful arm pull her right out of the claustrophobic tunnel. His sky-pine lantern was standing up behind him, imbedded in the soft ground of the primeval cave, lighting up her face. She could see the tiny silver specks swimming in his ebony eyes, sparkling at her from this angle. Ravaryn pulled her upright and close to his chest. Even if she had wanted to pull away, she somehow couldn't. He was magnetic. The more time they spent together made it harder for her to keep her walls up. Zee was softening towards him, as if her spirit, without her consent, was trying to fuse with him.

'Look around, Zee, and tell me you're glad you chose option B.'

He was so close she could smell his pine-bark scent mixed with the smell of his clothing. Zee tore away from his intense gaze and looked around. Her eyes adjusted without her bright green flames out in front of them. And she gasped at the beauty before her.

The cave opened up into an enormous clearing that glowed with stalactites of yellows, blues, oranges and greens, all dripping with the clearest water into an underground waterfall. A perfect crystal-clear spring. A turquoise lagoon of colour and light beckoned, and she listened to the water singing a sweet invite.

'This is extremely inviting after the heat, dirt and dust of the small passageways to get here.'

Ravaryn broke her awe-stupor as he started undressing in front of her. Zee's eyes widened in admiration for another reason: His chest was as if someone had sculpted every muscle. His fair skin almost glowed and looked as if it would feel like satin in the light from the cave.

'Come on, Zee, you deserve a rinse off after that.'

Magical white glow beetles flew around sculpted bonsai trees that sprinkled the edge of the perfect lagoon. The small trees were adorned with glowing blooms that illuminated the mystical space. Their blooms hung downwards like grapes on a vine. To think that the land above was poisoned maybe beyond repair, and underneath was this oasis, this paradise.

Zee's eyes roamed over Ravaryn's broad, sculpted chest without any shame, almost curiously. She had only seen a small number of boys or men in various states of undress, and none of them had looked like that. Zee spotted four large purplish puncture wounds that spread up from his right pec and trailed over his shoulder. They weren't fresh but they definitely weren't healed as though years old, unlike a few of the other raised white scars over his torso.

'Are those from the battle at the edge of the Rim?' Zee asked, interested as to how Ravaryn would explain it. Pretty sure already that's what they must be from.

'Yes.' He didn't elaborate, his mind clearly on something else. 'Will you come for a swim with me, Zemirahh?'

With that roll of his tongue, he was always luring her towards him. 'I shall. It's stinking hot in here, and I told you, you can call me Zee,' she retorted, pretending that he didn't affect her at all in the slightest. He just stood there, watching her, messing with her again. 'I'll meet you in there.'

'Are you shy, *Zee?*' His voice was like a velvet caress, and his smile glowed in the magical light of their surrounds, one side higher than the other.

Why was she hesitating? He was decades old, maybe even hundreds of years old. He had probably seen many, many women's bodies. But her heart still raced as she musted her bravery. She had nothing to be ashamed of. Zee stripped off her damp, dusty clothes all the way down to her soft black singlet top and underwear.

'Lead the way, Wings.' She raised an eyebrow, her heart utterly thrumming inside her chest.

His gaze did a once-over, making her stomach light up with the most unusual feeling, as if falling from a height but being caught at the very last moment.

'Your scars, Zee. They're... beautiful. You're a work of art.'

'Pfft.' Zee did an obvious eye roll. She was aware of her muscled legs, her flat, taught belly and too-large breasts that she was always forcing into tight hunting wear. She was skinnier than usual, her body now covered in swirly blackened scars, so she knew she wasn't a beauty. Not like the women in her village or like the girls in the cities with their hair perfectly placed and their faces lightly dusted with makeup to hide their blemishes.

'Do you say that to woo all the women in your life?'

'No. Just the ones I lure into dark caves and convince to come swimming with me.'

Zee's stomach did a little flip. Fear? Excitement? Gods, he was tall, and his eyes were sparkling with something. Mischief. What on Mother's earth was she getting herself into?

Ravaryn took Zee's hand in his own and led her down the winding tracks through the stalactites and into the cave's glowing grotto. Through a small maze of sharp pyres reaching up to waist height, the trail led down to the illuminated lagoon. It was absolutely breathtaking, and the *energy.* Zee could feel it, almost hear it like a drum racing faster and faster around her. This small isolated pocket was *full* of life and very intense vibrations. The ecosystem intensified every connection it must have worked very hard to create, and the humidity in the air made breathing a bit harder.

Ravaryn led her into the cool, shimmering water, which invited them in with the soft trickle of the falls on the other side of the pool. It was so nice to be treated this way. To be led, to be looked out for, even when she was aware that he knew she was extremely capable of looking after herself. Even though she had been prickly, bad tempered and grouchy this entire time, he had been there. Been patient. She felt her power whizzing through her body where Ravaryn's hand touched hers, and it felt absolutely invigorating.

'I'm sorry you lost him,' Zee said suddenly, referring to Caden whose body now lay in the Pheonix Forest. Bravely, Zee reached out towards his scars, the ones cascading over his shoulder, resulting from one of Kyeitha's creatures of the damned. Her finger gently traced along the jagged purple lines.

'Not as beautiful as your scars, are they?' He was so close, and his chest was firm but smooth under her fingers, just as she had guessed.

'I wouldn't exactly call my scars beautiful,' Zee said pulling away, her eyes looking down at her arms as her hands trailed gently over the top of the crystal water.

'They are truly lovely, Zee. I wonder if there's anything you've ever touched that hasn't become more beautiful by just being in your presence.'

Zee smiled at that. She was flattered, even though it was just sweet talk. 'Well, I did just touch you and, nope, nothing. Exactly the same. That face of yours, there's no helping it.' Her smile was wicked.

Ravaryn's deep laugh barrelled out. His eyes sparkled at hers, loving her sarcasm. Nature always found a way to overcome pain and heal Zee. For a moment, she felt a little bit like herself, even though she wasn't the same person that she was a year ago. She wasn't even the same person she was yesterday. Maybe this new version of her that was forming wouldn't be all that bad. Maybe the new Zee could learn to let her walls down just a bit.

Ravaryn followed her gaze as she looked down at her arm. 'No matter how darkened the exterior can become,' his voice was smooth and deep, his long fingers encasing her blackened arm, 'there is always light contained within. Like I said, you are a phoenix in the storm. Nothing, *nothing* in this life can dull your shine. You will rise again from this.'

It was as if he knew exactly what she was thinking, exactly what to say. Ravaryn drew so near that the silver specks seemed like little stars cascading across his midnight eyes. His hand slipped from her arm and moved slowly up through Zee's tangled hair to cradle the back of her neck. He tilted her face up to meet his with his other hand on her delicate chin.

Zee's heart was pounding against her chest, and resisting the urge to take quicker breaths just made it worse. He was so intense. She tried to peel away from that penetrating gaze, but she couldn't. No one was there, so she could make any choice she wanted. She could do whatever she liked, and deep down a little spark ignited inside her with a resounding *yes*.

He tilted her chin higher ever so gently, the warmth spreading, tingling on her cheek from where his hand touched the once-bronzed but now pale skin of her face. Her eyes met his again, but this time she didn't feel overwhelmed. A pulsing of want, a rhythm deep down inside of her, spread throughout her core. Ravaryn leaned down to meet her face, searching her eyes for a moment as if to ask permission, and they must have said yes. They probably pleaded in that moment *yes*.

He lowered his lashes as he gently brushed his warm, soft lips against hers, kissing her as if she were the most delicate thing he had ever held in his life. Her soft, full lips met his for the first time, and his hand grasped her hair as the kiss, the pull towards each other, deepened. He left her breathless when he finally pulled away to see her face again, to read her reaction. A rush of desire replaced the warmth that had filled her seconds ago.

'There she is,' he breathed. 'There's that powerful, gorgeous woman I first met.'

Zee felt her eyes glaze over. It was too much. It was too much of a reprieve from the life she'd been struggling to lead. Yet she knew in this moment that there was an intense energy, a connection, between them. As if they were somehow drawn to one another, no matter what the strange occurrences that had brought them together. Ravaryn knew her pain, as he himself had known deep pain and survived, surfacing on the other side of it. His body was pressed into hers as he gazed down at her, longing filling his features.

There couldn't be a more perfect moment. Pure happiness warmed her entire body and calmed her all at once. Just as she leaned a little closer, being braver, wanting more, she felt a flutter in her stomach. A blue light glowed bright between them, lighting their features from below. Her necklace. The stomach flutter deepened this time, and *not* in a good way. It morphed as something sinister swirled deep inside, and her smile faded.

'I- I don't feel so well...' Her eyebrows drew together, raising in the centre as her face contorted in pain. A second later, her arm was sparking with fury. She gritted her teeth and tried not to let out a moan of agony.

Ravaryn's gaze turned from elation to concern. 'Zee! Zee, what is it? What's wrong?' He gently gripped her shoulders, holding her as if she might faint.

His eyes were pinned on her face as she was pushed away from inside herself, forced away from the present. *NO! Not again!* were her last thoughts as she was flung into that dark place, the one she had been to before.

Before Ravaryn's panicked gaze, Zee's emerald eyes swirled to match the blue of the water around them, smattered with tiny silver specks. Black crept all the way from her forearm up her shoulder and spread like rotted roots to the base of her neck still supported in Ravaryn's hand. She was still in his arms, her body going slack for a single moment, then a sinister snarl crept across her face, a look that was foreign to her features. A look that didn't belong.

'Hello, Ravaryn, the half-breed watcher. Did you miss me?' The hissed words slid from Zee's mouth, upper lip curling over the predatory grin. They were followed by a bubbling laugh that burst from her mouth like a swarm of locusts, fouling the energy and air around them.

Kyeitha.

Dark Alleys

Aylenta

'That's it! Just a little further and you've got it, Tye!' Paxton yelled as Tye snaked along the thinning branch high up in the tallowpine, holding on for what looked like dear life. As he inched closer to the hanging sack filled with the raspor's honey, his body shook with the effort.

'Little bit more. You've got this,' Pax reassured. He had wanted to go himself but Tye had insisted that he had to rest as he was already injured.

'Got it!' Tye's wide grin beamed with pride, just as his whole body shifted and he dropped the bag.

Pax shot forward, skidding on the forest floor just in time to catch the bounty before it hit the earth and shattered the precious contents.

'Nice work,' Pax called out. 'Now slowly inch back towards the trunk.'

Tye not only looked like a forest sloth, he now moved at the same speed. Pax had to hold in his laughs with deep breaths as he watched his friend struggle, but eventually Tye made his way back to the trunk and back down to the forest floor. Pax gave him a hearty slap on the back.

The pair decided to check Diwa's first, as her cottage was the closest to their location and most likely the first place Zee would have gone, Pax hoped. He had never seen that fear in her eyes before. It was a gut-wrenching look that made Paxton's stomach clench with concern. Besides, they needed to let Diwa know what had happened. She was clearly the expert on all weird magical stuff, it seemed. Surely, she would know how to help Zee.

When they arrived in Diwa's hollow full of flowering gardens, the old woman was outside in the midday filtered sun. She was standing in the centre of the grove between her cottage and the entrance to the track, staring up at the sky. Diwa didn't turn around as the young men approached, but before they could announce their presence so as not to startle the old woman, she beat them to it.

'So wonderful to see you both.' Diwa spun and greeted them with her glowing grin and crinkly, sparkling eyes. She held out her arms and squeezed Paxton as he bent almost in half to receive her warm hug. 'And you dear must be Tyson Bramble!' She grasped him into a similar tight squeeze as his eyes widened.

'Yes, ma'am.'

'Ha! No ma'ams here. No lambs either for that matter! Would you two strapping lads like to come inside for tea?' Diwa did her crazy lady cackle while she held Tye at arm's length, taking in his features with her silver-specked eyes.

Paxton's insides instantly relaxed a little, and Tye laughed at her strange comment, a little uncomfortable with Diwa assessing his face so closely.

'We'd love to, Diwa,' Pax said. 'Is Zee-is she here?' His eyes were hopeful but his smile had faded.

'No, love,' she said simply. 'Now come inside and show me the spoils! I see you found the treasure stash that the raspors keep, not too deep!' she sing-songed.

Pax almost did a famous Zemira eye roll, and a small smile returned to his face. He knew that Diwa was aware something was up with Zee. Gods, he loved the old beetlenut. He knew that he would find out shortly – when Diwa was ready to tell him.

Tye's eyebrows connected in utter confusion, but he just followed the pair into the magical little cottage in the colourful grove. He was in absolute awe, having never seen so many strange plants: the shapes, the colours, the odd fruit hanging heavy on some of the vines. He had also never had raspor's honey before, and apart from being worried about Zee and her state, he was happier than he had been for months. The hard work and savings he had scrimped away was worth every second to finally see Aylenta, but not just Aylenta.

Tye admired Pax as he followed the strange Diwa along the track to the crooked, old timber door. Pax's unruly chestnut hair was tucked into a messy knot, shorter than it was when they had met in the mines. His strong muscled back would now have been fully healed from the horror he had endured. Tye wondered how the scars looked now. Had they faded? Did they leave a raised ridge that would forever stay with him? The deep tan of his skin shone in the dappled light of the forest. He moved with such athletic grace. Pax was always so sure of himself. So confident. Yes, it was definitely worth it, Tye smiled to himself as he followed them into the strange cottage enveloped almost entirely by an enormous fig tree's roots.

Sovereign City, Thorta

The young man's skull had made a delicious sound upon hitting the concrete wall in the dank alley, and the cracking was like a watermelon bursting open. Thaylon's huge hands bunched in the man's jacket and brought the now-still body up to his face. He looked closely at the worker's empty eyes and felt no remorse as he dropped the lifeless young man into a filthy puddle. Floating debris sprayed out as his body hit the ground heavily.

The incessant rain that had plagued Thaylon since reaching Thorta city had not ceased in days. He blinked away more drops as they poured down from above, soaking his sandy hair, now dark and slicked to his head, accentuating his hooded eyes and making him appear even more terrifying in the scarce light of the dark alley. A street lamp fuelled by the city's lighting supplies flickered intermittently at the entrance to the narrow alley between towering concrete buildings in the worker's district. The dilapidated half-crumbling buildings would be better than sleeping under a damp and cold bridge again.

Thaylon had promised himself to make haste to reach the western side of the Rim wall after indulging in a bit of freedom in Thorta's darkened alleys and danker parts of the city. He wanted to be in the far-west of Aylenta as soon as possible. And put as much distance between himself and the radiation wastes as he could. He was planning to draw little if no attention to himself or to make a trail of any sort that could easily be followed. This miserable city could go fuck itself.

He bent down and took a set of keys from the soaked body before him. Thaylon had been watching the man when he had left his small apartment on the bottom floor of the crumbling building. On his way to the night shift in the factories or lighting conversion works, he presumed. He was sick of being wet and cold and hungry. These little parasites were everywhere in this city. Humans. Thaylon's scowl scrunched his whole face, showing perfect teeth through his sneer. He pocketed the keys and proceeded to drag the body with one strong hand along the festering alley of rubbish, debris and scattering rats, dumping him behind a large pile of household waste.

He was contemplating taking an arm, a leg... or an ear. But thought against leaving a clear symbol that he had been there. Besides, the man was sure to have some foul form of human food in his apartment. He thought about all he had endured and the filth he was given to eat while under guard and slaving away at the edge of the Rim near the radiation fields. Anger ripped through his temples at the image of who had banished him to work alongside these lower life forms. *Fuck it.*

Thaylon kneeled down and withdrew a knife from his jacket pocket, deciding to give himself just a small treat. He roughly sawed away, making quick work of slicing a thick sliver of arm from the deceased worker, his blood mingling in the rainwater pouring down on the rubbish pile. The big man smiled to himself and chewed away at the raw delicacy he now delighted in. He didn't even bother to look back as he strolled from the alley and turned to retrace his steps from where he had followed the man just minutes before.

Fitting the small key into the crusty doorknob lock, he swung the door open and bent down to enter the small apartment. *Finally, a dry sleep,* he thought smugly to himself. *Why did I wait this long to take what I already deserve? I'll have to travel this way through the rest of the Rim. I deserve a little comfort after so many years without fresh delicacies such as this.* He took a long breath in through his nose as he held the piece of the worker's arm flesh to it, still dripping with watery blood but now free of the rain. *Hmm, why worry? Who's going to stop me? And by the time I reach him, there won't be a soul on the earth that can touch me.* A deep, gravelly laugh rose from his throat then he tore at the strip of human flesh he held in his hands, all perfect teeth now a dark shade of red. Thaylon didn't even bother to wipe the excess liquid from his mouth as he proceeded to investigate the rest of the apartment he had earned himself for the night.

Kyeitha's Threat

Lamiria

Ravaryn shook with rage. He had dreamed of slaying Kyeitha painfully and slowly for what she had done to him, his wife and his babe for *years*. But his heart had finally thawed. Thawed for the one in his arms, now possessed by that witch's darkness. His body tensed and his eyes almost bled black with the effort of restraining his dark magic, which Zemira had yet to witness. He wouldn't let it out; Ravaryn wouldn't risk hurting her, hurting anyone with it ever again. Not even for revenge, not even for Kyeitha. Zemira was too precious.

'What do you want?' he spat, his hand still behind Zee's head, not supporting it now but firmly holding a handful of hair to keep Zee/Kyeitha still so the former guardian couldn't do anything to harm Zemira's body while she was possessing it. The panic bubbled in his throat, mixing with revulsion and *hate*. His face slipped seamlessly into the mask he wore so well. He had learned from a young age and had perfected it, using it for years when he had become king inside the prison of the Rim world.

'Ravaryn, I thought you'd be overjoyed when you finally got your chance to see me again. Am I not what you were expecting? Well, neither is she.' Kyeitha's words slid like oil from Zee's rosebud mouth.

Mere seconds ago, he had finally had the chance to revel in the sweet warmth of her lips, which were now cold. A sour tang burned in its place. 'Whatever you think you're doing, you *won't* succeed,' Ravaryn bit out, his teeth almost cracking with the pressure to stay calm. 'She's too strong, and twice the elemental you ever were.'

He saw a flicker in Zee's face, a twitch. Kyeitha was losing control. She must have sensed her possession was fading. The amount of power it must have taken from Zee for Kyeitha to do this, to possess her, filled him with concern. Zee's face was already so drawn, and she was losing her battle with the pain every day. They had to reach the lake of life, and fast.

Kyeitha forced her eyes shut for a second as if keeping Zee out for just a moment more. 'She isn't Liara, Ravaryn,' she hissed. 'She may look just like her, her reincarnation almost, don't you think? But Liara is dead. Gone. And Zemira, this *girl*, she will never choose you once she knows what you are!'

Ravaryn's grip tightened painfully around the fist of hair he held, pulling her head back. A torturous laugh seeped from Zee's mouth. 'Go back to hell where you belong, you monster.'

Ravaryn's eyes burned, and his wings involuntarily sprouted. A dark mist poured from his skin from every cell holding in the fury that swelled around them both. The blue glow of the oasis waterfall and Zee's necklace was drowned out around them by his black rage.

Kyeitha laughed louder. 'I'll see you there, *demon*.'

Ravaryn growled, and he was absolutely menacing in the light of the cave's glow.

Kyeitha's words slid towards him like spider silk weaving in the air...

'Hair as dark as a raven's flight

Eyes that mirror the forest's light
Her hand will not be yours to take
The decision will remain hers to make
Demons will bark
Women will fall
And Zemira will be the key to it all.'

'What are you talking about!' Ravaryn roared.

Kyeitha's smile of satisfaction poured over Zee's features. Her eyes flickered green for an instant, swirling into the blue of Kyeitha's momentary possession. Just as the former queen relinquished her last hold over Zee's body, she whispered in a sweet voice that dripped with venom, 'Ask... your.... mother.'

Her eyes shut, and Zee's body went slack. Ravaryn's dark magic swelled around them, cocooning the pair.

'Zee!' Ravaryn shook her gently. 'Zee, can you hear me?'

The blackened veins crept back away from Zee's neck as if recoiling back into themselves, and the darkness withdrew into her left forearm. But she was unmoving. Ravaryn flew Zee's body from the water, placing her onto the smooth rock shore. There she lay, immobile, her necklace once again becoming dull. She was sunken. Drained. Almost lifeless. Over and over, Ravaryn frantically called for her to wake up.

*

Hands were held out in front of Zee's eyes, palms up. They were grey, and her head was light. Her body felt like it could float away on the breeze like a dandelion seed. A sweet smile of release spread on her face. She tilted her head back and breathed in a deep mossy earthen breath. The pain was *gone*. It was gone! Tears escaped her eyes, and Zemira relished the moment. She connected to the earth with every fibre of her being, her body finally feeling alive again.

After moments of floating, of just being appreciative for every second of freedom, Zee broke free of her trance and looked around. There was no sun, but she knew this place. She had been here before. No fear or anxiety could get to her here. Zee remembered the first time she'd visited this place in her spirit, just after the explosion in her village. Until she'd awakened in that hospital-like facility in Thorta.

Zee started to wander. The sun definitely wasn't in view, but there was no mist as such to block it, just a cloudy grey sheen overhead. There were strange vines interweaved all over the smooth pebbled ground. Unaware, a trail of blood blooms sprouted, unfurling dark flowers in her wake a she meandered peacefully through the still, dull land. She wandered until she reached huge ferns covering the sides of the trail, as large as any tallowpine from the forests back home. They made her feel miniscule, like a glow beetle flittering about in the dusk. Even bigger than the ferns, further ahead of her down the track, were mushrooms towering high above her head. They glowed a strange luminous pink. She held her hand out in front of her and summoned a small glowing flame with little effort with the same ease that she'd had before she was cursed.

Zee's whole life had been a guessing game with no real guidance. There was support and love, but secrets. And many, many things that had been kept from her. Withheld.

Unworthy a voice whispered. *Unwanted.*

No! Zee spun around but there was no one there. Blood blooms blossomed the size of her head behind her on the trail, growing larger and larger. She turned around to proceed back in the same direction as she was unsettled by the blooms' eerie black sheen. But Zee stopped abruptly as a woman now stood right where she had been, as if she materialised from the thick grey air around them. Zemira nearly walked straight into her as they stood eye to eye.

'Who are you?' Zee questioned brusquely, startled, yet not afraid. But also not entirely trusting of the stranger in this place she had only visited a handful of times.

'I'm a friend, my dear, so there's no need for you to worry. I've known you longer than you have known yourself.' The stranger emitted a kind smile.

Zee took her in. The woman had actual vines growing on her skin, and her hair was long stands of the finest little-leaved plants. Small ears like that of a fox poked out of the woven strands and twitched gently.

Her feet were bare, just peeking out from the velvet green of her mossy gown. They were paws, fur and claws, not human toes that peeked from under the fabric.

'I'm sorry, I don't think I know you. W-what are you?'

Her face was somehow familiar, but like nothing Zee had ever seen. The woman's eyes were deer-like and small, laced with beautiful long eye-lashes. Intricate antlers curved out from her woven-vine hair, littered with tiny pink and white blossoms. Zee couldn't be sure if the antlers were of bone or wood.

Her skin was a pale sage green, and her high, delicate cheekbones were littered with specks of glitter, almost as if the actual stars resided within her. Her aura shone around her like the first light of a fresh winter's day, clean, crisp and brilliant. The peculiar woman held out a hand, one similar to Zee's. Human, but not. Long, slender fingers entwined with Zemira's.

'Walk with me, my child,' the ethereal being gently coaxed.

There was an energy pouring from her that Zee could almost taste, like fresh meadows just after a summer's rain, clouds beckoning to burst. Zee tasted the sweetness of ripened fruit on her tongue. She didn't even second-guess the luminous creature, just took her hand and floated away with her down the track through the dark places, through the twists and turns.

Zemira felt light, at peace. If she had a choice to stay with this calm, light-filled woman, or return to the real world and be riddled with relent-less, excruciating pain, she would probably choose the former. She was *so* done with the latter... *so done.*

The Dark Rim

The Dark Rim, outskirts of Lamiria

The ominous grey mist hanging heavily in the air signified it was at least an hour past day break, although she hadn't seen the sun for years now through the heavy ever-present fog. But she had learned what each varying degree of light meant throughout the day. Sayde pounded the thick slate powder from the clay rocks inside a carved-out grove in a large boulder close to the entrance of the cavern some of the outcasts shared. Her dark vibrant eyes of the earth matched nothing here. This landscape had been drained of nearly all the rich colour of her home. She added a small amount of water into the well of finely crushed powder, creating a smooth paste. Her long, slender-yet-calloused hands scooped out copious amounts of the grey paste.

Sayde proceeded to cover her face and the exposed parts of her body with the clay mixture. When she was done, her luminous earthen eyes burst forward with a golden sheen, all the more visible due to the dulling of her body. She looked powerful and imposing. Her petite mouth stayed shut in their ever-present firm line, and her aristocratic nose inhaled even breaths. Today would be like any other. She smoothed back her pine-bark hair and secured its lengths out of the way with her nimble fingers. *We will make it to the black mouth, retrieve the catch and travel back safely. We will survive.* Sayde repeated the mantra to herself, like she had for years, as every time the retrieval would rest on her shoulders.

She grabbed the netted bag to carry the catch back with, rolled it up carefully and placed it inside her worn rucksack. Grey. Everything here was grey. Leeched of life. From the craggy hole-filled cliffs to the mist that never dissipated. The blackened sea and sands of midnight you'd think would be a nice break from the blandness. But no. Their eerie aura was enough to put anyone on edge. The sea's angry swell pounded viciously on the black beach.

The only light in her lifeless world was Noah. Every morning, his deep blue eyes were all Sayde looked forward to. He was like looking at a little piece of home, where the sky would bloom a luminous bright blue above her forest village back home. Noah's eyes made her heart ache. He also made her head ache at times with frustration, but mostly her heart. He was so boyishly handsome. So full of kindness and patience. How the time in the Dark Rim hadn't affected him, Sayde had no clue. He was tough. Made of something stronger than this place.

'Sayde, have I ever told you that grey is your colour?'

She looked up from where she sat at the entrance of the outcast's cave, barely containing the roll of her eyes.

'Yes Noah, just like every damn day.' Her face was unamused.

'Well, you look luminous all the same.'

A smile teased the corners of her petite mouth. Sayde drank in the summer sky of his eyes, and her heart raced. Noah was coated in the clay to mask his scent as well. Everyone who made the trek to retrieve the catch from the black mouth covered themselves the best they could. This way, they couldn't be scented and would hopefully make it back safely. Or make it back at all.

'You ready or what? Let's get this over with. I feel like a storm is brewing and want to get back before nightfall. I have a strange feeling about the trek today,' Sayde said.

'You always have a strange feeling about the trek.'

'No I don't. This is different. This is... I can't put my finger on it but I don't like it. So let's get this over with.'

Noah rubbed the back of his neck with his large palm, tilting his head down at Sayde. 'It'll be fine.' His gorgeous slightly crooked smile peeked out from the grey mask that was his face. 'Hey, we might even see the sea shiners today from the peak.'

'I swear you could make anything sound fun. Even the potentially life-threatening trek to haul back a catch of dunefish up the cliff and back to the cave. All without being tracked or scented by... you know what.'

'Oh, come on Sayde, my lady. Any day we're alive is a day to have fun.'

'Don't call me that!' Sayde swung her arm out playfully at him.

Noah twisted his tall, thin frame out of her line of fire. 'Okay, okay,' he soothed, hands raised, eyes crinkling. 'Whoa, down girl.'

Gods, he was infuriating. Lucky she loved him. From his annoyingly cheeky smile to his dreadlocked blond lengths of hair. Well, blond, when they weren't encased in grey. Which was rarely. To the way his eyes glowed when he gave her that look. When he knew he had annoyed her enough to forget that they were both stuck here. Imprisoned here.

Noah and Sayde had been outcast from Lamiria and their homes. Punished for ridiculous reasons by a mad queen who had lost her mushrooms decades ago. Sayde lifted her thin, wiry body from the stone in front of her. Years of minimal food had worn on them all. The outcasts. While she was still young, in a sense, her body could handle the strain. But her heart was growing heavier, even with Noah's light around to keep her sane

'Come on, Sayde, my lady.' Noah offered her a hand up, his voice gentler, less teasing and filled with care. He pulled her slight body up to meet him and searched her weary eyes.

'It'll be fine.' He lost himself in her russet gaze and squeezed her tightly. 'Remember, we make our own light.'

'A day with you in the Dark Rim is worth a lifetime free of it without you.' Sayde's eyes shined over. Noah. Her Noah.

He cupped her slender, ravishing face in his hands. She was even stunning when coated in the grey goop. Noah kissed her hard like he did every time they were about to make the trek. Like it was their last moment. Their last day together.

Sayde took a deep breath as her heart hammered in her chest. She forced her eyes to withhold the tears threatening there. She couldn't break the clay's smooth mask. She couldn't break... or she would never come back if she let it all out, if the tsunami of emotion was set free. Her rough hands squeezed Noah's muscled arms as she snuggled into his warmth. 'I know.' She forced a smile.

The wind whirled around them on the top of the crumbling cliffs as they carefully scaled down to the blackened stretch of beach being pummelled by the waves surging from the dark ocean. The mist still hovered, clinging in thick clumps around them and giving only a partial view of the landscape below. Sayde hated the descent. Small, furry spider-like creatures lived in these cliff holes. Crack creepers. The creepers loved to dart out at the absolute worst times, just as Sayde would be preparing to adjust her hold or lower herself using one hand's strength. A creeper would scurry its legs over her hand, sending a curl of revulsion up her spine. Causing her teeth to grit and her body to tense with the effort of holding on to the cliff's edge. Noah, as always, thought this was hilarious.

'They're harmless, Sayde. We're the ones using their homes for footholds.'

'They're disgustingly creepy! Foul little things,' she hissed into a hole right near her face, causing Noah to laugh out loud, throwing his head back.

'Shh, Noah, be more serious! That thing is out there.' Sayde's eyes smouldered.

Two sets of boot prints adorned the glistening black sand of the stretch of beach between Sayde and Noah's clan's cave and the black mouth. As they approached the mouth, Sayde's anxiety was thick in her throat, her nerves stinging. Her whole body was wired and on edge.

'We're nearly there,' Noah comforted, finding her grey-encrusted hand and gently squeezing it for reassurance and to share some of his warmth and strength with her.

Where he got it from? She had no idea. But she was glad that he shared it with her. He shared everything with her. If it weren't for Noah, Sayde wasn't sure she would have had it in her to keep going. To keep surviving in the Dark Rim. He was like a sunflower growing on a battle-field after a vicious war. One thing to hold onto. To keep safe. To love.

Sayde locked eyes with Noah as they reached it, the black mouth, where the caves and ocean met. They climbed up over sharp rocks that were almost like jagged teeth protecting the small circle of water inside the dark cave's mouth, a hidden grotto just up from the roar of the sea. The air around them stilled as they entered the opening. The atmosphere was instantly quieter here, and they were safer for now inside the cave system. They had reached their halfway point and were at least not out in the open. Sayde felt the jitters in her chest momentarily ease. She still had a disturbing feeling about the day, but for now at least they couldn't be spotted.

Sayde and Noah had reached the pebbled beach area at the back of the narrow cave, where the calmer water inside the deep pocket was still ominously black but at least it was calm. And eerily quiet. Together, they hauled the large nets in from the lagoon, a breeding area for dunefish that had always, thank the Mother, given them food. Today was no different.

Sayde struggled with her side of the larger net woven from the strong grass that grew sparsely near the caves they now lived in. The writhing bodies of the dunefish thrashed around in the net. They had long, thick bodies like that of eel, with fins littered randomly all over their charcoal lengths and golden underbellies, a mix of onyx and gold sliding in and around each other. They were almost beautiful. Almost, but not quite.

'It's a good haul today!' Noah beamed, struggling with the net. He started to slit throats, then Sayde took the dunefish and gutted them, keeping the innards to use again for more bait. Sayde and Noah were a solid team, not even needing to speak or communicate what the other wanted as they had done this many times before. They worked in unison, completing the task as fast as they could. But Sayde still couldn't brush away the ominous tingle low in her gut. Something was amiss, even more so than usual inside the Dark Rim. There hadn't been any sign of the creature that plagued their lives inside this prison they had all been unfairly outcast into. Unfairly was the understatement of the century.

'Alright Sayde, my lady. You ready?' Noah swung an arm out theatrically. His handsome smile added to his charm. He was truly gorgeous to look at, even in the mud mask. His tall, wiry, muscular frame that had once seen a bit more bulk was still extremely attractive. The Dark Rim hadn't sucked his soul out of him like it had for countless others. No, Sayde and Noah were survivors, they were a team. And they would make it out of this hellhole one day, together.

Sayde couldn't help the small smile that spread on wind-cracked lips, the grey mask slightly fracturing into small lines around her deep bronze eyes, wide as a newborn deer's. Some of her anxiety eased, maybe due to the trek coming to the halfway point. They had the catch, two large nets of dunefish each to haul back to the cave hung from their backs. They just had to make it back. Just like they had so many times before.

'I'm ready.' She tried not to think of the gross furry creatures skittering over her hands and feet as they climbed over the jagged rocks, all the while carrying the back-breaking weight of the dunefish. Then they were once again out in the open. The roar of the black waves pounded the shore and the mist hung overhead, hiding anything that may or may not be watching them... stalking them... hunting them...

Bone Orchard

In her dream-like state, Zee turned for a moment, noticing that the trail behind them was now laced with black blood blooms. How curious. She decided to ask the questions that had been circling in her mind. Like where are they? Why are the blooms sprouting behind them? How did this woman know Zee? Why is Kyeitha getting stronger? Why is she pushing Zee out of her own body, her own mind, once again?

Just as she turned back around to stare into the woman's captivating otherworldly eyes, Zee was ripped away from this strange world, as if a hole beneath her had opened up in the soft mossy earth. Zee fell, and the woman's long, slender fingers slid from her grip. She smiled down at Zee as she disappeared down into the darkness. She was torn from the dreamscape, a sharp ripple of pain echoing through her as she awoke in her sore body.

Gasping for air, she sat up rapidly, her heart pounding fiercely in her chest and her head spinning in pain. She glimpsed the glowing yet slightly blurred waterfall and crystalline pool in front of her in the illuminated grotto. She was back in the cave system, with a cloak of soft black velvet covering her. She tried to ground herself back in her body, back in the real world, back with Ravaryn.

'Zemira.' Ravaryn's unusually shaken voice broke through her disorientation. 'Zee... is it you?'

She looked up to see Ravaryn staring intently at her, his eyes wide. But he physically relaxed the moment he saw her emerald eyes once again. She was shaken and confused having been transported once again from her own body into another world.

'It happened again, didn't it?' she choked out. 'Are you alright? Am I okay?' She did a quick assessment of Ravaryn; he looked drawn but there were no visible injuries that she could see. She took a moment to feel her own body, past the ordinary aches and stinging thrum of pain in her arm. The mark of the hand print had black root-like lines still creeping from it, but they were unmoving. Her upper arm from the elbow up was thankfully unmarred.

It was then she knew she couldn't go on like this if the lake of life didn't heal her of this curse. She reached for Ravaryn. He took her hand and sat beside her, cradling her head against his bare chest. His hand seared through her hair to massage her head, to comfort her. His porcelain skin was so smooth and warm against her cheek. The embrace was so intimate, but it felt so right, like they had done this before. It was strange how comfortable Ravaryn now felt to her.

Zee spoke again. 'I need you to promise me something. I will *not* let her win. I will not let her make me suffer any longer. I need you to *promise* me that if the lake doesn't heal me and rid me of her, you will do what needs to be done.'

'Zee,' Ravaryn growled. 'It will work. You will be free, just hang in there.'

'*Promise* me, Ravaryn. You're the only one who can do it. Take your revenge on her; end her if the lake doesn't cure me. Promise me.' Zee lifted her head from his chest to stare into his ebony eyes. 'You owe me that much.'

She knew it was a low blow, that she was manipulating him, but she felt he did owe her. He had used her to help break his own curse, in turn getting Zee into this situation. She knew she was guilting him, but she was desperate for relief, desperate for it to end. 'Say it.'

'I promise,' he forced out, his tone sombre.

After embracing once more, they dressed, took one last look at the oasis and headed on through the cave system.

Zemira wanted to get out of these caves as quickly as possible. She trudged on, her pack feeling heavier with each hour. Over large, smooth boulders they trekked, translucent glowing creatures scuttling on the ceiling and rough walls around them, lighting the passages as they went.

'Stop.' Ravaryn all of a sudden extended a strong arm in front of Zee.

'Wha—'

'Shh.' He grabbed her and pushed her against the wall of the passage they were in. The ceiling was maybe double in height to that of Diwa's cottage and almost three times as wide. Zee was growing frustrated. *Why is he holding us up? I just want to get out of this cave system.*

As she was about to protest and push past him, Zee heard the crunching sound of large footsteps. Ravaryn lifted his finger to his lips and eyed Zee, motioning for her to stay silent. His expression was serious in the luminescent light. A deep, rumbling growl echoed loudly towards them, making Zee want to scramble. But she trusted Ravaryn's judgement; after all, he said he'd been through theses caves before. An enormous slow-moving creature plodded into sight, it's tough skin blending in with the bluish-grey alabaster of the cave walls. It was covered with moss, small fungi and tiny plants, a whole ecosystem upon its back. A huge head, like that of the ancient crocodile, came into view with hundreds of sharp, finger-sized teeth around the edges of its maw.

Zee froze, her eyes as wide as Diwa's teacup saucers. The creature plodded past as the statuesque pair made no movement or noise. Zee felt that her pulse alone racing inside of her body may have been enough to alert it to their existence. Another teeth-rattling growl came from the creature. All Zee could do was take in the strange apparition, its old eyes clouded over with a white sheen.

Zee thought of Kyeitha's creatures for a second and was drowned in a cloud of fear, but no. *This* being was obviously just adapting to the cave around it, having lived maybe for centuries within. Like many of the smaller cave-dwelling species, their eyes were all adjusted to the low light and mostly darkness of their habitats. It moved on, and Zee remained still as a corpse until Ravaryn moved first, letting her know it was safe to carry on.

'What on Mother's earth was that?' A chill ran up her spine like a small spider crawling up her bare back.

'It was an Armilandro. An ancient being.'

'How did you know it was coming?'

'I heard its oncoming footsteps in the cave ahead of us. I also have a certain sixth sense, if you will, when it comes to creatures.'

'Like you can read their minds or something?' Zee was curious.

'Something like that,' Ravaryn replied dismissively, moving on ahead of Zee.

'Wait. What? Really?'

He ignored her inquiry. 'Come on, we're getting close.'

Zee sensed he didn't want to elaborate on the strange ability right now, whatever it was, so she let it be. Far too exhausted to push the matter, she let him lead for a while through the labyrinth. Hopefully they would see the sun again soon, and if they didn't run into any more monstrous cave creatures, that would also be a plus.

'Not long now,' Ravaryn reassured in the eerie quiet of the cave. His silken voice soothed her agitated nerves. 'We're nearing the end of the tunnel and cave system.'

Zemira suddenly sensed an ominous energy. Her stomach roiled a little, just like in the blacksmith's den in the Borztan mines of Kymera. There was no luminescent glow from her necklace, which thankfully she remembered to check. She steeled herself for what was possibly ahead because this feeling was a familiar one.

'Something strange is up ahead,' Zee enlightened.

'What do you mean?' Ravaryn's eyebrow raised in question.

'You're not the only one with a sixth sense.'

They entered another large cavern. Over to one side in a small alcove were neat rows of human *bones*, hundreds of them, possibly amounting to dozens of individual bodies.

Zemira clutched her temples and shut her eyes tightly as her mind was bombarded with images. She could see them... see them all, their faces. Their energy within their bones was trapped. Each individual's own memories played out on the screen of her mind. Of loved ones... of *children* ... they were the bones of parents taken from within the Rim. She saw a small boy with chestnut curls, an impossibly huge smile and bright earthen eyes rimmed with gold. *Paxton.* Zee sucked in a sharp breath of shock. Pax was in one of the memories, so Zee grasped onto it. She could see him with his parents, see how happy they were, how they loved him dearly.

She watched as Kyeitha took his parents, leaving the small boy all alone. The Rim guardian killed them, in fact killed all of them in torturous ways. It was all too much, too gruesome, too heart-wrenchingly horrific. The forest queen, her grandmother, hadn't been keeping the balance. She had been *taking*... using the humans inside the Rim for their energy, their light, their *happiness*. Kyeitha had taken their away their life, their lifeforce, to create her army of the damned.

Zemira backed away from the mass grave, hot tears spilling down her furious face. These people weren't even buried, they were just waiting for her like a storage den... a bone orchard... a large amount of energy ripe for the picking. Disgusted, Zee felt the power in her arm begin to swirl. She hated Kyeitha even more now if that were possible.

'She did this.' Her voice was laced with the venom she felt. 'She's a *monster*.' Zee felt so angry at the murders, the absolute abuse of power. Of Kyeitha's distortion of the Rim guardian duty she was meant to uphold. Zee felt the urge to melt her own arm off. If Kyeitha wasn't purged from her soon, Zee was going to take measures into her own hands. Literally.

'I know,' Ravaryn said solemnly. 'There was nothing I could do, but I knew she had taken them. I called it the silent sickness. I tried to calm the people's hysteria. I even managed to rehome all the children. But it wasn't enough, it will never be enough. She's left deep scars all over this realm. But we will destroy her, Zee, and we will rid this world of her for good.'

They left the cave and the gruesome discovery far behind them. The mood was sombre, and they didn't speak for a long time. The sun barely warmed Zee's skin as the pair left the maze of caves for the daylight. But her relief was short-lived as they exited just before sundown. Zee's legs could barely hold her upright but she was spurred on by the immense rage churning within her, and the knowledge that the end was near. The real end for Kyeitha. The end to her own pain inflicted by the malevolent spirit. Zee used this anger and the adrenaline flooding her system to fuel her for the last bit of the trek to the temple of the Rim guardians.

Paxton's Disbelief

Aylenta

The tea in Paxton's dainty cup that Diwa had made him was a deep burgundy red and tasted of juneberries, lemongrass and raspberry. It was refreshing and calmed his sickening worry about what had happened to Zee. Diwa's concoction produced a warm burn in his throat and stomach, but not like Jill's whiskey had with its sharp, strong tang. Just enough to gently put his body at ease and make him forget the sting of the puncture wounds on his neck and ankle for the moment.

'Diwa, thank you for the tea, but please tell me if you've seen Zee. Was she here? Did she tell you what happened?' You always had to ask the right questions with Diwa to get the right answers. Or answers that were close enough for you to string together what information you wanted or needed. She was frustrating at times but Paxton never got annoyed with her like Zee sometimes did. He wondered how it would feel to have visions about people's fates, to see the world in an entirely different way from others. For Diwa, they had found out, was a seer before she was banished inside the Rim by Kyeitha, and nearly all her powers were stripped from her.

Her visions put her in an extremely precarious position of balance, of what to tell and what not to tell people to keep the equilibrium of their lives in harmony. Paxton studied Diwa calmly, who now sat opposite him at the old wooden table, surrounded by various odd chairs, all their designs and colours unique. All utterly Diwa. She gave him that warm, motherly smile that made her silver eyes sparkle from within and reached out a nobbly hand to squeeze his across the table top.

'She's not well, love,' Diwa said softly.

'I know.' Tears pricked at the back of Pax's eyes. 'I have been trying everything to help her, distract her. Cheer her up.'

'I know you have, dear man.' Diwa squeezed his hand in hers, her grip firm.

'There's nothing that anyone in *this* world could do to help her, that's why she's gone... with Ravaryn.

'What!' Paxton choked out his utter disbelief, chest tightening as anger flooded him. The calming effect of the tea he'd felt moments ago burned away in a second.

'You can't be serious?' he announced, taking his hand back from Diwa.

'I'm sorry, Paxton,' she said calmly. 'He is the only one who can help her now.'

'Help her? *Help* her! It's his fault this happened to her in the first place! Everything that has happened is *his* fault. I can't believe you let her go with him.'

'Paxton, dear, please calm down. It was the only way to help her. You must understand. Ravaryn did what he did to break a curse. He never intended for Zemira and Kyeitha to ever even meet. What transpired between them was meant to *be*. I'm sorry, I know this must be hard for you to hear.'

'Hard to hear...' Pax wanted to pelt the cup in front of him at a wall. He wanted to smash his fist into Ravaryn's face.

'Where are they, Diwa?' he asked through clenched teeth.

'They have gone to Kymera,' Diwa replied simply.

'I'm leaving, then. I'm going there to talk some sense into her. I know Ravaryn is your son and all that, but I don't trust him. I will *never* trust a man like him.'

Diwa's face sagged a little but she added no retort.

'How is your tea, Tyson dear?' she asked the wide-eyed Tye sitting adjacent to them, who was clearly too nervous and uncomfortable to contribute an opinion on the situation.

'It's umm... amazing actually. Thank you, Diwa. Do I taste a bit of histlethorn root in here?'

'Yes! Clever lad!' she remarked, as though pretending the heated conversation with Paxton had never occurred.

Pax was used to this, so he just ignored the pair and prepared to leave, his anger not subsiding a fraction.

'Pax, don't rush off like this,' Diwa said. 'Tye, I have something for you. Your mother has been ill, has she not?'

'Yes, but how did you know that?'

'Oh, the glow beetles tell me things,' was her offbeat reply as she proceeded to grab a small jar of powder from one of her tiny kitchen cupboards. 'I know you've got the healer's touch, lad, so give her a teaspoon of this in a steaming cup of tea every night before bed. It will take the water from her lungs and should heal her within the month.'

'Are you serious? My mother has had snow lung for almost two years now.' His eyes shone with hope.

'I know, love, but she deserves to see the man that you'll become. I promise there's no trick, just the right mix of Mother Nature's gifts, I promise.' Tye lunged forward at Diwa and squeezed her so tight that she burst out with a tizzy laugh.

'Oh, you're most welcome!' She then addressed Paxton before he could exit her cottage in annoyance and anger. 'Dear, I know you don't see it now and I'm sorry at what you must be feeling... but I know you will find Zemira when she needs you the most. Just please be careful. Take this.' She handed him a small vial, this one of liquid with a tiny cork holding it in.

'You'll know what it's for when the time comes.' Diwa clasped her hands in front of her stooped frame and rubbed them together, an action Pax had never seen before from her. He instantly felt bad for his outburst. It wasn't Diwa's fault.

'Diwa, thank you. I know it's not your fault.' He bent down and gently hugged her gently.

'I know, love,' she said, like always. 'I know. Now, I can tell you are eager to catch up with them, so take a woverbine to Ezerah city then you'll have to either coach or boat it the rest of the way to Zenya. Tye knows the way as he has just travelled this route to surprise you. I'm sorry, lad, that this visit is not what you expected and has been cut extremely short. But I will tell you something now: You have many more happy times in the future awaiting you here in Aylenta. I promise.' She winked and gave Tye the largest knowing grin he had ever seen. His heart filled with warmth and felt like it swelled two sizes inside his chest at her kind words.

'Now off with you both! And don't worry about Verena and Orion. I will handle letting them know,' she said as she ushered them out the door. 'I'm a popular soul and have another visitor waiting for me! Both of you, look after each other and steer clear of the fittle deer,' she cackled.

Tye gave Pax a look of confusion. Paxton just shrugged and shook his head a little as Diwa shuffled them both out the door. He pocketed the vial, and the pair thanked Diwa again. Then they were on their way.

Just as they reached halfway through the garden's twisting track leading up to the grove's entrance, she called out to them, 'Don't mind him. He does bite... but not today.'

They both had no idea what Diwa was on about as they waved and turned around, leaving her magical garden. When they reached the peak, Tye skittled backwards with fright as he came face to face with two glowing yellow eyes. They belonged to the largest wolf he had ever seen, his black coat camouflaging him well in the forest's low light.

Pax grabbed his arm from behind and ushered him past the big wolf, giving him a wide berth on the track and instantly knowing that Diwa's warning had been about him. This wolf was the exact opposite to Orion's in every way, but so similar that Paxton couldn't tear his eyes away as they passed. The pair let out the breaths they had been holding as they got further away from the sentient wolf.

'Mother's earth,' Tye gulped. 'That's the biggest bloomin' wolf I've ever seen, Orion included.'

Pax smiled a little. 'I have a feeling our trip is only going to get stranger from here on out,' he warned Tye, and the pair set off for Kymera, a place Paxton had put firmly in the past. A place he had *never* wanted to see again.

Lake of Life

Lamiria

Finally, they had reached the outskirts of the meadow that led to the temple. Zemira's legs could barely hold her weight, and she teetered and stumbled. Ravaryn had caught her before she'd face-planted into the soft, sweet grass and wildflowers that carpeted the ground. The full moon had just risen and cast a bright glow over the landscape, making it shimmer with even more magic if that were possible.

Ravaryn ignored her complaints as he carried her the rest of the way. She was too weak to even protest after a while. The thicker forest track at the end of the meadow passed by quickly. She was feeling dizzy, and the pain in her arm was at an unbearable level. If she'd had more energy, she would have been able to suppress some of it, pretend it wasn't there, but now she felt as though she might pass out.

'We're here.' Ravaryn gently laid her down at the edge of the water to the lake of life. Zee rolled her head to the side and saw the stone throne metres away, up on the open pergola of the temple's expansive veranda, with a view to the lake. That is where she had sat, Kyeitha, her *grandmother*. She had tried to kill Zee's father, her own son. She had tried to kill Zemira. She had stolen people from inside the Rim, murdered them to create her dark magic. Dark magic she'd used to torture her own creatures, ready to wage war on the very humans contained inside the Rim world that she had been destined to protect. Destined to care for, to watch over, to *love*. Zemira hated her with every fibre of her being. That witch was finally going to die.

'Don't forget... your promise...' Zee forced out, turning her head to meet Ravaryn's onyx eyes.

They shined over a little as gave a small nod. 'I promise.'

'Okay then. I'm ready. Let's do this.' She knew she should feel more apprehensive but all Zee felt was relief.

Ravaryn scooped up her frail body into his arms. Zee winced at the agony her body was vibrating with. *Just a little bit longer. Just a little bit more. I can take it.*

He walked her into the water at the edge of the lake. The moon watched over them, directly adjacent the lake's edge and the stone throne behind them in the now-desolate temple. There were a few scattered millowisps hopping from lily pad to lily pad. As if sensing the strangers in their pond, they floated their little bodies over to investigate the two entering into their waters.

One tiny creature hovered so close it came to rest a small hand on Zemira's cheek, its yellow and purple wisps of light glowing around her face. Zee felt a spark of warmth as the tiny creature placed the miniscule hand on her cheek, and the glow remained there after it removed its delicate palm and floated away. Ravaryn just watched, his face unreadable. Was he silent with awe as Zee was? She couldn't tell. He seemed tense, much tenser than usual.

'You ready, Zee?'

Zee mustered up her last reserve of strength and forced a smile. 'Ready, Wings.'

And with that, Ravaryn lovingly lowered her body down into the water.

'Take a deep breath,' was all he said as his dark eyes locked onto hers.

She took one last look at the tall, handsome man who had promised to help her get here. To help heal her, to help break her curse, without any hesitation. Then she forced her eyes shut, drew the deepest breath she could muster and gave herself to the lake as the water pooled over her face. Ravaryn's arms never left her body, and he was now chest-high in the water. Zee felt her whole body engulfed in the cool, healing liquid, and she surrendered to the calm peace. She felt as though she were falling asleep, but once again she found herself in that familiar yet unusual dark place. There was no pain, and Zemira couldn't be happier.

*

Ravaryn dragged Zee's body from the lake. He had only submerged her under the cool water for less than half a minute, but she appeared unconscious. The mark on her arm started to seep black into the surrounding tissue, and her head came up, eyes opening and looking around, searching the surroundings. She took in the temple, the lake, and then Ravaryn. His hand was on the pummel of his borenium sword, his mind quickly calculating the situation. *Was it her? He had promised.*

He would not let Kyeitha win. He would not let her return. For a moment, there was recognition in her emerald eyes. *Oh, thank the Mother.* But then she was gone. Sparkling blue flooded her irises, and the black poison spread fiercely from her arm, travelling upwards. A harsh, heartless laugh left Zemira's mouth.

The lake hadn't worked.

Ravaryn knew what he must do. Kyeitha had won.

He had promised.

Five drawn-out words left Zemira's throat in Kyeitha's voice. 'You... don't... have... it... in... you.' Her sneer was venomous.

Black mist swirled from Ravaryn as he reached for his borenium sword, pulled it from its sheath and swung it overhead with such force that all he saw in that split second was the look of shock Kyeitha gave him from Zemira's delicate features.

'Wrong again, Kyeitha.' And the sword hit true. Blood sprayed from where it had connected with Zemira's lithe body.

Kyeitha screeched with anger, her darkness dissipating along with the blackened lines of rot that led from Zee's arm to her throat.

A blue mist spread through the air and twisted away, and she was gone, up into the night. Ravaryn paled as the realisation hit him.

What have I done?

He had promised.

Disbelief rattled him to his very core. He couldn't believe the lake hadn't healed her. Cold spread through his body, into his very being.

What have I done!

He reached for her then to stifle the bleeding. It poured from the wound, staining the earth beneath her. Ravaryn firmly cupped Zemira's arm just below the elbow where he had severed it from her body. He projected his dark power around it, cocooning it. Her arm crusted over with a black stone-like casing, as if it had been cauterised. But Zee was lying there, still and lifeless. Ravaryn howled in agony; it was like Liara all over again. His heart felt like it was being ripped to shreds, his throat burned and his eyes misted over with tears laced in agonising pain. He moved closer on his knees, gathered Zee into his arms and held her to his body, her blood on his hands.

'I'm so sorry, I'm so sorry.'

A massive force from behind him connected with his skull, cracking his head with such a hard impact it rendered him instantly unconscious. His body slumped forward over Zemira's immobile body in his arms, away from the direction of the blow. The pair were now both unconscious in a pool of Zee's blood under the light of the ever-watching moon.

Part II

The Watcher Intervenes

Zee was still there in that strange world where the darkness had taken her again. She was trailing through a grove of glowing mushrooms as little flying lizards flittered from under the mushrooms' large umbrella under-bellies. They darted out in front of her when a small beetle made the unfortunate decision to glide through the peculiar grove. Zee looked be-hind her to see if the blood blooms had followed her again as they had last time, sprouting larger than she had ever seen them before in the real world. And there she stood, the earth-woman, with a friendly expression on her face. No blood blooms were to be seen.

'You are back, my child.' She didn't look old enough to be calling Zee a child but was so spellbinding with her different attributes from animals. Nature also grew from her as if it was a part of her actual being.

'Where are we?' Zee mustered enough composure to actually ask some questions this time, rather than just basking in the euphoria of not being in constant pain.

'Why, we're in this grove of cauldron mushrooms, of course,' she said simply.

'No, I mean where *are* we? Like, are we in a different world or something? This place feels different. Weird, but familiar.'

'There is only one world, child, and we are in it.' The woman smiled a little, her delicate, elongated fingers reaching forward and motioning for Zee to follow her deeper into the grove.

This woman, this *being*, reminded Zemira a lot of Diwa for some reason, never giving direct answers. Zee knew how to deal with this: Ask very direct questions if she wanted specific answers.

'Last time I was here,' Zee spoke, deciding where to start, 'there were blood blooms growing as if they were sprouting because of me... following me. Why was that?' She felt cold and alone when mentioning the blood blooms but she didn't know why.

The woman grasped her hand as they walked side by side now, and held it gently. A warm, soothing sensation spread up Zee's arm and into her body, calming her from the inside out like a cup of Diwa's warm tea and a hug rolled all into one.

'They grow from great loss. You've been suffering, dear, as you've lost a part of yourself.'

'How did you know that?'

'I know everything about you, Zemira. Since the day you were born, you were destined to change this world. To heal it. To unite it. To bring peace.'

Zee was surprised she wasn't more shocked at hearing these words. Was it because of the soothing magic the being was clearly using on her? Or just the environment around them? Or was she actually hallucinating?

'Am I dead this time? Every time I've found myself here, I have suffered an injury. But this is the longest I've stayed in this place; the longest I've been able to speak with you.'

'You're not dead, my dear, at least not yet. But you do have to wake up soon. I won't give you false hope; you have a hard path ahead of you. But I didn't choose you for no reason; I chose you because you are *strong*. *Determined.* You're tougher than you could ever imagine. There is something much more powerful than your gifts that you've been blessed with:

determination. It's never giving up, no matter how hopeless a situation may seem.'

'I don't want to go back. My arm, the pain. I don't think I can take Kyeitha being inside of me any longer. She's changing me, *destroying* me.' Tears slid down her face.

The woman took her slender fingers and stroked Zee's cheek, pulling Zee to crouch down with her as she kneeled on the soft moss-covered earth. When Zee's tears hit the ground, a cauldron mushroom bloomed in its place.

'How did you do that? How does the magic work?'

'It's your magic, dear, *you* did it. All magic is tied to your emotions and feelings, Zemira. You are most powerful when you are passionate. Whether it is for good or bad, happiness or pain. You are still powerful, but you must choose which you decide to rely on. Kyeitha unwisely made her choice.'

Zee watched as the small mushroom sprang up from the earth before her eyes and started to glow as if it had just materialised out of nothing. 'I've been taking my powers for granted. The people inside the Rim, they needed me. I destroyed their peace, the entire way their world functioned. And the magical beings, the forest people of Lamiria, I killed their queen, their last Rim guardian. In one action, I set two worlds into absolute chaos.'

'Yes. Yes, you did, my dear, and I am proud of you.'

'What are you talking about? I've caused fear, pain. *Death.*'

'You are not looking at the bigger picture, Zemira Creedence. Sometimes we all have to do things we don't want to do for the greater good.' As she stood, her gown followed her, and it was as if it was barely even made of fabric.

Zee then looked closer. Tiny plants, a miniscule world of miniature blooms, small insects and glowing buds, all interwoven, swayed as she turned. This was a being of extreme grace.

'How is it that you know me since I was born? I've never met you before. Who are you?'

'I know all my children.' Her smile lit up her delicate features. 'I am the Mother.'

Zee was dumbstruck, and her mouth hung slightly open in awe of the realisation. She felt her eyes widening without her permission. 'As in... Th- *The* Mother?' she stuttered.

The magical being laughed. 'You may call me Gaia if you like.'

Zee felt lightheaded, as if the small millowisps from the lake had squeezed themselves in through her ears and were spinning around in her head like a vortex.

'How can this be? How can *you* be? Here? The ancient ones, they destroyed you. They killed you, poisoning you and almost the entire earth.'

'Ah, yes. They did indeed destroy themselves, but they are still *children* though. My children. They didn't know what they were doing.'

'You don't blame them?'

'They are children. It wasn't their fault, dear one.'

Zee mulled over Gaia's answer and digested it as they walked out of the mushroom grove's glow and into a dark, barren land.

'These are the deadlands outside of Lamiria and the Rim.' Gaia gestured with her hand, sweeping it out before them. The blackened soil and dark clouds went for kilometres and kilometres, further than the eye could see.

'How could you forgive them, the ancient ones?' Her confusion was evident.

'I am a mother. There is nothing in this universe that my children could do that I could not forgive. You will help them, Zemira, you will help them all. To rebuild, to regrow the world anew. You can sprout pure life from your being, if you will to do so.'

Zee backed away, overwhelmed by Gaia's words. But she was implying that she expected Zee to do so.

'I-I can't. I can barely even survive.'

'You will do just fine, child. I will see you soon. Oh, and please look after Ravaryn as he is your balance. No matter how dark he may seem, there is always light within.'

'Wha—'

Zee opened her eyes and she was in a bed with a thick, soft blanket wrapped around her whole body. She could barely open her eyes, but sensed there was someone at her bedside, watching her. Large yellow eyes met hers when she looked around, and a scar ran down the side of a face she did not recognise. As a smile spread across his features, she stared into those eyes for a moment longer. They never left hers, and sensing no immediate danger, she let sleep take her, wholly and deeply.

*

Aytac had left the old woman's cottage and passed by the two young men. One he had seen before, but the other with paler skin and auburn hair he had not. He let them be. They were neither in his way nor obstructing it. The leads he'd found had led him to the strange cottage in the Black Forest. And indeed, the leads had been correct: she was a seer. Diwa was partially insane from what he could gather, but that didn't matter as she had given him answers.

'You cannot break the prison's Rim wall,' she had said, but had told him exactly where the Dark Rim was to be found. It was another Rim, a prison of sorts. Diwa had also said she was sorry that there was no way the magic could be broken. *Sorry!* She had been *sorry* about his sister... his twin sister.

His heart ached heavily with guilt and longing for his twin. The old woman must have been telling the truth; otherwise, how could she have known? But to say there was no way to break Kyeitha's prisoners free? He wouldn't take that for an answer. After all, he'd seen things no one in the last five centuries of Lamiria and the Rim world had seen: He had seen a guardian defeated. A wall destroyed. A girl break a curse, break the way of a world. The girl, or rather young woman, who now lay unconscious in front of him. She had yet to wake. Her injuries... her arm... Gods, hopefully she would survive. And that traitorous scum, the king, he would pay for what he'd done to her. Luring her to the temple, why? Just to try and end her after she had freed him and his entire world? Ravaryn hadn't even put up a fight after Aytac had smashed his head with such force, fuelled by his sudden rage and unexpected feelings of worry for the young woman.

Zemira.

The Rim Walker.

She had proven that she could walk through one Rim world's walls, and then destroy them altogether, so maybe she could do it again. Maybe she was the key to getting his sister back. Then he could stop. Then he could finally *rest.*

Maya Village

Lamiria, north-west of the temple

Zemira woke to sun filtering through a large, open window. Birds of all kinds and colours imaginable flocked and fluttered through the perfectly lit forest surrounds she could see from her bed. It appeared that she was floating in a tree's canopy. As she took in her surrounds, she noticed she was in a house, or a room from what she could guess, that was high up. The ceiling was made of thickly thatched grasses and the wall of tree trunks, timber and bamboo. The bed was soft, and her body felt light and... and *pain free*. Her head was almost dizzy, and Zee had the strange urge to giggle.

She went to push herself up to sit against the pillow and back of the bed where she lay, when an unfamiliar sensation rippled into her brain. *Oh, Mother Earth.* Her hand. Her hand was *missing*. Her heart pummelled in her chest rapidly as panic swept through her. How was she going to... going to hunt? Climb? Dress? *Anything?* Zee wanted to scream. To cry. But her head was all fuzzy and she couldn't feel her emotions properly, so she took a deep breath and the worry melted away. At least she was still alive.

Then she realised the agonising pain was gone. Kyeitha was gone! Zee wasn't in Gaia's otherworldly realm. She wasn't in the deadlands with her as she replenished her earth. Zee was back in her body in the real world and wasn't in pain. Relief flooded through her. Then another thought popped into her mind. *Ravaryn.* Where was Ravaryn? He had kept his promise, and her heart swelled. He had actually done it. She was missing her arm but she was still *here. Alive.*

He hadn't kept his promise in the way Zemira had imagined he would have as she thought for sure that she was not going to survive Kyeitha. That Ravaryn wouldn't have taken any chances with the queen potentially taking over Zemira's body as a vessel. Taking her over completely, and returning. But he had taken the chance to *save* her. So why wasn't he here? And where was here? Why would he leave her now? Zee felt a small pang of sadness. Had he left her? His part of the deal being over? Was she once again alone?

A tall man entered through the doorway into the circular room. For one second, she felt hope flutter its small wings in her gut, but as the form entered fully, Zee realised it wasn't Ravaryn. This man had a stern look and a scar down one side of his face. His dark brown, almost black, hair was not quite as deep as Ravaryn's. It was much longer and tucked messily behind his ears, and his eyes... those yellow eyes. Zee had seen them before. He had been watching over her, sitting next to her bed, in her barely conscious attempt to awaken.

'You're awake,' he stated in a deep, steady voice, sliding a tree stump towards the bed and seating it next to her.

'It seems I am,' she replied cautiously. 'Where am I? Who are you, and where is Ravaryn?' Zee struggled to sit up with one hand. Her left arm was wrapped against her chest in a clean white cloth, holding it in a sling of sorts against her chest.

'You don't mess around, do you?' He smiled, easing the serious look from his features.

Zemira thought it was hilarious all of a sudden how his huge form was perched upon such a small seat next to her low bed. A giggle slipped from her mouth; she hadn't felt this happy in her body... well, maybe ever. She just looked into the stranger's piercing sunflower eyes and waited for him to explain, all thoughts and worries somehow evading her mind for the moment.

'Ahh,' he said, that grin of his widening a little. 'That would be the sunstream vine flowers.'

'Sunstream vine flowers?' *What on earth was he on about?*

'A few small flowers in bloom make an extremely potent painkiller and leave you with a feeling of immense euphoria. We had to give you a brew when you arrived. We didn't want you to awaken in any pain. It seems from your current state,' his eyes wandered to her wounded limb tucked under the blanket before him, 'that you've been through a hell of a lot of late.'

'We?' Zee questioned.

'Yes, the village healer and myself. You're in Maya Village at the far east of the guardian's temple. Most of us came here to avoid Kyeitha's reign. To stay away. To hide and be left in peace. I, however, have only just returned. I was kept away, forced to be Kyeitha's right hand for years until you, Rim Walker, freed me. The village people are elated upon hearing that you are here. You're a hero, Zemira Creedence.'

Oh, Mother. 'Please don't give me any more of those flowers. My head fells like millowisps are flying around in there.' Zee giggled again.

Aytac almost laughed, but he seemed to hold it in.

'I'm glad that you're free of her. I'm glad I helped someone. What is your name?' Zee asked, composing herself. He was handsome in a rugged way, not like the chiselled line of Ravaryn's jaw and midnight hair.

'Aytac, my lady.' He bowed his head.

'Ha!' Zee burst out a laugh. She felt ridiculous again. 'Lady. I'm no lady.'

Aytac's smile returned.

'Where is Ravaryn? Have you seen him? I need to know he's alright.'

131

'Alright?' Aytac looked confused. 'My lady, he is in the holding cells awaiting punishment for what he did to you. He attacked you at the lake, and if I were not there to intervene, I don't know that you would have survived.'

'Attacked me?' *Oh no, it must have looked like that.* 'He didn't attack me. It's not like that. Please take me to him immediately! You don't understand.'

'Please, my lady, calm down,' Aytac placated.

'I'm not a lady, and don't tell me to calm down! I must see Ravaryn now,' Zee ordered. Her right hand burst into green flames and sweat beaded on her brow.

'Okay, okay.' Aytac rose and motioned with his hands out in front of him, as if trying to soothe an animal, all the while the amused expression stayed on his face. 'I will take you to see him, but please extinguish that,' he asked gently. 'You will be out of sorts for a few hours more. The effects of the sunstream flowers can do strange things to your emotions, but they do wonders for pain.'

'I don't need anything for pain. I'll cope.' Zee gritted her teeth and tried to stand from the bed. Her head spun but she ignored it well enough. She *needed* to see Ravaryn.

Aytac just watched her stand and struggle. Then he proceeded to lead her from the room.

'Take it easy, Rim Walker, or we will definitely need to give you more sunstream if you fall from the walkways.' Aytac led her out into the open onto a very high walkway.

Zee's eyes squinted a little as they adjusted to the sun's brighter presence outside the room. She gripped a smooth, slightly twisted wooden railing and was amazed at how high up they actually were. Before her lay an entire village in the trees, where thick woven pathways of living roots and branched railings connected the structures together. Sphered shapes carefully woven from branches and plants like little bird's nests were nestled everywhere inside the trees' centres.

'What is this place?' she asked in awe.

'Maya Village,' Aytac told her again. 'Hiding place for deserters of the mad queen. After I take you to see your friend, I have a proposition for you. A deal. One that I think you will be most interested to hear. One that will benefit us equally.'

Zee didn't answer. Her body was floating, and she was relishing the absence of pain and the fairy-tale village before her. She felt as though she could float away on a cloud but was also anxious to be reunited with Ravaryn. She didn't know why, but it somehow felt wrong to be without him. And she needed to speak with him, to piece together what had really happened after she had been submerged in the waters of the lake of life. Zee wasn't angry for some odd reason. Maybe it was the sunstream? Or maybe she was just happy to still be alive. Or was it that fact that Ravaryn hadn't left? Would he if he wasn't stuck here though?

They reached a hut-like cage at the base of a huge rainforest tree, having followed spiralling stairs that led all the way around the thick tree and down to the forest floor. Zee had stubbornly stumbled most of the way down. Inside the hut there he lay, bloody and beaten with his hands bound behind his back to a centre pole in the middle of the muddy structure. His head was bent forward, hair dangling messily in front of his face.

'What is this!' Zee demanded. 'Untie him at once!' She felt her magic ignite inside of her, coming to life in her veins. Her head spun and she had to steady herself against the entrance to the hut.

'Ravaryn.' She lurched forward, stumbling to the ground. 'Ravaryn, are you hurt?' She reached for his face with her right hand.

'Why are you here?' His harsh, gravelly voice greeted her as if he had not spoken for days.

'What do you mean? Are you wounded?' Zee bent her head to look in-to his downcast eyes. They were shinning, the ebony within, with unsteady emotions.

'Untie him!' she ordered Aytac again.

He lifted his outstretched arms. 'As you wish.'

Ravaryn slumped forward from the pole as the metal chain was un-clasped from behind his back.

'Ravaryn look at me. What happened to you?'

'What happened to me?' he croaked out. 'How could you seriously be worried about me? After,' he almost choked, 'after what I did?'

'Whatever do you mean?' Zee was lost. 'You did it,' she said slowly. 'You kept your promise. I'm here, aren't I? You saved me. You freed me from *her*.' A giddy laugh slipped from Zee's mouth. 'We did it.'

Ravaryn looked at her then and raked two large hands through his tangle of thick curls. 'Are you mad? Has he not told you what I did? Zee I-I cut your arm off. I-I-...' He looked as though he was about to break.

Had he been torturing himself this whole time? Tears welled in his eyes. He didn't look well. 'You did what I asked you to. I thought you would have to kill me for sure,' Zee replied. 'But here I am. I don't blame you for anything, Wings. I'm fine. The pain, and the agonising darkness and emptiness, are gone. I feel like me again. *I thank you.*' The last word came out quieter, gentler.

Ravaryn's deep eyes welled and grew wider. He looked as though he was in shock. He said nothing.

Aytac just stood by and watched the pair.

Ravaryn started at her for another long moment, digesting what she had just said, then rose unsteadily to his knees and embraced her in a crushing hug. He held her there while time slowed, breathing her in, ab-sorbing the nearness of her.

She didn't even blame him.

He pulled away and brought his hand to her cheek, encasing it so gen-tly. Then he looked down at her chest where her left arm was wrapped and bound to her in a sling.

Ravaryn lifted his onyx eyes to meet Zee's deep forest ones. 'I am *so* sorry.'

Zee gave him a look of reassurance, communicating her forgiveness without a word. Then she spoke. 'Hey, enough of that. A promise is a promise. Now if you don't mind, can you please carry my weary arse back up that huge tree, because I swear to the Mother if have to face those stairs, I truly will be devastated.'

Ravaryn let out a ragged laugh. 'Anything for you.'

A Mother's Worry

Black Forest, Aylenta

Something is not right!' Verena seethed as she paced back and forth before the fire, wearing a track into the woven mat on the floor with her bare feet.

'She should be back by now! I still can't believe she left with *him*!' Her fists clenched at her sides as she let out a growl of frustration. 'Gods, I *hate* that man!'

Orion rubbed his tattooed hand over the deep tanned skin of his face and watched his wife have what seemed like her hundredth meltdown this week.

'Verena, please. Diwa said it would take them at least two weeks at *least*; we can't just go rushing in to save her anymore. She's a grown woman, and for whatever reason,' Orion's sculpted muscled shoulders slumped over as he leaned forward on his elbows at the table in the cottage kitchen, 'she *chose* to go with him. She also chose not to tell us, and will have her reasons. Diwa also said that it was meant to be, that we wouldn't have been able to help her anyway. Zee probably didn't want us to worry about her and now you're more worried than ever. This isn't what she would want.'

'Diwa! Sometimes I swear that woman is a menace! She's always telling half-truths.' Angry tears spilled from Verena's eyes as she chewed down hard on the inside of her cheek.

'Come now, my love, *please*. Diwa would never put Zemira in a situation that was bad for her and you know that.'

'Yes, but that was before I knew that... that *man* is her son!'

Orion slid his wooden chair from the table, and it screeched slightly in protest against the stone floor of the cottage. He came to stand in front of her by the fire, two large palms on her shoulders. She looked up at him, her verdant eyes still angry, but some of the rage dissipating when they met with Orion's deep emerald gaze.

She leaned forward and rested her head against his firm chest, her head fitting neatly under his jaw.

'I'll go,' he said softly, caressing the lengths of silken hair down her back, attempting to placate her. 'I'll have Diwa show me a vision, and I'll go find our little wolf. Not that's she's so little anymore.'

Verena nodded against his chest. 'Thank you,' she murmured.

'Please... *try* not to worry too much.'

'That's what mothers do,' Verena said simply. 'We worry'

Orion watched the flames flickering inside the fireplace as he held her, calming her wild spirit.

'I can't lose her...' Verena choked out, her anger crumbling into fear.

'Shhh... you won't. I'll find her. Remember that she is strong, she is brave and she's a survivor. Also, Ravaryn doesn't have the nerve to let anything happen to her.' He swayed his wife in his arms, soothing her worry the best he could, knowing it was laced with the grief from them losing the baby, her pain still raw and fresh.

*

Orion left their cottage on the hill later that afternoon. He didn't need much as he would travel as Wolf, hunting on the way before finding Zemira. He padded down the worn track to Diwa's, leaving a calmer but still miserable and anxious Verena behind. He had offered for her to come to visit Diwa as well, to have a chance to see Zemira in one of her vision clouds, but his wife was still too angry with the crafty old woman. Which was fair enough. But she had reassured Orion that she would try to be calm and focus on the fact that he was going in search of their daughter.

Diwa's door creaked open as Wolf made it nearly half way through, its edges laced with pops of colour from blooms opening in the sun's caress. Flittering butterflies gently enjoyed their nectar. Diwa stood in the door-way with a knowing smile on her face and a greeting of open arms.

'Come in, Orion dear.' She smiled, but her voice sounded a little tired

Orion noted the difference from her usual exuberant tone and entered into Diwa's fig-strewn home. Tea and cake were sitting at the old wooden table, ready as always. He shifted in the small space, taking his human form, his head reaching the roof of the small dwelling as the tree roots tickled his shimmering silver hair. Diwa followed in after him, leaving the door open as it filtered in warm afternoon light.

The shifter slid into the wooden chair, this one a deep burgundy in colour, faded and cracked with time. It was decorated with a design of a twisted wood sphere in the centre of the back. Diwa was forever moving the old chairs around the table, all differing in size, colour and pattern. Orion had no clue why she did half the things she did, so he didn't bother asking. He just took a seat in the sturdy chair and greeted Diwa with a slightly forced smile.

'I'm guessing you know why I'm here then.' He eyed the still steaming cup of honey-coloured translucent tea and the delicious looking cake iced with golden icing and asylum flowers.

'Yes, love.' She slid her own sunshine yellow chair out from the table and took a seat. The seat was adorned with a thick pillow to prop her up a little higher so she didn't appear to be as small as she sat opposite him.

'You want a vision. You want to see her before you go and check on her... as she's taking longer than expected, is that right?'

A warm grin spread over his handsome face. A more genuine expression laced with humour at Diwa knowing the exact bloody reason he was here. Gods, she was incredible. 'Yes,' he replied politely.

'One condition,' she cooed, a little more energy back in her face.

'And what would that be?' Orion said, a brow raising slightly, making the tattooed area of his face shift with it.

'Enjoy your tea and carrot cake first, please.'

He chuckled now, his shoulders relaxing into the back of the wooden chair a little. The back of it was almost tall enough to support his large frame.

'Alright, fine. A hard bargainer, as always.'

Diwa replied with a laugh. It masked her tired demeanour from before but not entirely.

She then cleared the table, and the air in the cottage seemed lighter and less stagnant with the two having conversed, reconnecting a little. Most of Orion's animosity disappeared as he could never stay annoyed at Diwa for too long. She was just too darned lovable, and it wasn't really her fault that Zee had chosen to leave Aylenta in search of healing, even if it had been with Ravaryn.

How destiny was strangely weaving them all into each other's lives hadn't gone unnoticed to Orion. Life was strange, and the way it worked even more so. Diwa placed the empty plates in the small sink that looked out to her gardens and placed the teacups gently on the bench beside it, careful not to bump or knock the still-settling tea leaves that clumped at the bottom of them both. They would be left to dry for her to inspect and decipher later after Orion had left in search of Zee. She shuffled back to the table and took up her spot again opposite Orion, his emerald eyes following her slow movements. She placed both her hands on the table, palms upturned towards the ceiling of her cottage, and smiled a cheeky grin at Orion.

'Hands this time, please love.'

Orion complied and engulfed her child-sized wrinkled palms within his own broad tattooed ones. Diwa's smile faded, her eyes turned cloudy and her head tilted back as if she were studying the roots creeping across her ceiling. The cottage turned unnaturally dark, and she squeezed Orion's hands firmly. An otherworldly fog spun from where they were clasped together, and slowly but surely formed a ball in the air, suspended perfectly between the two of them and hovering above the table. It went from foggy grey to deep amethyst to a mossy green colour, and smaller spirals of fog spun around more rapidly on the inside of the sphere then formed into figures, two figures to be exact. They stood, their backs facing Orion, in front of a body of water. Millowisps scooted around them, and Orion realised that the figures were Zee and Ravaryn standing before the lake of life.

Diwa took a gasp of air and let go of Orion's hands, blowing out a forceful breath through the vision, as if trying to blow the image from the air.

'Dee, wait.' Orion's plea was too late; the image was gone. His heart sank a little as he had barely seen his daughter. He couldn't tell if she were okay, only that she was still with the king and that they had made it to the lake.

Diwa took her hands back abruptly. 'Oh sorry, love.' She waved a hand in front of her face, almost feigning a cough.

Orion lifted a disbelieving brow.

'This weary old vessel isn't what it used to be, you know,' she deflected.

'Is that so?' Orion countered.

'Well, did you see her?'

'Yes. It appears they have made it to the lake, but heaven knows why it has taken them this long. I'm going to go check and retrieve her all the same. Verena is worried sick.'

'I know. I know.' Diwa nodded, clasping her bumpy knuckles together in front of her. 'Just... be careful.' Diwa's large silver eyes pleaded.

'Of course, always.' He got up from the table and circled around to give her a warm embrace before he left on his journey.

141

'Thank you. Thank you for always being there, for *all* of us. I don't know what we'd do without you.' Orion placed a gentle kiss on Diwa's wrinkled forehead and left the charismatic cottage in the flower hollow of the Black Forest.

*

Diwa sat at the table after he had left for a long while, digesting thoughts and images from the future, before she got up to check on the teacups. Hers was a small brown cup that depicted seeds underneath the earth sprouting and reaching towards the top of the cup in search of sun. Inside the teacup had formed the shape of a six-petal flower.

'Hmm.' She flexed both her brows then placed the cup down and looked into Orion's. She had given him a white cup that had a flock of birds migrating from one side of it to the other, all floating over a body of deep blue water. At the bottom of the cup, still shifting in tiny movements, the tea leaves clung together in the form of a four-limbed creature, not quite human. The figure's body was made up of tiny spheres clumped together, as if it were a solid creature made entirely from rocks. She sensed trouble.

A Deal is Made

Maya Village, Lamiria

Zemira was shown around the picturesque village after Ravaryn had scooped her up and flown her back to the high walkways above the holding cell, gently placing her on the bed. He hid this grimace of pain at his own injuries, his hand lingering longer than usual on her own.

After she'd awoken, he had not left her side for a second while Aytac led them through the village. The small bird nest-like dwellings were truly magnificent inside. The craftspeople of this tribe were something to behold. Every single piece of this village was made by gifted hands. Art was carved into much of the wood work, telling stories along the way, making the place seem even more magical if that were possible. Zee was brought to the centre of the village. All the while, Ravaryn lingered closer to her, more protective than usual. He eyed Aytac suspiciously, and Zee could feel the tension there. After explaining to Aytac the situation that he had come upon at the lake of life, and what he had gathered had happened was wrong, the man was more understanding but still very cold towards Ravaryn.

However, Aytac treated Zemira with attentive care, explaining as they made their way through the village how it came to be. How the people were happy and thriving without a ruler overseeing their lives. The children were displaying more and more rare powers. There were even morning lessons to help teach the young ones how to wield their magic.

'We have children exhibiting elemental powers, but only one, unlike you, Zemira, having the gift of them all. Most of them are very adapt with the earth and are able to manipulate plants and trees, but we have some more attuned to water, wind and weather. The older shifters were wary at first, as most young ones take after their parents and have the gift of shifting, but times it seems are changing. We've learned that elemental magic is just like shifting, or any other skill. Practice, practice and more practice.'

Zee inwardly felt a little... small. She had never been brave enough to try the extent of her powers, as always having to hide or fear her mother's wrath had made her unsure of herself, almost ashamed of what she could do. What she contained. She had never fully mastered any of her gifts, just guessed and hoped for the best, stumbling along in the dark on her own.

'We're here.' Aytac held his bulging, muscular arm in front of him, almost bowing to Zee and motioning towards a doorway on the far wall closest to the tree trunk he had brought them to. They'd moved through the village by now, some of the village people whispering as they went past. A few gasped as they took in the sight of them. Zee wasn't sure if it was at her or Ravaryn, but they were all wide-eyed yet respectfully bowing their heads slightly as they passed.

'Sahara awaits you, Zemira. She is our village healer, and she may be able to heal your current predicament.' Aytac gave Ravaryn a look as though he were looking at something that went rancid months ago and needed to be disposed of.

Ravaryn held his stance, and Zee felt like he was about to actually growl at the other male. She felt his anger seeping from him in a thick, invisible mist.

'I ask you something in return though,' Aytac continued.

Oh. There's a catch...of course there is, Zee thought.

'I need your help. I need you to help me free my sister and many others that were taken and unfairly punished by the queen. Only you can free them, Rim Walker. If Sahara can help you, will you do it? Will you come with me to free them?'

That wasn't what Zee had been expecting. She instantly felt bad for her quick judgement. She had judged Aytac wrongly and had instantly thought that he would have wanted something for himself. But instead he wanted her help to free others. Zee felt a spark of compassion ripple through her veins, trying to move towards Aytac to soothe his pain. She felt his sorrow. Of course she wanted to help rescue Kyeitha's prisoners. It sounded *right*. It sounded like something Zee was made for.

'I would be happy—'

'Zee,' Ravaryn cut in, guiding Zee towards him and spinning her away from Aytac. 'Wait. You don't know what you're agreeing to; it could be dangerous. It could be a trap.'

'I want to help in any way I can to wipe Kyeitha's touch from this land, and I will willingly do so.'

'Just please think about it first. We don't know if they're telling the truth.'

'Wings, thank you for your concern but I can make decisions for myself.'

Ravaryn glared daggers back at Aytac's smug face. 'As you wish,' he said to Zee.

She winked at him. Her weary, sunken face actually had a small spark back to it. An ember just hanging on inside, waiting to return. That was the first time he had seen her, truly seen her, since Kyeitha had riddled her with pain.

Ravaryn let her arm slip free, and she ducked inside the woven cloth of the doorway and entered into a room carved within the biggest tree

Zee had seen in her entire life, leaving Aytac and Ravaryn behind to wait for her to return.

*

Zee's skin zinged with a peculiar sensation upon entering into the darkness of the healer's chamber, like fluffy caterpillars were crawling all over her. The room was full of items: shelves, books and unknown jarred creatures floating in some kind of clear liquid. Dainty glowing flowers emitted a welcoming yellow light. They hung from the low ceiling and were placed haphazardly around the room in vases and strung up around some of the shelves. Smoke swirled in the air as some kind of incense burned. A fragrance Zee couldn't quite put her finger on filled her nose and blanketed her senses further.

After a minute or so of looking around the space and trying to decipher if a person was present at all, Zee called out awkwardly. 'Hello? Anyone in here?'

There was no answer so she ventured further into the room. The floor angled downwards, and more of the glowing flowers were strewn around on various objects as she proceeded further into the hollowed-out trunk. It grew darker, and the misty smoke grew thicker, lingering in a dense cloud on the narrowing ceiling. Zee eyed some of the objects on the timber shelves, noticing one and trying to distinguish what the peculiar metal thing was. Its smooth black finish shone in the light, and she reached forward with her right hand to pick the object up. It was a perfect rectangle with smoothed edges, thin and very light. One side of the metal shone silver, with a small fruit depicted in its centre, and the other side was a reflective black surface. In the centre on the bottom of a dark black screen was a perfectly round circle, a button. Zee placed the object down and went to press on the circle.

'*Don't touch that!*' A shrill scream startled Zee and she spun around to see a tiny woman standing before her, her dark skin blending into her surroundings, large eyes locked on Zee. She had dreadlocked white hair piled high on her small head, making her face look even smaller. Beads and small pieces of shiny metal adorned her. The woman lifted a bony

146

hand and pointed at Zee's face, and a row of bangles chimed together down her forearm, making a soft jangling sound.

'That is an ancient relic. It poisoned the ancients' minds. It has great power and is very dangerous.' Do. Not. Touch!' she scolded Zee like she was a small child. 'Come, sit!' She swiped her long, skinny arms in front of her, motioning Zee further into the cluttered space.

'Sit where?' Zee answered back, equalling the woman's energy. 'There's so much stuff in here I can barely walk, let alone sit.'

'Oh, pish posh, keep going!'

Zee felt uncomfortable with the woman behind her and shepherding her forward like cattle. But she proceeded through the smoky space and thin walkway. Ahead was a small open area with more of the illuminating yellow flowers hanging from the ceiling. A circular space was clear of objects and clutter, and large floor cushions were placed around in a circle atop a beautifully patterned mandala mat. The woman motioned to a large, soft pillow adorned with intricate hand-sewn designs of beautiful flowers and strange snails trailing over vines.

'Sit!' she commanded. 'You feel very peculiar,' the woman stated, creeping down to sit opposite Zee in the space. Dried plants hung from the ceiling in bunches, and bones of animals dangled along with the glowing flowers.

'I feel strange?' Zee replied, amused. 'I do feel strange, actually,' she agreed. 'Whatever sunstream flowers are, I don't think I'll be having any more any time soon.'

'Not the flowers, *you*. You are not of this world. You are half.'

Zee had an underlying feeling that she understood what this odd woman was saying. She reminded her a little bit of Diwa.

'Are you a seer?' Zee asked the healer. She sat with one hand resting on her crossed knees.

'I see things, but I am not a seer. I see possible futures, instead of the actual events, and you, young woman, have many, *many* possibilities,' she crooned.

In the dim light, Zee noticed she had markings on her skin, scarred tattoo patterns in black, similar to her own. One was creeping around her neck, and others wove around her long, thin arms.

'Those markings, they're like mine. I've only seen one other person with them. How did you get them? I mean, how are they made? Mine just appeared, but it felt like I wanted them there somehow, and then they just *were*.'

'They are stories, marks of strength. Instead of lingering on the negative force of the actual injury or pain, you were able to force your body to deal with it and move on. There is great strength in being able to change, move on quickly, accept, survive. Not all have such a gift; therefore, your magic has rewarded you with a sign of strength for everyone to see. We were made by the Mother from the ancients' souls when the world was reborn after the Oxygen War. You possess genes, *gifts*, from a small group of warriors that lived on an island close to the bottom of the old world. They used to mark their skin in patterns to tell stories, and these markings were a great honour to have in their tribe. You have accepted the injuries that happened to you and moved on without anger, resentment or regret. A rare gift indeed. They're beautiful and you deserve them.' She lifted a thin eyebrow, admiring Zee's small facial scar that crept out from her hairline near her eye. Then she leaned closer, eyeing her as if she were trying to look into Zee's very soul. Zee forced herself not to recoil backwards from the intensity of the woman's gaze.

'Hmm,' she harrumphed.

Zee remained still and changed her mind. *Nope. This one's definitely stranger than Diwa.*

'I am Sahara, as you already know, and I'm going to help you heal that... mishap.' She righted her thin frame, beaded hair and numerous dangling earrings following her as she circled her arm in the air towards Zee's bandaged arm against her chest.

'Mishap?' Zee replied. 'I'm not sure if you've noticed or not, Sahara, but I'm missing an arm!'

'And I'm missing my jar of pickled snake heads but you don't see me complaining now do you?'

148

Great. I'll probably leave with two heads instead of an arm.

'Look, I'd love you to heal my arm and I've already agreed with Aytac that if you can help me, I'll try to free the prisoners. I'll help in any way I can, I promise.'

'Oh, I know you will help,' she rattled on, 'but I'm not going to heal your arm.'

Zee's heart sank and she eyed the healer, confused. She was happy to be alive, but life with one arm... well, that was definitely going to be a challenge to say the least.

'*You are.*' Sahara barked out an ear-grating laugh, and leaned back to straighten herself, smiling with teeth that looked like they had been sharpened to points, her dark eyes glistening with excitement.

The Sunserpent

Alvion Sea

Salty air swept over Paxton's sun-bronzed face as he stared out at the perfect day that shone down upon the Alvion Sea. This voyage was so different from the last time he had seen the same waters, when he and Zemira had crossed in Winifred 5, Warwick's rusty old boat. He wondered if she were still sea worthy? Was Winny still transporting goods to all three territories? Keeping the peace treaty that held the three nations together even after the Rim wall had been destroyed? Or had she succumbed to another vipen attack? A lethal one? Or had she just fallen apart from rust holes and taken on to much of the sea to sink to her watery tomb?

The boat that glided over the water he now stood on was so different. It was built from smooth wood and had thick material sails, and it was *huge*. It was maybe three times the size of old Winifred 5. Tye had known just where to go and had explained as they abruptly left Kali Village exactly how he had travelled to visit them from Kymera. He had saved and planned for every detail of his trip for months to surprise them.

Pax hunched his shoulders forward and leaned on his elbows that supported him on the railing on the edge of the Sunserpent, his hands clasped in front of him. His chest squeezed a little with guilt at cutting Tye's trip so short, but he was consumed with worry for Zee. She had changed. She wasn't the happy-go-lucky girl she had once been, shrouded by mystery. Sure, the shrouded-by-mystery part was still there in bucket-loads. But the happy-go-lucky? He wasn't even sure who she was anymore. He knew he still loved her with all his heart and would do anything for her to keep her safe. She was his family. His only family, and he would not lose her too. His gut shifted uncomfortably at the thought of being unable to help her. He hadn't been able to do a damn thing. And he hadn't been the one to blaze on in and save the day. Unlike *Ravaryn*.

His fists clenched together, causing his skin to pale as a scowl settled on his face, the calm of the ocean breeze and the sun from a moment ago gone. His body shook with a chill, and he felt a small itch as he stretched further forward, pulling at the raised scars that littered his back like the raised land of a freshly ploughed field. The King of Kymera was responsible for so much suffering. He had done so many despicable things. How *could* she? How could she have gone with him? She wasn't in her right mind. No. The sickness had overtaken her. He just hoped that she would overcome it, that she wouldn't let it win and become like *him*.

A shoulder nudged against Pax on the helm of the Sunserpent's deck. Tye's large smile lit up his face, and he had been in such high spirits the whole trip. Tye hadn't lost his childlike excitement, even though he had grown up immeasurably. He looked like a young man now, and could act appropriately according to the situation he was in. But he kept that bright open part of himself just for Pax, it seemed.

'Isn't it awesome?' Tye asked, taking in a large breath and standing tall to let the sun warm his freckled face and fiery dark hair. 'I think I could be a sailor one day,' he admitted. 'Always moving. Never staying put, never having to worry about frost toe or snow lung or to have the cold weigh your body down.'

'I'm sorry about your mum, Tye.' Pax rubbed the back of his neck where his hand usually found tight, rigid muscles to soothe. 'I didn't know she was sick.'

'Thank you. There are so many people in the lower levels of the village that get it. They usually recover after a few months of rest and care. But-but...' he stammered, 'she was heartbroken when I disappeared. I think that's what has really done a number on her... *me.*'

'Hey, it's not your fault. It's the damn king and his mines that he saw fit to run and stuff with innocent people.'

'I never would have seen her again if it weren't for you. And Zee and Orion,' he added.

Tye stared out to the horizon, his eyes glazing over a little. Pax knew that look; he was replaying things they had both witnessed and endured in that place in the past. He clapped a comforting palm on Tye's shoulder. 'I can't wait to meet her, Tye. Your mum. I can't wait to meet them all. And I can't wait to see her recover once she takes that brew Diwa gave you.' He smiled a little at the thought.

'You really think it'll work?'

'That woman and Zee are pure magic. It will *definitely* work,' Pax confessed. His smile stuck and spread to Tye as well.

'Yeah, she's one hell of an old woman,' Tye agreed. 'They both are, actually. I've never met anyone like them, definitely no one in Kymera is anything like those two.'

'I don't think there's anyone in this entire world like them,' Pax replied. His brow relaxed a little just thinking of the things he'd witnessed Zee do. The power she contained. She was strong, and she'd make it through this... whatever was going on with her and her magic.

The large metal bell on the ship's deck started to ring and resound out to all the boat's passengers, signalling that lunch was ready.

'Come on, let's go eat before we're left with the scraps again. I'm glad we make port tonight as I don't think I could handle one more day of meat slops stew.' Paxton's nose involuntarily scrunched at the thought of the thick bowl of Mother-knows-what that was served to them at every meal. Tiny floating squishy sea creatures, chunks of tentacles... and Pax was pretty sure whatever grease was left over from cooking other meals, all stirred into one large pot. His face turned green at the thought.

Tye just laughed. 'Agreed.'

The pair made it below deck to retrieve their portion, along with the rest of the crew and passengers on their way to Zenya, Kymera's capital and largest port, which connected it to the other two territories. Zenya, where the king's ice castle stood, and hopefully, where Pax would find her. See Zee again. He just hoped she was doing better and that whatever Ravaryn could do for her *had* helped her. Had healed her. And he hoped that Ravaryn hadn't sunken his claws into her any further than it seemed he already had.

An Elder Elm Seed

Zee had awoken to the sounds of an orchestra of birds serenading the entire village as the sun rose. She'd had trouble getting to sleep, whether it was the visit with Sahara or how strongly she'd felt about seeing Ravaryn bound and beaten in that mud cell, she wasn't sure. Or maybe it was that he had insisted on sleeping in her room on the floor beside her.

She rolled over onto her right arm. The dull ache permeating from her severed arm still bound to her chest was beginning to become louder. But she invited the pain; it was nothing like what she'd had to live with while Kyeitha's spirit was inside her, poisoning her. No, this drumming ache was steady and bearable. The sunstream flowers' painkilling effects must be wearing off then. She tried to move as quietly as she could, not wanting to wake Ravaryn. His large form was facing away from her on the floor of tree house, his scarred, muscled back facing her. Why had he refused to leave her side and insisted on staying close to her? To protect her?

He didn't trust Aytac, that much was obvious, and he didn't trust the deal Zemira had made with him and the village healer. Ravaryn had warned her after her visit to Sahara. *There's something he's not telling you. It won't be as simple as finding a hoard of prisoners and just simply freeing them. I know you want to play the hero but you have to think straight, Zee.*

His words had hurt. After all, it wasn't Ravaryn who was missing a part of himself. A part of what he was. Zee had been a hunter, an adventurer, a gatherer, and physically fit and free all her life. No, she couldn't do it; she couldn't live with part of herself missing. She was a nothing or everything kind of woman. If there was a chance, a slim chance the healer could somehow help her to become whole again, she had to do it. She had to try. Zee would take the risk. She had always powered on straight ahead into things, it's just the way she was. No point in wasting time thinking and worrying about what will be. Just get it done. What's the worst that could happen?

'I'm curious. You have a beautiful vista of an ancient rainforest filled with bird life and a morning sunrise right in front of you, yet you choose to watch me sleep?'

Zee jumped. 'I wasn't watching you sleep!'

Ravaryn's deep chuckle warmed her insides. How long had he been awake just lying there? How was he always two steps ahead of her?

Ravaryn stretched his mouth-wateringly masculine body and sat up, clasping his muscled arms around his raised knees. His black curls tumbled down across his forehead. *Mother,* how was it he looked that good in the morning? It wasn't fair. His bare chest was enticing; he had slept only in his black fitted pants that hung dangerously low on his sculpted abdomen. A hunger rose inside of Zee just looking at him, as if a deep rolling wave was starting to rise low inside of her.

Ravaryn just watched her as he usually did, and then smiled that gorgeous smile that also looked a little threatening at the same time. 'How'd you sleep?' was all he said, ignoring the bloom of red Zee knew was all over her cheeks.

'Terribly. What about you?'

'Like a newborn fiddle dear wrapped in its den, knowing I got to sleep in here right next to you.'

'Ugh, how did Mazda deal with your *pleasantness* in the mornings all those years?'

Another laugh rumbled from Ravaryn, making him shine in the morning light filtering through the canopy outside.

'You should think yourself lucky, Zee. I don't share my 'pleasantness' with just anyone.'

Zee blushed. Those stupid glow beetles flittered around in her stomach again; she'd have to figure out how to get rid of that ridiculous feeling. 'Well, I have a big day ahead of me, so if you don't mind, I'd like to get up, get dressed and get on with it.' Zee tried to calm her racing heart and thoughts of Ravaryn's perfectly sculpted body in front of her.

'Right.' Ravaryn held her gaze, smile dropping a little. 'So you're going to somehow gather these three things the healer has told you that you need. That she is not going to heal you... you're going to heal yourself... *and* you're to somehow gather, what was it? A seed from an Elder Elm, ten teeth freely given and something dear to your heart, all by yourself, without any help? Even though you should be resting and healing from a severe injury.' His eyes now shifted away from hers, skimming across the bound and bandaged arm, regret and shame shining in them.

'I'm not leaving your side, Zemira,' he stated, darker, quieter.

'It has to be me to retrieve them,' she explained again.

'Right, so you're somehow going to scale the tallest tree known to grow in these forests, an Elder Elm, and make it all the way to the top to harvest a seed – with one arm?' He raised a quizzical brow. 'Do you even know what an Elder Elm looks like? And the teeth? Didn't she stipulate that they had to be freely given? How on Mother's earth are you going to procure ten teeth from someone or something that you can't even communicate with? You'll lose the other arm for sure...'

'Look,' Zee huffed, 'you can come with me, but I have to do this alone. You don't understand. I need to try, if there's...' she paused, searching for the right words. 'If there's any chance I can have it back,' she gestured to her arm bound to her chest in its sling, 'I have to try.'

Ravaryn paled a little, guilt streaking his features, making him look instantly older. 'I understand, but I'm helping you. This was my doing, and I'm going to make it up to you, I promise.'

'I know you will,' she said, a flutter in her throat. Because somehow she did know... she knew he would stay by her side no matter what... and she wanted him there. She wanted him with her. The thought was terrifying. Something her mother had once said rang in her mind: *The closer you let someone to you, the worse it will hurt when they leave.*

The pair had a breakfast of exotic fruits and dried meat delivered to them by a small blonde girl with beautiful dark skin, the contrast of that along with her fern-green eyes made her stunning, Zee thought. She was quiet, bowed quickly at Zee, and rushed from the room before she could even thank her. Zee had struggled more than she had expected trying to dress herself that morning, wincing in pain at every movement of her missing arm. She ignored the rush of emotions waiting to pour from her at the slightest sign of weakness, like a swarm of rattlebees just waiting to attack from their hive.

Ravaryn had dressed and left the room, stating he was only leaving briefly and wouldn't be gone long. It warmed Zee the way he spoke to her, told her things that he really didn't need to. She guessed where he was going, to talk with Aytac, to gather as much information as he could before they left to collect the items Sahara had told Zee she would need. Zee forced down most of the food, not really tasting it, but knowing she needed to eat. Her usual appetite had gone for the moment as she had too much on her mind. The wooden door opened just as Zee was attempting to put her boots on. Ravaryn entered, bending his head to fit inside the frame as he entered the room.

'You ready for this?' He arched a brow and did that half smile he saved just for her.

'As soon as I figure out how to get these boots on.' Zee's face contorted with frustration, her green flames threatening to melt them as she struggled.

Ravaryn moved quick as a flash to kneel in front of where she sat on the bed. 'Please, allow me.'

Zee just admitted defeat and nodded slightly.

He gently lifted Zee's feet and slid them into the dark boots Mazda had made for her. The act was strangely intimate as he was so *gentle*. He took his time relishing the fact that Zee had surrendered and let him actually help her do something. His long, elegant fingers moved swiftly with the long laces, tightening them on each boot, his palm coming to rest on the back of Zee's calf when he finished. He looked up and asked, 'Better?'

Zee could feel the heat radiating from his hands through her boot into her skin. 'Better,' she murmured, remembering how close she had let him get to her in the underground oasis, how she had been so *free*. How he had felt so smooth and warm close to her skin. Her face moved closer to his, her eyes dreamy with the thought, and Ravaryn leaned in to her. Time slowed down—

'Morning,' a deep voice boomed through the doorway to the room, breaking the intimate moment in an instant.

It was Aytac. Ravaryn scowled. Zee pulled back. What had she been doing? Was she really going to kiss him again?

'I wasn't sure how long it would take you to find what you seek for the healer,' he explained. 'So I have a small pack of a few days' worth of food and supplies for you both.' He eyed Ravaryn, almost choking on his name.

And just like that, the tension was back in the room, this one of a completely different kind. Zee stood, her head swimming a little, but she felt okay, lighter in a way that she hadn't been for nearly a year.

'Thank you, Aytac, that's very kind of you.' She reached for the pack and swung it over her right shoulder, glancing at Ravaryn as if to say *bite your tongue, be nice*. Ravaryn met her gaze and raised his brows as if saying *I'll behave*, before grabbing the pack straight off Zee and swinging it over his own shoulder. She just rolled her eyes smiled politely at Aytac, setting off out the doorway and leaving the two men behind. She stepped into the warmth of the morning sun, breathing in the fresh air, the sounds of the birds and the promise of a new day without the burden of that crippling darkness swimming around unwanted in her veins.

*

159

Sweat threatened to drip into her eyes as she stared up at the behemoth of a tree. That was an Elder Elm? How on earth was she supposed to scale that with one arm? The sun had heated up and sweat and nausea were sliding through Zee like a water snake slithering through a stream. She felt like slumping down against the trunk and going to sleep. Ravaryn's dark eyes followed her.

'Please tell me you're not going to try and scale this giant with your bare... *hand*. I spoke with Sahara this morning, Zee, and she alluded to the fact that yes you had to retrieve the items, but she said nothing to indicate that my helping you would hinder this in any way.' He reached for her hand, sliding it inside his large palm, and moved in front of her.

'Let me help you. Please. It's the least I can do.'

Zee locked eyes with his, those silver sparks taunting her in the midday sun. She felt defeated in more ways than one.

'Alright,' she admitted defeat with an outbreath.

A smile crept over Ravaryn's face. Within a second, he scooped Zee up in his arms, forcefully but gently. His large black wings sprang into view behind his back as he snapped them powerfully in one swift gust to fly them upwards. Ravaryn now hovered calmly with an annoyed Zemira in his arms.

'Now all you have to do is coax a seed from one of the Elder blooms and retrieve it. Still all by yourself, I'm just assisting you with... locational issues,' he winked.

Zee rolled her eyes and felt like pinching his hard chest beneath her body to expel some of her frustration.

'Fine.'

'Fine what?' he prodded.

'Fine, you can help.' She relaxed a little and took in the view. Gods, she loved this. Flying. It was incredible. The gentle breeze brushed over her heated brow, refreshing her from the thick humidity of the forest floor below. Her spirits instantly lifted like magic. 'Alright, what do I have to do?'

'I thought you'd never ask,' Ravaryn smirked. He swooped down to the outstretched thinner branches of the tree.

'Where are the flowers?'

'They are hidden,' Ravaryn said. 'Camouflaged in the foliage, their petals are the exact shade of the tree's leaves, so you have to spot the clusters instead of the usual signs of a bloom like colour or shape. The seeds are rare and very powerful, and small leamuras, little possum-like creatures, feed on them, so the tree hides its bounty in plain sight. You have to be stealthy and gentle as at the slightest sign of trauma, the petals will bind so tightly around that seed that the tree will have poisoned it just to protect it from you.'

'That's a bit overdramatic, isn't it?' Zee countered.

'Not at all. Sometimes we have to be violent to protect what is precious to us.'

Sometimes I guess we do, she thought.

'How do I coax the seed out?'

Ravaryn gave a mischievous grin, making Zee's stomach flutter a little and her throat constrict.

He leaned close to her ear and whispered, 'You tickle it.'

'What? Are you being serious, because if you think this is a joke, I swear to the Mother I'll—'

'It's not a joke, Zee, calm down,' he chuckled. 'Look, there's one.' He glided closer. 'Summon a gentle breeze first.'

'I need my arm,' Zee said awkwardly.

'You do.'

'You drop me and I swear you'll regret it.'

'I won't drop you. I promise.' As if to reassure her, his strong arms squeezed tighter around her body as she removed her right arm from around his neck. Being cradled with no hold on him, Zee's heart started to race a little more.

She mustered a gentle breeze to rustle across the tops of the Elder Elm's leaves, all reaching upwards to the sun. Zee spotted the cluster of leaves that opened out from each other in a beautiful round arc of deep green petals, the insides shining like silken gold in the sun.

Ravaryn hovered above the bloom that was opening. 'I'm going to get close enough so that you can reach the bloom, but whatever you do, don't bump it. You have to tickle the centre of the small fruit-like orb in the middle; it should crack open and the seed will present itself within.'

Zee took a deep breath. There was absolutely no way that she could have ever done this on her own. Did Sahara know how difficult this mission was? Ravaryn sure had. What was her deal, the crazy old beetlenut. Zee shoved the thought away and focused on the opening bloom just below her. She reached down as far as she could, cautiously.

Her long fingers stretched towards the beautiful orb. It looked soft, like a sphere covered in smooth gold peach fuzz. An intoxicating smell filled her senses, like fresh juneberries mixed with summer rain. She tickled around the surface as gently as she could while Ravaryn braced her, trying to hold them both as steady as possible hovering above the bloom. The core started to crack a little.

'It's working.' Zee reached further down as the cracking continued, and tiny stigmas wriggled out to reveal the centre, where there lay a tiny seed, a glowing green ember within. Its shape was like that of a teardrop, and Zee reached into its centre deep in the flower's middle.

'A tiny bit lower,' she requested.

Ravaryn's arms strained, his wings a perfect gentle beat as he brought her slightly lower. Zee grasped the seed, warmth shooting into her veins with a feeling of the sun's first morning rays and the crack of a storm rolling around within her.

'I've got it!'

Just as Ravaryn went to pull Zee away from the flower, it snapped shut, encasing her hand. Her necklace shone with blue light, and a sharp screech came from something underneath the flower. Crawling up to pry at the flower now encased around Zee's hand was a vicious little creature clawing at her. A leamura.

Zee emitted a yell of fright upon the creature suddenly appearing and the flower snapping shut over her hand.

'No,' Ravaryn forced out through gritted teeth. 'Don't let that thing bite you, Zee. Their bite is poisonous.'

'Now you tell me! My hand is stuck!'

Ravaryn struggled to stay steady and to not pull Zee away from the tree, as the force of the flower would not yield an inch. Like a Venus fly trap with its prey, Zee was stuck.

The leamura's ears were fluffy, with large black rings around its bulbous eyes. If it hadn't been screeching and clawing at Zee, her hand trapped within the flower, it would be almost cute. *Almost.* Grey and green fur covered the fierce little thing in a spotted pattern down its back. Its ears pointed back like a vicious cat as it hissed and screeched at her, but it didn't attack yet. It just clasped onto the flower encased around Zee's hand, holding her hostage. Ravaryn looked down at it, his head resting close behind Zee's.

'What's it doing?' she asked.

'Calling for help.'

'Help? Help with what?' Zee replied, her voice an octave higher, the trapped feeling getting the better of her.

'Well, this is why I told you to be careful. Leamuras don't actually eat the Elder Elm seeds; they eat the creatures that get trapped in them that are lured by the beautiful perfume. Usually birds, serpents and skimper frogs,' Ravaryn explained matter-of-factly.

'What!' Zee exploded. 'Why didn't you tell me that before?'

'I didn't want you to worry.'

More leamuras scurried up the tree from below. Zee could see their movement through the gaps in the foliage. The one clutching at her hand screeched its battle cry to alert the others to its find. Zee panicked as more and more came up the tree, their sharp little teeth gleaming with sinister smiles.

More and more circled around her now on the top of the tree, clinging to branches all around and screeching at her, their little faces multiplying rapidly as they prepared to pounce.

'Hell no!' She took a deep breath and screamed back in the foul little creatures' faces. Her trapped hand ignited in a burst of green flames, and the leamuras were blasted back from her. They were sent flying through the air and crashing back into the canopy of the trees. The Elder bloom sizzled and disintegrated in a crusted pile of ash, and Zee's clenched fist was released. Ravaryn righted them in the air, pulling Zee up and away as she swung her fisted hand back around his neck, hanging on tight. Her hand was still warm against the skin of his neck. A flicker of emerald flame glowed in her eyes as she puffed a little, calming herself.

'Got it,' she said, facing him again.

Ravaryn smiled. Well, that was one way to retrieve an Elder Elm seed.

'You good?' he asked.

Zee nodded. 'I'm good, Wings.'

'Alright then, on to item number two?' His handsome smile was on point in the sun's light, annoying Zee for some unknown reason. He was enjoying himself.

'I have an idea.' Ravaryn smiled wider and took off in a smooth medium-paced flight.

Zee tightened her fist, clutching the seed. *Okay, that was easy-ish.* Her heart still raced, disagreeing in her chest. The warmth of the seed inside her palm penetrated into her, its magic eliciting beautiful images in her mind of forests fresh and green. She felt the power within it, the power the tiny vessel contained. *Maybe this would actually work?* One task down, two to go.

The Armilandro

Northern Lamirian Forest

Zemira tried to focus on the warm air coursing over her skin as Ravaryn's wings swept them over the northern forest of Lamiria.

'We're here.' His breath was warm as he came closer to Zee so she could hear him over the wind's static around them. It shot a tingle up her spine, that velvet voice near her skin.

They landed gracefully in a small clearing. Ravaryn carefully placed Zee down and helped her to right herself, her balance still unsettled with her body having lost one of its limbs.

She opened her right palm to glimpse the glowing seed that they had successfully procured. 'There's so much power in it, I can literally feel it pulsing. It's incredible.'

'So much power in such a small vessel,' Ravaryn replied, smiling back at Zee.

She pocketed the seed safely away and looked around. 'Where are—'

Her words were cut short as she did a 360-degree intake of their surroundings and spotted the entrance to a cave behind her, a familiar cave.

'You've got to be kidding.' She eyed Ravaryn, unimpressed. 'I hope you're not suggesting we have to go back in there?'

'Unless you have a better idea where you're going to get ten teeth freely from, please by all means, lead the way.' His crossed arms stayed in front of him as he tilted his head and waited for her response.

She groaned in defeat. 'What are you suggesting?' She actually felt a pull inside of her towards the cave, like it remembered her and invited her back.

'There's a certain someone who lives in these cave systems that you've already met, and he may be willing to give you some of his 'spares' if we ask nicely,' Ravaryn explained.

Recognition blossomed on Zee's face. *Is he talking about the Armilandro?*

'You don't mean... are you mad? That thing will eat us both in one go and pick his teeth with our bones before the moon even has a chance to come out!' Zee's heart fluttered with panic. That was by far the largest and most terrifying thing she had seen, worse than the vipen, and three times larger than a woverbine.

'We may have an advantage.' Ravaryn raised a brow and did that gorgeous half smile. 'When it comes to bargaining with him.'

'How do you even know it's a him? This is nuts. We need another idea. I'll bargain with a floxel or something if I have to.' Zee turned to storm off into the forest, Ravaryn just watching her calmly, his smile not leaving his face.

'You will not be freely given anything unless you can ask for it, and I have a feeling Sahara knew that. The last time I checked, as powerful as you are, you cannot communicate with creatures.'

Zee stopped in her tracks. He was right. Why was he always right? She hated not being the one with the answers. She hated not being right. Gods! When she was with Paxton she was always right, she always had the answers and knew what to do. Ravaryn confused and infuriated her. 'And you can?' she retorted.

166

'It just so happens you're in luck.' He raised his eyebrow arrogantly higher.

'You can talk to creatures?' she stated sceptically.

'In a way... yes.'

'Why are you just telling me this now?' She felt her anger rising for some reason, which was silly. Why should she feel angry? It's not like he owed her anything.

'You never asked,' was all he said, tone neutral.

Zee was taken aback. 'It's not exactly something that I make a habit of asking people.'

'Well, maybe you should. You think that procuring seeds and teeth to heal a missing limb are normal, but asking someone if they can communicate with animals is ridiculous?'

Exasperated, Zee found some shade near the entrance of the cave and slid her back down its wall to rest. Ravaryn followed her and came to sit with her on a nearby boulder, using it as a seat.

'I have,' Ravaryn began, 'a unique set of gifts. I'm not like other shifters; most of them have one primary form that they can shift in and out of. Like Aytac. His form is a black wolf. Fewer shifters from stronger lines have two forms that they can shift in and out of like your father. I have an animal form, but it's not what you would commonly find in this world, and it's something I'm not particularly sure you would ever want to see.

'I learned from a young age that I could partially shift portions of my overall primal creature, like my wings, keeping my true form hidden. And I have other powers that no other shifter I have ever met has. I don't tend to elaborate with just anyone on these things, Zee. I am, believe it or not, a bit more secretive and untrusting than most as I don't know where these attributes have come from and don't quite understand my powers completely myself. I believe they might be something to do with my lineage. I don't know who my father is, and you know my mother. We both know if there's something she doesn't want you to know there is no way to get it from her. Frustrating as she is, I believe she has kept my father's identity from me for a good reason. I was just starting to develop and control some of my more volatile powers before Kyeitha's curse. But, yes, I can communicate with creatures, and it's honestly one of my more favourable skills. Chester, my duellerat, is one of my closest companions. And that vipen on the night you crossed the Alvion Sea, the one who took a lock of your hair, it was sent by me.

Zee stared at him, open-mouthed.

'There are many things I regret and could have done differently but to be honest with you, I'm more like you than you think. I'm still learning the extent of my powers as there's no one to teach people like us. We have to stumble through this world discovering who we are by ourselves. Sometimes I used to feel like the only person in the world; I felt I'd never make a connection with anyone, and that no one would ever understand how I felt. I felt *lost*. But there's one thing I've learned that's helped me through it all, even after...' Ravaryn stumbled, 'even after I lost them, Liara and Aida. It is to never give up, to never stop fighting no matter how dark the night becomes.'

Zee stilled in her position against the cave wall. Not knowing what to do or say, her heart constricted at the pain in Ravaryn's voice. He had never mentioned their names.

'I-I'm so sorry.' The words spilled quietly from Zee's lips. She was so moved by his honesty that he had told her such intimate details about himself. About his family that he had lost. She rose awkwardly to her knees and shuffled over to him on them.

Ravaryn lifted his head and wiped his face roughly, sweeping away the emotion there. Zee slid between his seated legs and wrapped him tightly in a one-armed hug. 'You're not alone. I have no idea what I am or what I'm supposed to be doing either.'

Ravaryn hugged her back firmly, holding her there almost selfishly. Her scent, the warmth of her so close to him, it was intoxicating. He buried his head in her hair and rested against her shoulder, unable to pull himself away. 'Thank you,' he said simply.

*

The walls of the cave system moved with glowing life as they got deeper into the caverns. Strips of glow worms hung like decorations.

'I can sense him up ahead,' Ravaryn announced.

Zee was relieved they didn't have to search any deeper into the tunnels. It definitely wasn't her favourite place. The confined spaces, the limited light and the memories of the trapped souls she had found in the bone orchard all contributed to her discomfort. They walked quietly through the ancient lava tubes that opened up into a larger cavern, lit brighter with the luminescent glow of small mushrooms coating the walls. Huge stalagmites reaching to their partners made Zee fell like they were in the giant mouth of an ancient god.

'His den must be near. I can feel him close by.'

Zee's necklace instantly began to glow a bright blue warning. Just as Ravaryn searched around the cavern they had entered, Zee felt a huff of warm breath blow closely and powerfully against her back.

She spun around at the same time as Ravaryn. The Armilandro's crocodile-like maw snapped at her. Zee dove away from the terrifying creature and landed hard on the damp floor of his musty cave. He snapped furiously, following her scent, large milky eyes making him even more menacing. Zee scuttled back to safety through tightly packed towers of stalactites, her heart pounding in her chest. Her wounded arm throbbed against her chest; she must have opened the wound when she landed hard against it. She hyperventilated as the Armilandro smashed its way into the maze to reach her. *Great.* They'd walked straight into his den, it seemed, and they hadn't even known he was there. How was a ginormous blind old creature so stealthy?

'RAVARYN! About now would be a great time to ask him, don't you think!' Zee screamed. She army-crawled further into the tightly packed spikes of earth around her, grimacing through the pain as she tried to get away from the Armilandro. She heard a deep, rumbling roar that felt like it came from the depths of the earth itself. It wasn't from the Armilandro, yet the sound resounded through her like thunder, turning her bowels just a little to mush.

The Armilandro stopped its attack on her, and she heard a roar of its own as its huge feet pounded away from her through the rubble it had created trying to reach her. Zee crawled into a tight space and wrapped her free arm around her, her breath rattling. She heard guttural sounds emitting from a distance away. *Another point to add to the 'I hate caves list,'* she thought.

A moment later she heard Ravaryn calling for her.

'I'm here!' she said her voice strained.

Within a second, Ravaryn was there, his hand outstretched to her. 'Are you hurt?' He wrapped her fiercely in his strong arms.

She felt small, and a little overwhelmed. 'I busted my arm a bit, but I'm still breathing. Stars, what on earth was that other deep roar? Are there two of them down here?'

'I'm so sorry. I could sense him near but didn't realise he had come up behind us. No... no there's only one. He's willing to talk; he was just caught unawares by us intruding into his den. Armilandros are very territorial.'

Zee was still shaking a little. 'So he's not going to try eating me again?'

'No, he's willing to talk if we leave.'

Zee swallowed deeply, her dry throat full of cave dust along with the rest of her. 'Then let's do this.' She gritted her teeth in an effort to ignore her arm. 'But I swear to the Mother if he eats me, I'll chargrill him from the inside out.'

Ravaryn chuckled. 'I'll let him know that.'

He helped escort Zee out of the rubble of the attack. They stepped into the cavern's opening in the centre area that was sparser with less stalactites, and there he was. Massive, muscled body with clawed feet and giant gaping maw. His thick-plated leather hide was covered with moss lichen, and the tiny ecosystem Zee remembered from the first time she laid eyes on him was still intact. That terrifying maw was open, and he was so still, which made him even more terrifying. With those useless milky eyes, he was like a creature that had indeed come from the underworld. In his stillness, he knew exactly where the pair stood, and he was listening. The smell of musty swamp and dead moths lingered heavily in the air. The creature made a deep rumbling growl that rolled out from his belly as if he were saying, 'I haven't got all day.'

Ravaryn began, holding Zee's upper arm to support her. 'Armilandro,' he spoke loud and clear. 'We are sorry to disturb you. We have come here not to try and harm you or take from you, but to ask you to give something of yourself.'

A loud angry-sounding roar came from him.

'What did he say?' Zee whispered.

'He said it's laughable that we think we could harm him. And asked what we want of him.'

He addressed the Armilandro again. 'We seek ten of your old teeth, and we cannot take them without your permission. Can we please have your blessing, ancient one?'

A few more rumbled growls exited the beast. Zee's liquid legs had solidified slightly. She was in awe now more than ever of Ravaryn and his powers.

'He said he will give us ten teeth from the floor of his den if we do something for him.'

'Do what?'

'He wants us to take the bones of our others that *she* left here. Their souls are loud, he says. They bother him. He wants us to take them away from his caves and bury them in the earth where they belong. He said they need peace.'

Zee realised what the Armilandro must have meant. Kyeitha, and the bones they had found passing through. The bones of the humans. Pax's parents. Kyeitha had taken them from the Rim and murdered them, leaving orphans in her wake.

'Tell him we agree, and we thank him,' Zee told Ravaryn with respect.

'He can hear you.'

'Thank you for your teeth. We will put the bones to rest far away from your home.'

The Armilandro made one last roar and lifted a huge foot, then turned and began to plod away to the other side of the cavern. He came to rest in a flat smoothed-out area that Zee hadn't noticed before, then circled like a monstrous cat, curled up his body, shut his milky eyes and seemed to go to sleep. He blended into the pale grey surrounds perfectly, looking like a statue from an ancient civilisation, carved from stone.

'What did he say?'

Ravaryn translated the last sounds for Zee. 'He said don't ever come back as next time he will make us into a meal.'

Zee swallowed hard. 'Right.'

'Over there.' Ravaryn pointed to Zee. 'I'm guessing you should do this on your own.'

She walked over to a pile of what looked like bleached driftwood from a distance. Once she came closer, in the dull light of the cavern's glow small blue scorpions scuttled away from a large pile of bones. They were big enough that they could have come from a woverbine. Zee crouched down and started to search through the skeletons, and sure enough scattered on the ground through the piles of bones were teeth. It didn't take long for her to amass ten, which she pocketed. She then returned to where Ravaryn stood, eyeing the sleeping behemoth one last time before they left his den.

'That is something I never want to do again,' Zee admitted.

'Me neither.'

'What do you mean? You're the one who could talk to him.'

'But that didn't mean I was sure he wasn't going to eat us.'

Zee shook her head in disbelief. 'You're such a bluffer. You act like you're all-knowing and have it all together, but you don't have a clue, do you?'

Ravaryn laughed loudly at Zee's mockery. 'Don't tell anyone, will you. It'll ruin my reputation.'

Zee's mood lightened at his humour. He could be funny sometimes too. She couldn't wipe the impressed smile from her face.

*

They retrieved the bones from where they lay on the dusty floor of the cave. Sadness now filled Zee as she helped Ravaryn move them to the leaves of an elephant-ear plant that she had conjured. He dragged the large-wrapped parcel of bones and souls attached to them deep into the forest for her, just as the sun was setting and the Mother's moon began to shine in the sky. Zee spread her right hand's fingers down on the earth in a beautiful part of the forest that felt peaceful and calm.

The earth shifted around the bones inside the leaves, and they sank into the ground as Zee moved the earth around them, burying them deep. She panted a little and sat back on her knees once she was happy with her efforts.

Ravaryn silently watched her. When she used her magic, she glowed with a bright light that he had seen in no one else. His heart swelled when he watched her; she was ethereal, beautiful, pure energy.

Silent tears for Kyeitha's victims streamed down her face as she wished them peace and stared up at the moon. Ravaryn came to sit beside her and stared up at the deepening night sky with her. The forest had come alive around them, and to Zee's amazement, orcles started to pass by them in the forest's night. They were creatures from Diwa's stories, stories that she'd told Zee when she was a child. Their big, billowing bodies filled with water at night as they collected seeds to travel to the deadlands and plant new life.

'They're real.' She smiled through her tears. 'Diwa used to tell me stories of made-up faraway lands when I was young. Stories of mud munchers and orcles, fairies and demons. I guess she was telling the truth all along. I don't think I've ever seen anything so beautiful.'

'Neither have I,' Ravaryn agreed, watching the orcles planting seeds right before them in the freshly disturbed earth that the bones now rested in. He stole a sideways glance at her sitting on the forest floor next to him in the moonlight.

After a peaceful while of watching the orcles sow their seeds in the glowing moonlight, Zee spoke. 'Do you remember her stories well?' Her voice was soft, melodic.

'I remember them all,' Ravaryn answered

'Which one of them was your favourite?' Zee's shoulders were relaxed, and her focus was far out on the woods before them.

Ravaryn made a sound as if he was preparing himself to admit something dear to his heart. 'I have to say the fairy-tale about the fae and the demons.'

'Oh, that one always made me a little sad.'

'A romantic deep down, are you, Zee?'

'No!' Zee retorted, suddenly embarrassed, knocking his shoulder with her own. 'It's just sad that they fell in love with monsters. Tell it to me, would you?' She missed Diwa. Ravaryn's connection to the old woman no longer made her jealous, just made her feel closer to him in a way.

'It'll be nothing like a story from Diwa, but I'll try my best.' His voice was as soft as deep silk. 'Once upon a time, the earth was destroyed by its children. The Mother wept, her heart poisoned and weary, then she took her lost souls and gathered them, every last one, and she used their energy to create a safe haven for the last surviving humans, so they would be protected from the outside poison and damage. And to keep them safe from themselves. Then she called forth other beings, the forest folk, to watch over and protect them. The day the old world died, the destruction was so loud and so unbearably terrible that the impact split the very fabric of this world, and the realm walls cracked, opening doorways into other worlds previously unknown.

The Mother tried desperately to heal the cracks in the walls, tried to close all the doors before anything could opportunistically slip in. She sealed them, but some beings had already slipped through. Some were benevolent, like millowisps and floxels, but some were not – like the larkadens and vipens. Some were not beasts or creatures at all: two fae and two demons had walked through the walls and entered our world. The queens were not yet queens, and they became the Rim guardians decreed by the power of the Mother. Their powers were used to protect the forests and the forest folk outside the Rim, and to watch over the humans inside and keep them safe. These queens helped Mother Earth regrow, replenish and heal from the earth's destruction. But now Mother Earth was young, reborn after the blasts, and she didn't know her creatures as well as she thought. The queens were lonely.

One day two newcomers visited from a distant land. The fae queens both fell in love, in their own time, with the two men. Handsome as they were, they were both charming but otherwordly, different. And unbeknownst to the women, secretive and manipulative.

These men tried to marry the two fae queens, claiming the realm needed kings, but the queens refused. There was no such thing as marriage in their world. The queens had ruled and chosen who they would be with, which should have been enough. There was no need to surrender themselves to the men through marriage as their love should have been enough.

The men became angry and tried to steal the fae queens' powers, tried to steal their thrones from underneath them, breaking their hearts and their trust. The women banded together to stop them, but when they confronted their lovers, the men's true selves were revealed. They transformed into the demons they had been all along, having tricked the kind queens.

They fought. The queens won, but their hearts had been broken, the deception fracturing something deep down in both of them, but each differently. Having both fallen pregnant, they raised their children alone, never to know they had been fathered by demons. Mother Earth tried to console her fae guardians as they felt guilty for not foreseeing the danger. But the women healed in their own way and moved on, protecting the Rim world and becoming the first Rim guardians.'

Zee sighed. 'See, it's sad.'

'Not all fairy-tales have a happy ending.'

'Then it's not a fairy-tale, is it?'

'No, I guess not.'

A Beastly Encounter

Dark Rim, West of Lamiria

The mist hung low and thick to the glittering black sand of the dark shoreline. Their previous footprints from the morning were still partially visible, but the crashing waves were encroaching further and further up the beach. Creeping towards the cliff and devouring their previous track. They walked closer towards the overbearing craggy cliff's edge that towered up above the dark cove, their feet sinking in to the glistening dark sand with each step as the weight of the dunefish burdened them.

There was enough to feed the entire cave of outcasts for a few more weeks when rationed out perfectly by the old leader, Flinder. Flinder's body may be weary and worn but his mind and wit were as sharp as a freshly whet-stoned dagger. Noah and Sayde struggled across the beach as quietly as they could, Sayde's anxiety going into overdrive. But there was nothing she could do to speed the last part of their trek. They couldn't go any faster, couldn't be any quieter and certainly couldn't prolong the inevitable climb back up the vertical, sharp-stoned grey cliff back to their cave. Back to safety.

Sayde's eyes darted around in the mist that lingered above the dark water crashing onto the beach before them. Salt spray hung in the air, and her shoulders burned with protest at the weight she was carrying. Noah, sensing her anxiety, grabbed her hand as he walked along slowly beside her, reassuringly squeezing it and catching her attention.

He raised a quizzical eyebrow at her, and Sayde knew exactly what it meant: *Calm down. Your frowning will give you wrinkles.* She tried to shake away the worry. He was right. He was always right. She just needed to chill. She could see up ahead the end of the short stretch of coastline that was in between their cave and the black mouth, where the dunefish resided safely away from the larger, more terrifying creatures that inhabited the waters of the Dark Rim's sea.

They reached the steep cliff, stopping for a short break to prepare physically and mentally for the climb. It wouldn't be the first time one of their clan members had rushed the last leg of the trip and ran out of energy, too physically exhausted to hang on to the windswept cliffside with the weight of the catch attached to them, so fell with exhaustion to their deaths below. Their bodies always disappeared into the night as creatures found the free feast.

Noah glanced at her through the cracked clay mask, his cerulean eyes sparkling. She couldn't wait to get back, deliver the catch to the clan and sneak away to the stream at the back of the cave tunnels to bathe all of that clay from his strong, muscled body. Her cheeks flushed underneath her own clay mask at the thought of her hands sliding over his body, and she gave him a reassuring smile back. All that worrying was for nothing. Her stomach growled uninvited into her thoughts, now thinking of the fish she carried. Mother's Earth she was hungry!

The pair gave each other a sweet, reassuring kiss, the kind that lovers who know each other inside and out did. Then they started the torturous ascent before them. The mist moved in around them as they ascended higher.

Sayde looked up above her; the top of the cliff was in sight. As she looked for another hole to grip, that's when she saw it... the blood on her palm. *Stay calm. We're nearly there. Just a little bit more.* She pulled herself higher, gritting her teeth. Fear made her look out to the mists behind her. A loud rumble pounded the eerie sky behind her.

'Sayde, CLIMB!' Noah yelled.

The blood now dripped down her arm from the cut to her palm.

'GO!'

Sayde's heart pummelled inside her chest. She forced her body upwards as quickly as she could, pushing it as hard as it could go. Noah climbed faster and was now at her side. An orange glow caught her eye in the shifting mist behind her, a dark shape moving within it. The clouds were illuminated with orange as the mist barrelled towards them.

'Climb, Sayde, *climb!*' Noah roared, not bothering with a quiet tone any longer.

Sayde couldn't speak as her throat was constricted with fear. *It's coming.* Every cell in her body pushed her on. The cliff top was barely in sight through the mist that swelled around them. A screech so ear-piercingly close it reverberated inside her, shaking her very soul. She was frozen... actually frozen in fear. Somehow, she had known, she had *known*. From the mist, a burst of fire blazed towards them, mixing bright orange light with opaque grey.

Noah locked eyes with Sayde. 'Look at me,' he commanded. 'Never forget that you make your own light.'

Black talons the size off daggers shot out of the mist behind them. Noah's words brought Sayde back to reality, forcing her out of her terror and upwards. They were so close, so close to the top. With a cry of effort and a final adrenaline-fuelled push of might, Noah heaved Sayde up over the edge. They had made it! Sayde spun around to grab Noah's hands to haul him up with her. She saw two glowing eyes rimmed with gold directly behind him in the mist, orange flames swirling inside them as black-taloned claws seized Noah's body. They constricted tightly around him in seconds, and he was torn from the cliff, from Sayde's grasp.

Their eyes locked as time slowed down. His eyes said a goodbye...
then monstrous black wings pounded the air, tearing him away into the
mist of the Dark Rim. The scream that ripped from Sayde's throat echoed into the vastness, leaving her all alone on the precipice of the prison.

Sunstream Flowers

Maya Village, Lamiria

Ravaryn and Zemira returned to Maya Village later that night to find the young girl with dark skin and stunning eyes waiting outside their room. Her eyes grew huge at the sight of Ravaryn, his dark wings surely looking menacing in the moon's glow as they landed on the timber platform at the entrance to the room.

'I've prepared a bath for you,' she murmured, talking straight at Zee, maybe not brave enough to look Ravaryn in the eye.

Zee had grown used to his appearance but she still couldn't forget how intimidating he could be, or how stunningly handsome. His dark eyes shone in the night like he were a part of it, just like it were a part of him. His stance alone with his muscled build was enough to scare anyone.

'Thank you,' Zee replied.

'There's some thippleberry salve and sunstream flowers for you too,' the girl added, eyeing Zee's blood-stained bandaged arm strapped to her chest.

'What's your name?' Zee forced a smile at the sweet girl.

'Mirabel.' She straightened with pride.

'Thanks again, Mirabel. You must be tired waiting up for us like this. Please go and get some rest.'

Mirabel smiled shyly and nodded, then dashed away down the roped wooden pathway that connected their room to all the rooms and homes of Maya Village together like an organic, living thing. A spider's web connected high in the rainforest canopy. The village was truly gorgeous at night. Small orbs were filled with the glowing flowers Zee had seen in Sahara's den, and they hung suspended throughout the village like little millowisps hovering in place to light the walkways and rooms of the people here.

Zee and Ravaryn entered the bird nest-shaped room to see a wooden tub was filled with water and herbs. Two parcels of food wrapped in banana leaves sat on the bed on a wooden tray. Salve and a cup of water were on the small stand next to Zee's bed, along with the sunstream flowers. She crinkled her nose up at the thought of having to take them to ease her pain. But she was tired and her severed arm was absolutely pounding now.

'Thank the Mother for Mirabel. I don't think I would have been able to muster the energy to find food tonight after the day we've had.'

They sat on the woven floor of the room and ate the meal that had been saved for them: boiled grains, roasted root vegetables and dark meat all covered with an exquisite blend of citrusy herbs. The view out of the window was of a bright moon in a cloudless sky littered with a million stars. And the shining lights of the village flickered through the forest like the glow beetles from home.

After eating, sleep felt so close that Zee's eyelids drooped and her limbs felt like lead. She lay back and gently rested her head on the floor.

'Any other time I wouldn't intervene, but if you don't wash and salve that wound it will fester, and you'll be in a worse predicament than you find yourself in now.'

She groaned loudly. 'I know... but I don't want to move...'

'I'll help you bathe if you like.'

Zee's eyes shot open at that comment. 'In your dreams.'

'As you wish.'

Ravaryn gazed at her with that arrogant smile, the one he did just to annoy her. She crawled over to the tub and used it to stand up, whipping the light material screen that separated the room in two.

'You peek and it'll be the last thing you see,' she warned.

'With my honour as a former king, I swear I wouldn't dare.'

'You were a terrible king!' Zee countered.

Ravaryn laughed from behind the screen. 'Exactly. Now I know you're extremely capable, but my offer still stands. It must be hard to... to adjust.'

Zee struggled to undo the bindings on her arm with her one right hand. She was so weary, and he had already seen her down to her undergarments in the underground oasis. So what? Was she that proud? Hell no. She would not struggle, not anymore. She was done taking the hard road.

Zee came out from behind the screen and headed straight for the sunstream flowers, placing one in her mouth and swallowing it down with the cup of water.

'Fine,' she said flatly.

'Fine what?' Ravaryn cocked his head.

'Fine, you can help me undo this bandage.'

'You'll have to ask me nicer than that,' he stated.

'Don't worry. I'll go get Mirabel,' she seethed.

'You'll fall over with exhaustion before you find her,' he pointed out, crossing his arms in front of his chest.

'Why do you have to be so difficult?'

'Ask me nicely.'

You pompous arse.

'*Ravaryn.* Will you *please* help me?'

His smile was devilish 'Of course. All you had to do was ask.'

He was in front of her so quickly she almost stumbled back. His long, slender fingers worked gently on the binding that held the bandaged arm to her body.

183

He started to unwrap the sling then the bandages around her torso, slowly. Zee could feel his fingers grazing against her ever so slightly, sending sparks into her at every contact point. All of a sudden, she wasn't so tired. Her mouth felt dry as Ravaryn just kept to his task, delicately unwrapping her injured arm.

'I'll leave this last covering on. Try not to get the wound wet. I'll salve it and dress it for you once you're done.'

Zees legs were tuning to liquid, and her head started to feel a little light. The pain from her arm was ebbing away, and she felt happiness and warmth seeping over her. Ravaryn stood so close to her now, and her head could fit perfectly under his chin if she tried. She leaned forward, rested it there, and it felt good. It fit. Ravaryn tensed for a second and then relaxed against her.

'How are you feeling?' he questioned.

'Funny.' The word came out as a giggle.

'Ah, that would be the painkillers kicking in.'

'Ravaryn, can you help me?' She lifted her head and looked him straight in the eyes, her face dangerously close. She wanted to kiss those lips. They were so soft and inviting.

He swallowed. 'Seeing as you asked so nicely, how could I say no.' Ravaryn started to carefully take her shirt off, his eyes never leaving hers, then he helped her out of her pants.

Zee smiled with a confidence that was rare for her when it came to men. 'I want to feel clean. Can you help me with - everything.' She looked down at herself, gesturing to the rest of her clothing.

Ravaryn actually looked pained. 'Zee, I don't think that's a good idea. You threatened earlier that if I peeked a glance at you, it would be the last thing I'd see. Now you're asking me to undress you?'

Zee's instincts threatened to embarrass her, but the feeling didn't come. 'I won't kill you in your sleep, I promise.' She rolled her eyes as heat pooled inside of her. 'So what if you see me? I'm sure you've seen hundreds of naked women before.'

'Hundreds?' Ravaryn laughed. 'What on earth do you think of me, Zemira?'

'Please help me. I want to be clean and wrapped up in that bed so I can sleep today away.'

He looked into her eyes. Searching. 'Are you sure?'

She nodded, meeting his ebony gaze.

He slid his hands down to the cotton singlet she wore and gently eased her out of it. His hand brushed Zee's bare breast, causing a soft moan to escape her.

Ravaryn swallowed hard. 'I will remind you that you asked me to help you in the morning when you are likely ready to kill me again.'

'I know,' Zee said, her head light and her heart so free she felt like a dandelion seed ready to float off into the wind.

Next he slid her out of her underwear and stood in front of her. 'Gods, you're beautiful.' His eyes sparkled silver in oceans of ebony, growing even darker as he looked at her. 'If you hadn't taken that sunstream, I don't think I'd be able to stop myself from taking you over to that bed and making you mine,' he growled.

Zee swallowed, warmth flaring deep inside of her, a pulsing throb that wanted him too. 'I'll remember that,' she whispered.

'So will I,' he stated, his voice deep and laced with desire. 'Now let me help you into that tub before I can't help myself.'

Zee smiled and obeyed.

Ravaryn helped her into the tub, careful not to wet the wound that was all that remained of her left arm below the elbow. He felt shame and guilt well inside of him whenever he looked at it.

Zee saw the sorrow his face. 'You shouldn't feel bad. If you were someone else, someone weaker, I'd be dead. They wouldn't have had the guts to do it, and Kyeitha would have won. I think she would have stolen my very body from within me.'

As he began to soap her body, she purred, 'I think I could get used to this.'

'I doubt very much you'll be saying that in the morning.'

'I'll make you a bet.' Zee's voice was light and teasing.

Ravaryn raised an eyebrow, amused by this carefree Zee. As he washed away the dust from her skin, forcing himself to *only* wash, he wanted to do so much more. She was so carefree, so happy when she wasn't in pain. He was concentrating fiercely on his task, yet his mind desperately wanted to touch, caress and stroke the parts of her body he had only been given permission to wash. He took a deep breath.

'I bet you a flock of floxels that I won't care you saw me naked in the morning! Haha!'

Ravaryn's laugh rumbled out from him. 'I will take that bet and counter you your very own duellerat, *if* in the morning, you don't want to strangle me with your remaining hand.'

Zee laughed and fell backwards, sliding a little more into the tub. 'I've always wanted a flying pet! I love to fly. I love the feeling of being in your arms, the wind streaming around us, like we're the only two in the world.' Her eyes were dreamy.

Ravaryn stilled, his heart pounding. Her words penetrated him deeply as he felt the same way when she was with him and cradled safely in his arms, the world below them.

Thinking it was a good time to get her out of the tub, Ravaryn held the large towel out to her. As she stood up, the water cascading down her body, she smiled at the look of restraint on Ravaryn's face,

'Gods, you torment me, woman. Come here.' He wrapped her lithe body in the towel and helped her from the tub. 'I'm not sure I can handle this unrestrained Zee.'

'Why not?'

'I think I like her even more.' He led her over to the bed and helped her dress with every last ounce of restraint his entire being contained. As his hands shook, he wanted so much to let them explore, to play, to please. But instead he sat her down on the edge of the bed. Her dreamy forest eyes just looked up at him, huge in the glow of the flower orbs hanging from ceiling.

'I have to dress your arm now, Zee.'

'Okay.'

'It shouldn't hurt as the sunstream seems to be doing its job, but... you haven't seen the wound yet. It may be a little confronting.'

She just shrugged. The sunstream was definitely doing its job.

Ravaryn clenched his jaw. Very carefully, he unwrapped Zee's bandaged stump. The skin on the wound was black and stone-like from the magic he had conjured that night to stop the bleeding. Zee just watched him work. Neither said a word as he applied salve to the wound and bandaged it back up with the fresh material that Mirabel had left them.

'Thank you,' Zee said sleepily, unperturbed by the sight of the stump.

Ravaryn stilled. 'You don't need to thank me. I'll be expecting my floxels in the morning.'

A tired laugh bubbled from Zee. Ravaryn's heart swelled. It was one of the most beautiful things he had heard in a long time.

'Will you sleep next to me?' Zee tilted her head to Ravaryn, locking eyes with him. Very clearly through whatever euphoric fog she was swimming in, she was asking him to say yes. She knew what she was asking.

'I don't think that's such a good idea.'

'I mean it. *Ravaryn*, please sleep next to me. I don't want to be lonely anymore. Just hold me for a bit.'

Ravaryn froze, trying to decide what the right thing was to do. He longed to hold her, to comfort her, to have her all to himself, but he had made so many mistakes in the past. He didn't want to make any more.

Zee outstretched her right hand towards him. 'Don't make me beg.'

That nearly broke him. Consequences be dammed, he needed her comfort too. She hadn't called him Ravaryn like that, *not ever*. Once, it was all he had dreamed of. When they had met, she had hated him with her very core, and all he had wished was to hear his name like that from her. She knew what she was asking even through the sunstream fog.

Ravaryn slid into the bed beside Zee. She rolled over, and he moved in behind her, spooning her perfectly, his large body fitting against hers like it were made to be there. He moved a muscled arm under Zee's head, and the other cocooned her to him as he rested his warm palm against her stomach. Zee moaned a little with the warmth and comfort that trickled into her at his touch, at being held, at being safe. 'Do that again and I won't get a second of sleep.'

Zee sleepily replied in a whisper, 'I won't do that again, not until you ask me to.'

Ravaryn groaned and squeezed her tighter against his rigid form. 'I'm serious.'

'So am I.' She gazed at the moon, her heart fluttering and her body tingling as if small fish were gliding through her veins. She couldn't remember a time when she had ever felt like this. Content. Protected. And not alone.

The Healer's Den

Birdsong gently coaxed Zemira from the dream world. She felt like she had slept for days, and something warm and solid was wrapped around her. *Ravaryn.*

She tensed for a moment, then relaxed as she remembered asking him. She'd wanted his help, and she'd wanted him close to her. Was it really that bad to need help? Zee rested her head back into his arm. Had they both slept like this all night? The comfortable bed dipped in the middle with their combined weight, and Zee felt so warm as she snuggled in to him. She felt the smallest of movements from Ravaryn still wrapped around her.

'You awake, Wings? Or are you pretending to be asleep to see if I barbecue you or not.'

Ravaryn let out a sleepy mumble. 'I'm awake. I was just trying to pick what colour I wanted my floxel herd to be.' His voice thick with sleep, and he was still hugging Zee to him, waiting for her to panic, or be horrified with embarrassment. Or worse, to throw him out of bed and attack him.

Zee smiled and stared out at the beautiful morning unfolding before her. Calm and serene, the energy of the day matched her own, and she felt almost *peaceful.*

'Well, that's too bad,' she replied, remembering her bet. Her smile grew, imagining what the look on Ravaryn's face was. 'Because I was just picking out a name for my duellerat.

Ravaryn laughed behind her, then squeezed her tightly against him.

'Are you trying to crush me now?' she teased.

'No.' He buried his face a little closer into her silky midnight hair, and said, 'I'm just savouring this moment before you realise what you've said and change your mind like all good women do.'

'Lucky for you that I'm not a good woman, and you're not getting out of it that easily. I think I'll call him Thor.'

Ravaryn just held her against him, his body pulsing with want, wishing this moment would last.

'Thor it is, then.'

She wasn't embarrassed that he had seen her naked. It was far more intimate a thing for Zee to have asked for help and bare her weaknesses to him. She felt proud of herself. Sure, she had been affected by the sun-stream flower, but it only gave her the blind courage she lacked to ask for help. It hadn't made her judgement waver. She had meant what she said the night before. And she liked the way Ravaryn had reacted to seeing her naked body, the way he could barely restrain himself. He was fun to tease like that, she realised, and she was glad she had finally let someone in. That he was the one here with her. But they would have to get up soon. Today was the day that Sahara would hopefully be able to help her.

*

Mirabel had shown up with breakfast for them and informed them that the ceremony would be held at dusk. It was also the Mother's Moon Festival. The whole village was in a flurry of movement, preparation and excitement. Mirabel took Zee to her home to prepare her for the celebrations, along with her three sisters, mother, aunts and grandmother. Zee felt happy and light at being included in such a large group of women. They flurried around her, arguing what colours suited her most, what materials would complement her skin and what shades of Luna mushroom paint to adorn her skin with. Unlike the festival back home, no one here wore masks. Paint was to decorate the skin and face, made from the special glowing mushrooms that the villages back home had decorated the town with instead of themselves.

Zemira felt magical by the time that Mirabel and her sisters had finished with her. Her long hair was fashioned in the most intricate of braids, making her heart ache for Diwa. Bright yellow and green neon paint was patterned over her skin. A deep green and bright summery yellow fabric cascaded from her shoulders like a cape, striking against her midnight hair. Skirts hung elegantly over the black pants that she insisted on wearing; she may be letting them dress her up but she still wasn't keen on dresses. The short top left a bare strip of midriff, making the outfit feminine and breezy. Zee felt like a warrior goddess. They had even wrapped her wound covering with bright material. She then helped the women prepare the food and special parcels full of sugary treats and fruits.

Mirabel's grandmother, Belladon, showed her how to weave and thread the dried leaves to tie the parcels. 'We have passed this skill down to our daughters and our granddaughters,' she explained, her voice sweet and musical.

Zee struggled with her right hand, frustration burning in her chest the longer she tried and the more she continued to fail. A trickle of panic crept into her after a while, and her right hand burned as small flickers of emerald flame licked at the perimeter around her skin.

A worn old hand slid towards her, coming to rest upon her own, but hovering above Zee's until the tiny flames calmed and disappeared.

Zee felt a sting of emotion trying to force its way out from behind her eyes. *How was this even fair!* she fumed inside.

'Shhh.' Belladon's voice was steady, as if she could see the internal struggle Zee was going through. She squeezed Zee's hand and caught her eye. 'Look at me, dear. You are not *broken*... you are not *less*... you are still you. And you are not a burden, not to anyone or anything. No matter what happens today, no matter whether your physical body is healed or stays as it is, you are still *whole*.'

She gave Zee a watery smile. 'Trust me, us oldies know things. This moment, like every other, *will* pass.' She squeezed Zee's remaining hand tighter.

Zee rubbed her fingertips across the bridge of her nose, pinching tight-ly, not wanting to smudge the gorgeous decorations of the paint on her skin but needing to soothe her frustration and tension there somehow.

'Thank you,' Zee replied after digesting what Belladon had really said. It sat heavy in her heart. *She's right. I'm still me. I'll get through this. I'm not less.*

'You're a true miracle, Zemira, and I just wish my Flinnigan was here to see you weave your powers and heal Kyeitha's poison.' Belladon spoke with such faith, as if she already believed Zee could do it.

'Oh.' Zee hesitated, still not comfortable with taking compliments and feeling sadness for Belladon's lonely tone. 'Has Flinnigan passed?'

'I hope not.' Belladon sighed 'He was taken away. I now believe he might still be alive in the prison, the one Aytac says you have promised to find and free the survivors.' Her troubled face shone with hope again and her shining old eyes stared right into Zee's very being. 'Thank you,' she said, her voice filled with emotion. 'Thank you for all that you are.'

Her smile breathed life back into Zee as her hand slipped away back to her work. Zee continued with more concentration and determination for the task, weaving the parcels of food as best she could in her current state. Would this possibly be her life from now on if she was unable to heal and regrow her arm? Fear beat steadily in her chest. This was a mas-sive feat that lay ahead of her. Her heart swelled as she realised she wasn't just responsible for healing herself anymore. She could help heal the pain of an entire village if she was strong enough, and the weight of that sat uneasily on her shoulders. Her mind wandered, as it often did these days, to Ravaryn. Where had he gotten to for the day?

As if Mirabel somehow guessed her thoughts, she offered an answer. 'All the men go to their own ceremony to prepare for the celebrations.

They visit the steam baths to cleanse their bodies and their souls. It is a sacred ceremony so that they always remember to treat their mothers, sisters, wives and daughters like the Mother Earth – with respect and love.'

Zee felt an uncomfortable swirl inside of her at that word. Love. It was a dangerous thing. She shook the feeling away.

'Come on, its time. Let's go!' Mirabel glowed with excitement, the orange and reds of her outfit making her look like a fire sprite ready to ignite. She was truly gorgeous.

Zee thought of Mazda and how much she would love this and the difference in the traditions, the colourful clothes, delicious food and the buzz of excitement in the air. Zee followed Mirabel through the spiralling walkways of the village home to the centre, where it seemed hundreds of people were gathering in the open structure where Sahara's den was tucked into the trunk of the ancient forest giant.

*

Mirabel led Zee through the crowds of colourfully adorned villagers. Thankfully she blended in well and not too many people stared at them in passing. The noise of the crowd talking, laughing and shifting about in the space was so foreign to Zee; she'd never seen so many people before in her entire life. Mirabel pulled her through the crowd by her right hand, and before Zee knew it she was standing in the centre of the chamber before Sahara. Ravaryn and Aytac were also there, along with a line of young men either side of the tiny, wrinkled woman.

Zee locked eyes with Ravaryn. He was dressed in black, but white and black paint adorned his skin. Black patterns around his eyes made him look menacingly even more handsome. He didn't smile, but he didn't look away from Zee's gaze. His dark eyes seemed to reassure her all the same.

Aytac stood on the other side of Sahara, also towering higher over her. He was dressed in black and brown simple clothing with striking red paint crisscrossing over his skin in an arrowhead pattern. He looked handsome with his yellow eyes shining back at her. She took a deep breath, stepped forward and looked down at the healer. Sahara's hair was beaded with bright greens, blues and oranges, and feathers sprouted haphazardly from the nest high in her head, contrasting with her white hair. Bright yellow paint dotted her dark skin, catching in the wrinkles and making her look like an exotic flower in bloom.

She smiled at Zee with her sharp pointed teeth and announced, 'We begin,' stamping a wooden staff at the same time, her loose pieces of beaded hair clinking together with the mass of bangles on her thin arms. Her voice seemed to project over the crowd, and everyone stilled. They then started to sit in rows surrounding Zee and Mirabel in the centre of the open area.

'Good luck,' Mirabel whispered, her voice full of anticipation. She squeezed Zee's hand before dashing off into the crowd, no doubt to find her sisters.

Zee felt her stomach lurch, and her temples pounded even though the crowd's noise had dispersed. She looked to Ravaryn who stood still along with the other men, his large hands clasped out in front of him. As Zee searched his gaze, he gave her a reassuring wink and a quick smile. She relaxed a smidgeon as the crowd became quieter still.

'Sit, child!' Sahara commanded Zee.

She obeyed and came to sit crossed legged, still facing the healer with the swarm of eyes at her back.

Sahara began to pace around Zee, talking loudly to the entire gathering. 'The Rim Walker has come to honour us with her presence. She has freed us of the mad queen's reign, but in doing so she was infected by her hate. She has lost part of herself. Today, we will witness whether or not she has the courage to heal herself from this poison, from this infliction that has burdened her! She has promised if I help her find the way, she will find and free our loved ones. Free them from Kyeitha's hidden prison and return them home to us!'

The crowd boomed with cheers and yells of joy, clapping their hands together and making Zee flinch at the sudden noise. She was glad she was not facing them. She stole another glance at Ravaryn. He was steady, calm. He was reassuring her just with those midnight eyes. *I can do this. He looks calm... this will be fine.*

'Teeth are the strength to regrow the bones, the seed is a spark of life with the power to grow rapidly and create new life! An Elder Elm seed is an object of power. What is your third object?' Sahara's rattly voice echoed out over the entire village. 'The third object is one of great sentimental value and memory so the body doesn't reject the new limb.'

Zee pulled at her necklace holding the moonstone from Diwa, and the knot in the woven band snapped. She took one look at it in her palm and handed it to the tribe's healer as she circled back around in front of her.

'And lastly.' Sahara smiled down at Zee and took the necklace from her outstretched palm. She came now to stand in front of Ravaryn. 'A lock of hair from the one who took away the poison.'

Ravaryn's brow creased in momentary confusion. Sahara had not mentioned this, but he quickly complied, bowing down to her short frame. She produced a small knife and hacked away at a shiny onyx curl.

'Woven together, these guides will show you the way. They are ingredients, Zemira Creedence of the Rim; they will not heal you, but you must use them and the great power within yourself to heal your own body and soul of this burden.' Her hands gestured in circles towards Zemira's arm.

Sahara sat before Zee and laid the objects out in front of her on the mat. The Elder Elm seed in the middle, surrounded in a circle by the Armilandro's teeth, the necklace open around the seed. She sprinkled Ravaryn's hair over all the objects as a young man came forth and handed her a large wooden cup. She took it and handed it to Zee.

'Drink and we will see what you are made of, Rim Walker. Drink every drop and we'll see if Gaia deems you worthy.' Sahara's grin grew huge, her sharp little teeth menacing, her eyes growing with excitement.

Gaia?

Zee took one last look down at her missing arm, then glanced over at Ravaryn. His eyes shone with concern and guilt as she downed the contents of the wooden cup. She nearly gagged half way but forced the mixture down. It was thick as though someone had pummelled a swarm of caterpillars in a bowl and sprinkled it with aniseed and swamp water. The foul, thick syrup hit her stomach as if it were alive, and sluggishness spread into her body, her limbs and then to her eyes. She felt them shutting against her will just as Ravaryn came forward to catch her.

Zee's eyes fluttered as she tried to open them, but they were as heavy as stones. She sat up and realised she was in front of a pond scattered with lily pads and millowisps.

'Hello again,' the sweet voice sang from beside her.

Zee turned herself around and there she was. *Gaia.*

Zee was not sure what to say or how to start explaining why she was here, or how.

'She's gone.' Gaia smiled, tilting her head to the side, her deer eyes wide. Small pink blossoms adorned her antlers this time.

'Yes...' Zee guessed she was referring to Kyeitha's spirit. 'But so is my arm.' Zee went to hold out her left arm, but as she did, her mind connected with the image before her eyes. 'It's – it's there.' Her right hand slid over the perfectly intact arm free of scars, free of tattooed stories. Just her plain old arm.

Gaia laughed. 'Where did you think it had gone, my dear?'

'It... it's gone in the real world,' Zee tried to explain.

'This is the real world.' Gaia tilted her head to the opposite side. 'Can't you tell where we are?'

Zee looked around again. They were sitting right in front of the lake of life, where they had initially tried to heal Zee's arm in the first place.

'I don't understand.'

'In your mind and in my realm, this is how you see yourself: whole, strong, capable, powerful. You have so much power inside of you that you've forgotten about. The pain has blocked it from you. But you're free of all that now.

'But how can I take some teeth, a seed, a stone and some hair and use it to regrow a limb in the other realm? The physical one?'

'How did you bring your father back from the verge of the underworld?' Gaia questioned.

'I used his memories, his powerful energy from them. His... happiness.'

'Sooo,' Gaia prompted. 'There are hundreds of people in that gathering with you, child, and they all wish you well. They all believe in you. *Ravaryn* believes in you. You can use their hope, their energy to heal yourself. Focus. You've done miraculous things before.'

'How do you know all this? I mean I was just there... and now I'm here with you.' Zee trailed off, confused.

'I am the Mother. I am part of every living thing. I have eyes and ears everywhere,' Gaia reassured her as she rested her long, moss-coated fingers on Zee's hand. 'There is one thing that you will take though if you use those objects to heal yourself. They will become a part of you. Ravaryn's hair... he will give you a part of himself, and forever you will both be connected.'

She looked deeply into Zee's eyes now, her star-speckled cheeks sparkling, her luminescent eyes mesmorising Zee. Gaia was so beautiful, stunning like the sun on a summer's day. 'Something you know you may already *have* will be yours forever, something that you can't give back.'

'What is that?' Zee said. She was starting to feel dizzy.

'Ravaryn's heart.'

'I-I.' Zee paled.

'I know it sounds like a lot, but power like that to regrow something that was taken from you takes sacrifice from the one who took it.'

'But this isn't fair. What about Ravaryn? He didn't take *it*, he took away *her*... he saved me from her. I can't just take something like that away from him. He deserves to decide who he is going to love.'

Gaia laughed. 'That's very true, my dear.'

'What's so funny?' Zee asked.

'Oh, my child, it's you! You don't see what's right in front of your very eyes.' She squeezed Zee's hand tighter, amusement twinkling in her eyes. 'You don't have to worry about asking permission, and you don't have to worry about taking his heart. It already belongs to you, my dear. He's already decided.'

It already belongs to me? Zee didn't know what to say to that. She couldn't think straight. How could this be? How could he love someone like her?

'Why wouldn't he love someone like you?' Gaia's fingers caressed Zee's face.

'How did you know I was thinking that?'

'I know what every one of my children are going through. I know what every plant, bird, fish and creature on this planet feels and thinks as you're all a part of me.' She released Zee's hand and face. 'I have many things to regrow, and much land to heal. You know what you need to do. If you ever need me, you can find me in your sleep. I will always be here for you. You're one of my favourites.'

Gaia rose to her pawed feet and started to glide away along the edge of the lake's waters. Millowisps swept through the air to follow her, and flowers bloomed a trail in her wake.

Zee sat staring out at the water, at the lily pads in bloom. *It already belongs to you...*

A memory stole its way into Zee's mind.

Zee sat close to her mother on her bed in the cottage as Verena cradled a small bundle wrapped in cloth as she wept over the baby's still form. Zee wept beside her mother, feeling her pain.

After Zee didn't know how long, Verena came back to her a little, back to the real world she must have desperately wanted to escape from at that moment.

'We'll bury her near the chamomile... she'll sleep peacefully there,' Verena managed through her sobs.

'We'll make a beautiful garden surrounding her, Mum, where her soul will rest peacefully. Dad is out there right now making the perfect spot.' Zee tried to comfort her mother the way Verena had comforted her. But Zee wasn't a child anymore, and her mother needed her now. Verena looked so small and broken holding her stillborn baby.

Zee wrapped her arm around her mother and rested her head on her shoulder next to her as they stared out the cottage window to the garden before them. Orion

198

dug meticulously in the centre of the wildflowers. 'You have us, Mum. You have me and you finally have Dad back. We'll always be here for you, and we'll never forget Zandara.'

Zee looked down at the bundle in Verena's lap, cradled gently.

Verena squeezed the baby to her chest again as more tears fell.

'Tell me, Mum... how did you know? How did you know Dad was the one?'

Verena's eyes cleared a little and a small smile tugged at her top lip. 'Something deep inside you awakens. A fire ignites that you never knew you contained, and it burns only for them.' Her eyes watched Orion out in the garden, and Zee turned her head to catch that look, the one Verena had only for her father.

'It fills you with a strange sort of magic, a warmth and a light like you've never felt before, and when you're not around them, it's easier for you to feel the cold. You feel... you feel as though a piece of you is missing. You feel alone. That's how you know, my love, that's how you know what love is.'

Bramble House

Zenya, Kymera

The air seemed to drop ten degrees just on sighting the glowing city of Zenya ahead. The clouded sky darkened the day as the Sunserpent glided into the rougher waters coated with icy debris, caressing the dark bay ahead. Paxton didn't know why, but he was nervous to be meeting Tye's family. And of course he had nerves spinning in his gut at the prospect of facing Ravaryn again, his last encounter replaying in his head and leaving a sour taste there. But it would be worth it to see Zee after what had happened. It felt like such a long time ago, but only a week had passed. He just hoped to the Mother than she was better, that whatever magical illness had taken hold of her had been healed.

The boat roughly came to port into the frozen bay full of ships, and the chill in the air from the snow frosting every surface made Paxton's heart race. His body had suffered this cold before. The mines flashed before him, and his back rippled where the old scars lay healed but never forgotten to his body and mind. Tye came up from below deck and produced a thick, furry moscow coat for Pax after sliding his own on, hood and all.

'You never get used to it.' Tye smiled, his cheeks reddening from the frigid wind already. 'I was born and bred here and it still gives me a swift kick every now and then when I forget who's boss.'

Pax took the coat gratefully. He loathed the cold... there was only one thing he hated more, and it resided in the dark towering pyres of the ice castle looming before them in clear view of the port. The sky pines stretched high above the pair as they made their way from the Sunserpent's deck and down the rickety ladder back to solid land, albeit frozen.

Tye's excitement to see his family again was contagious. Pax could practically feel him vibrating next to him as he led them through the crowded village at the base of the snow-covered trees. People were everywhere selling wares: sky-pine seeds for igniting fire, moscow jackets, hooded coats, mittens, scarves. Small shops carved into the bases of some of the tree trunks sold warm bread, the scent pulling on Paxton's stomach, his mouth watering. He hadn't eaten anything but cook's slop soup for days. Fresh bread sounded amazing right now. Meat roasted over small cooking fires threaded through metal sticks, and the scent wafted in the open air, the small grill pits exuding warmth and heavenly aromas, making his mind wander from his worries.

'Tye, I know you're keen to see your family, but can we please stop for a bite? My stomach is going to kill me if you don't as this stuff smells *incredible*.

'I was just thinking the same thing!'

'What do you recommend? That meat stick thing looks good.'

'I recommend everything!'

Pax liked that answer, and his chestnut eyes shone with excitement back at Tye. 'Let's go, then.'

The pair devoured every snack along the food-vendor road that meandered through the food district of the village. They also grabbed a fresh loaf of humseed bread, some small jillabee berries from the west of Zenya and a nice-sized silver trout for Tye's family for dinner that night. The sun was still hidden, but Pax could sense the afternoon was reaching dusk as the village lights sparkled brighter and the clouds above became denser and greyer. They tracked through narrow alleyways with homes littered closely on either side, some of the doors painted different colours. Some were adorned with Kymera's symbol, a snowflake centred around mountains and a sparkling night sky, all made from thick heat-capturing bricks, unlike the houses and cottages in Aylenta that were all made from trees, milled wood and thatched grass rooves.

Pax's stomach had thanked him with all the food he and Tye had indulged in, but now he felt the cold even more. His cheeks stung and his nose burned with each frigid breath; his limbs were heavy, and sleep became all too tempting. A night with a bed that didn't swing from the ceiling of the ship's deck above would be most welcome.

'Nearly there,' Tye said, as if he could sense Pax's discomfort. 'The drop in temperature is a warning that night is coming.'

'Oh, great,' Pax said wearily. 'It's not just me then.'

'Nope. We'll be ice biscuits in another hour or two if we stay out here. But we're home now! See that deep blue door on the far right? At the end of the lane? That's home.' Tye slapped a hand on Paxton's back and raced ahead like a school kid keen to get inside.

Pax couldn't help but smile. He envied Tye already for the home and family he had, and he hadn't even met them yet.

'They don't know we're coming,' Tye informed him after the small run up the lane as they approached the doorstep. 'It'll be a bit of a surprise for them. I have to warn you though, my family can be, well... you'll see.'

'I think I can handle it, Tye,' Pax reassured. 'If I can handle Diwa, I can handle anything,' he joked.

'Don't say I didn't warn you!' Tye said. He slid an intricate metal key from the front pocket of his pack and used it to open the deep-blue wooden door.

Paxton entered into the high but narrow brick building, Tye shutting the door behind them and locking it quickly to save the heat from escaping into the oncoming night. The warmth inside the house instantly warmed their frozen cheeks. A small fire crackled in a fireplace, and a sky-pine seed could be seen in the centre exuding its warmth and heat from within the flames.

'Anybody home?' Tye called out cheerfully, hastily removing his boots, mitts and moscow coat and dumping it all on a bench inside the entrance to the dwelling.

Pax followed suit and removed his too, the heat already radiating deliciously around him in the warm air. There was no sign of anyone in the front room, so Pax followed Tye into the kitchen area and placed the bag of food and goods they had bought for dinner on the table. The table was painted a deep blue, the same as the front door of the family's home, and the chairs were all a bright cheery yellow, the colour of buttercups. Then an ear-piercing scream tore into Paxton, making him jump slightly.

'Tyson!' The screech emitted from a smaller female version of Tye, from what Paxton could gather as the blur sped towards his friend and embraced him in a vice-like hug. The redheaded figure nuzzled her little face into Tye's torso, and a messy ball of red hair was all that stuck out from his stomach.

Tye squeezed her back, his freckled hands rubbing her head like a puppy, a happy sound coming from deep in his throat. 'Juny-bug!' he greeted her warmly. 'Pax, this is Juniper, my little sister. Juny, this is Paxton Raker.'

Her eyes were half-blue, half-green he noticed when she turned to look at him. Paxton couldn't quite tell which colour they possessed more of, but they widened in awe as she took him in. She then lunged forward and embraced him just as she had her big brother. Pax's face showed his awkwardness at the unexpected gesture. He mimicked Tye and patted her small head as he hugged her back, lifting his heart a little.

'Thank you,' she squealed. 'Thank you for bringing Tye home.'

He had a feeling that she wasn't referring to the exact moment that they were in right now. He felt it in her words that she was referring to the past. Paxton smiled warmly down at Juniper, and she beamed back.

He took in the rest of the narrow space, and something else shot forth at him as he turned to his right. He saw a flash of fur and a long body almost like a serpent's shoot out *through* the wall towards him. Paxton

204

raised his hands in defence at the last second, and the creature's direction changed as it hit the dinner table's surface, spinning around madly. 'What *is* that thing?' he laughed.

It had a long ferret-like body, dainty clawed paws on short legs, and frills that fanned out around its round face. The frills were covered in fur but the edges were laced with small feathers. From what Paxton could see, it looked a lot like a furry axolotl. It hissed at him and its feathered little ear petals fanned out around its neck like a frill-neck lizard, shaking in a display of annoyance, Paxton guessed.

The creature spun in circles around the table and the bags of food, fast as any ferret would be, then it leaped off the table straight for Juniper, its coloured fur changing from brilliant white to a deep purple, blending in perfectly with Juniper's jumper as it twisted itself around her neck.

'This is Edgar!' Juniper replied excitedly, as though the awful creature was a cute little kitten and not a vicious-looking furry snake. 'He's a sparalinx, and he owns this building, sort of. It's kind of his territory, and he can morph through the building walls and cracks in the bricks. Eddie usually comes to visit around dinner time,' she explained as she searched in the bag for something to offer him as he nuzzled into her neck like the perfect living scarf.

Finding the loaf of bread, she tore off a little chunk for him. 'There you go, Eddie,' she cooed, her voice coated in affection for the strange creature. 'You be a good boy. This is Paxton.'

The sparalinx grabbed the chunk of bread with his two front paws, unfurling slightly from around Juniper's neck, and nibbled on it like a river otter with a clam while its eyes narrowed on the newcomer to the house.

'He's our friend, okay? So no leaping from the walls to scare him, no hissing, no eating his hair,' Juniper instructed.

'Eating my hair?' Paxton almost choked as he watched the creature, the pair in a stare-off. He'd decided already that he was not a fan of the building's wall-leaping, camouflaging 'owner'.

'Sparalinxes sometimes eat people's hair when they're new to a building, but Edgar won't do that to you.' Juniper scratched lovingly under Edgar's neck.

Paxton just scrunched his nose at the creepy hair-eating thing.

'There's a whole neighbourhood over on the west side of town and everyone who lives there has really short hair! Their sparalinx is a cranky old one and eats their hair while they sleep!' Juniper's eyes shone with amusement.

A chill ran through Pax, gooseflesh rippling through him at the thought of something eating his hair while he slept, and he had the urge to tie his shoulder-length chestnut hair safely behind his neck.

Tye leaned forward and gave Edgar a rough scratch on the top of his head, 'Alright, Ed, off with you for now.'

The sparalinx shoved the chunk of bread in his mouth, leaped from Juniper's neck and disappeared through the wall to go and harass one of the other families in the neighbourhood for some treats.

'Where are Mum and Dad, Juny? I want to surprise them as I've brought something more than just Pax with me.' Tye's excitable energy resonated perfectly with Juniper's.

'More surprises!' her voice hitched again.

'Yep.' Tye laughed.

'Come on, then.' Juniper grabbed Tye and dragged him through the homey kitchen that led to a narrow hallway with doors either side. 'Mum's in bed sick again, and Dad's gone to work. You just missed him.'

Tye leaned back to explain to Pax as he was pulled down the hall. 'Dad's a baker, works nights.'

'You didn't tell me you had a sister! She looks like a mini you.' Pax said, confused, but also happy to be in a home filled with warmth and excitement, to be included in this joyful moment.

Juniper then pulled Tye into a dark room, and there wrapped under a mountain of blankets was Kyra Bramble, Tye's mother. She turned her head as if in pain, eyes opening like she had just dozed off. Then she realised who Juniper had pulled into her bedroom; her face was ashen but her strained smile was luminous, like a rainbow had just presented her with a pot of gold.

'Tyson, honey,' her voice rattled out of her like she hadn't used it in months.

Tye leaned in and hugged his mother gently for a long minute, breathing in her rose and geranium scent. He was happy to be home again. He kneeled down next to the bed, and it was then that Kyra noticed he wasn't alone.

Pax stood awkwardly in the bedroom's doorway, not sure how to feel about being included in such an intimate moment. He cleared his throat and as he was about to introduce himself, Kyra's voice whispered, 'Paxton, it's so wonderful to finally meet you. I can't believe I get to finally lay eyes on the man who saved my boy.'

Tye's cheeks reddened, and he was glad he was facing away from Pax.

'Nice to meet you too, Kyra, ah Mrs Bramble.'

'Oh, my stars, *please* call me Kyra.' Her deep blue eyes were darker than Tye's and her hair lighter, with streaks of strawberry blond sticking out messily from the pillow her head rested upon. She coughed out loud, another ragged sound, her voice thick with sediment. She sounded so sick.

Paxton added. 'Kyra, I'm not sure what Tye's told you, but I think you should know he's the one who saved *me*. Not the other way around. I wouldn't be standing here right now if it weren't for him.'

Her bony hand squeezed Tye's strong one, her eyes shining fiercely with pride at her son. 'That sounds like my young man.'

'I have something, something to help with the snow lung, Mum.' Tye took in a deep breath in. 'I have a cure.'

Kyra's eyes glazed over a little, her thin pale brows knitting together. 'Whatever do you mean?'

Tye could see she was confused, and he didn't want to risk stressing her or burdening her with anything else. Rather than explain everything, he made the snap judgement to just make her the tea and elucidate if her condition did, in fact, improve. He rose from his kneeling position and placed her fragile hand back on her blanket.

'You'll see, Mum. Pax and I are going to cook us all dinner. Juny, you want a job?'

'Yes!' She uncurled from her cat position on the bed and bounced off towards the doorway.

Tye directed her to the kitchen, away from his mother so she could rest. 'Pax and I bought jilllabee berries at the market today. They're in a bag on the table.' Juniper shot out the door, ducking under Paxton and racing off into the kitchen to find the treats.

'I'll be back in a moment, Mum. Just call out if you need anything, but I've got some tea I need you to try straight away.' His smile was huge, showing all his teeth. His mother was going to be alright, and he would actually use his talent as a healer. Tye was going to save her. He mentally ran through the list of actions to make the brew to perfection for his mother. His body tingled throughout and he thanked the Mother he'd met Diwa.

In the kitchen, Juniper's sugar rush from the jillabee berries or just from having her brother home was far from annoying. She was pure joy, laughter and happiness wrapped into a wild bundle of spindly limbs and wild red hair, and she filled the small home with an aura of comfort, the opposite of her wild energy. As if the outside world and all its worries and negative going ons couldn't reach the Bramble house. As if she were a little guardian protecting the happiness of the whole family.

She instantly made Pax wish he'd had a younger sibling as she buzzed around them like a rattlebee while they made dinner that night. He rubbed a hand over tight spots at the back of his neck as he watched Tye prepare the tea for Kyra. Pax, Tye and Juniper ate in the kitchen while Kyra remained in bed, drinking the brew Diwa had given Tye, and some broth made out of the silver fish they'd bought at the markets.

That night, Pax slept soundly for the first time in weeks on the floor, nestled between Tye and Juniper's bunks either side of each other. Juniper had talked nonstop, then instantly became quiet when she fell fast asleep, her head on her pillow and her little legs tucked in underneath her body with her bum raised in the air. Pax smiled. She was a whirlwind of six-year-old chaos, but she was adorable.

'How come you never told me you had a sister?' Pax asked, a little hurt. Maybe Tye wasn't as good a friend as Paxton thought him to be? Maybe he hadn't trusted Pax enough to let him into his sacred home life until now?

'When I met you... when we were in the mines... the worst thing I could imagine happening wasn't that my parents would never see me again... it was that Juny wouldn't know what had happened to me. That she would be alone and think her big brother didn't love her anymore.' Tye's deep voice cracked at the admission.

'I couldn't even think about speaking her name in that horrible place. I couldn't let myself think about her or talk about her at all; otherwise, I would have broken down, spiralled hopelessly. It's not that I wanted to keep her a secret or anything, but after Zee and Orion saved us, it was just so surreal that we were free. And that they had powers, I mean, Orion literally shifts into a wolf! I just didn't think about it, and I didn't have a chance when I came to visit you in Aylenta. The day I got there... Zee ... it's been a bit hectic.

'On the trip across the sea, you seemed a bit down, Pax. Your nightmares, I didn't realise how bad they still were. I guess I thought Juny would be a nice surprise. She has a special gift, I reckon, she can light up any room she enters. Her energy is contagious. I don't want you to feel left out or anything as you're family now, and you'll always have us. If Mum wasn't so unwell, I swear she would have leaped out of that bed and tackled you to the ground with hugs and kisses the way she talks about you – after I told her everything about the mines.'

Pax chuckled at the mental imagine of Kyra Bramble racing towards him and tackling him in motherly hugs. 'It's all good, Tye. I was just curious is all. I get it now, thanks. I'm lucky to have you, and your family. It means a lot.' He felt his heart swell three sizes bigger as he rolled on his side and squeezed his pillow tight under his head. 'Night.'

Later that night, Paxton woke in a sweat and jumped as he heard sounds coming from another room. It took him a while to remember where he was, then he instantly relaxed as he heard Juniper's sweet snores and Tye's louder not-so-sweet ones. There was shuffling and a noise in the kitchen. Maybe it was Tye's father returning from work? Or it could have been Kyra, up from her bed. Maybe she was already feeling a little better?

Pax relaxed and stared at the ceiling in the dark, worry gnawing at his stomach just thinking about Zee. Was she okay? Was she healed? Had it gotten worse, whatever magical hold Kyeitha had over her? He hated the fact that he couldn't help, that he had no magic and possessed no knowledge that could aid Zee, but mostly he hated that face of the man she was with. Would she now trust the slimy liar? The king's smooth voice still reverberated in Pax's ears sometimes as he'd held the knife tight to his throat in that powerful grip... *Try anything and this boy will have an extra orifice that won't serve him well...*

Pax rubbed at the raised scar on his neck, anger burning in his chest. He'd get Zee back, he'd get her back and as far away from *him* as he could, magic or not.

Rock Guardians

Lamiria

Orion's wolf paws pounded on the cool mossy earth as he ran through the heart of the neon forest between the old Rim world and the mountain pass that was the gate to the guardian's temple in Lamiria. He tried not to rush as he wanted to give Zee the time she needed, and he didn't want her to be unhappy to see him. And honestly, he wasn't looking forward to the confrontation with Ravaryn.

Wolf ducked and weaved through the glowing foliage, its strong energy calming his unsettled heart. He could have flown over the forests in eagle form and made it to the temple faster by far, but there was something about being in this form, as Wolf, that he needed right now. Images of a bright, happy smile complete with sparkling emerald eyes filled his mind. It was as Wolf that he had been at his best, he had been a good father and had been Zee's best friend, her protector, her confidant.

How his missed his hunter, but realised he also missed the girl she used to be. You only get that one precious chance to be a good parent, and deep down in his heart he felt he had done his best. Zee was strong, she was caring and she knew right from wrong. At least he was confident that she did.

Little glow beetles began to flitter about as the moon peered its face into the sky. The forest air was still and warm, but coming to life all around him. He spotted a large fiddle deer in the distance, its antlers glowing with white flowers that bloomed in the moonlight. It huffed out a sharp breath, maybe scenting the stranger in his territory. The deer's majestic grey coat shimmered with a metallic pale blue shine.

Wolf would reach the gates by morning if he kept up his gentle pace, and he knew that he should be more concerned, he *was* of course still concerned, but he knew a different side of his daughter to the one that Verena did. He had been in the fortunate position to see her grow, to *truly* see her grow, when she thought no one else but him was around to witness it. He'd seen her do some reckless but extremely brave and amazing things. He'd seen her speed and accuracy when hunting. Her kindness and empathy, her growing earth powers fighting their way to the surface, desperate for her to wield them, to let them break free.

Yes, Orion would find her soon enough, and hopefully she would be more herself again. *Healed.* The moon watched over him as he made his way through the light of the forest, the mountainous gates growing nearer with each hour.

Wolf travelled late into the night, taking in the neon forest and enjoying its beauty and some of the creatures he hadn't seen for many years. Finding a soft patch of wild mint to rest in that was nestled in a thicket of large figs and sparse lily pillies, he rested then awoke to the sounds of bird calls layered upon each other, signalling that dawn was here. He stretched his long, powerful legs, still in Wolf form, and emitted a large yawn and growl of sleep as his muscles flexed inside him.

He arrived before long at the mountainous entrance that led into the meadows of magic inside the entrance to the temple in Lamiria. He cautiously sniffed the air, scenting messages in the breeze. The atmosphere was steady, mist still lingering close to the forest floor, having not yet risen with the sun's warmth for the day. The forest grew wary as he watched it, shifting around to take in the gap between the rocks, the thin valley lined with a mossy carpet that led through the mountain pass. The gates. The walls were high above the narrow track and laced with ferns, moss and tiny earth spirits that whizzed in and out of the cracks in the walls. Between the boulders, their translucent green and brown bodies, similar to millowisps but more like dragonflies without legs, glided through the air.

Wolf had made this trip many times before, and the rock guardians had never bothered to stop him. He would pass through the narrow valley to the other side, then all that was left was to cross the meadow, and he would be at the temple, where he would find Zee. Hopefully she and Ravaryn were still close by, and she would be healed and whole.

The thick mist hung heavily in the air as he made his way along the path. Moss cushioned the pads of his paws, and condensation settled on his thick white coat. The mist grew thicker in the pass, making it harder to see the path ahead. All he thought about was seeing Zee again, and he didn't even notice the walls narrowing, the rocks slowly shifting silently around him until it was too late. Until they were almost crushing him. Until the guardians had risen out of the very walls before his eyes.

The rock guardians had awoken.

They shifted, causing grating, crushing sounds as they scraped against each other, debris falling all around Wolf in the mist. The way ahead was blocked all around him by earth and rock, and he was claustrophobically caught in the narrow gap of the pass as the guardians rose before him. A voice like thunder overhead boomed from the rock closest to him. Wolf shifted his stance, backing up a little but not retreating. He stayed as Wolf for the moment.

'WHO DARES ENTER?' the voice boomed.

Why would they rise now? It didn't make sense. Wolf had come and gone many times before, all visits unwelcome by his mother, Kyeitha, the now-dead forest queen. So why now?

Realisation struck him like a slap. No. This must have been why Zee had taken so long. Because the rock guardians were protecting the temple and the queen's lands. How had she gotten through? These guardians knew there was no queen now seated on the throne. This was not going to be good.

A growl emitted from Wolf's throat, and he shifted into his human form. 'I am Orion, son of Kyeitha, and I wish to enter into the meadow pass.'

'THE QUEEN IS DEAD!' the voice this time came from the other rock guardian, its tone so loud that it rumbled through the walls of sentient rocks around them, cascading them down upon Orion. He had to dodge them until the landslide eased. The huge rocks still stood unmoving before him, blocking the misty path.

'WE MUST PROTECT THE LANDS.'

And that was it, the conversation was over, and a gigantic hand made of rock swung directly for Orion. He just managed to dodge the granite fist as it smashed into the ground where he'd stood a second ago, leaving an indented mark in the mossy path. The second guardian behind the first shifted the rocks that formed his monstrous body, then rolled and rumbled to elongate them, making his limbs longer and thinner. It then started to scale the narrow walls of the valley path, creeping rapidly up to and around Orion like a giant spider. It leaped in the air and landed behind him, blocking him in between the two rock guardians, and morphed back into its thicker, more solid form.

Orion took in the situation and in a split second shifted to Wolf, leaped up onto the wall and darted between the two. Their fists of rock followed him, pummelling into the walls of the pass, the earth-shattering boulders barely missing his every move. He leaped and spun away from each swing but knew he couldn't escape the blows forever. No matter how agile and fast he was, inevitably he was going to get struck sooner than later, so he ran vertically up the crumbling wall between the two enraged rock guardians. Then Wolf leaped straight for the first one's face that blocked the way to the meadow.

The rock guardian behind him followed just as Orion had hoped, with a powerful fist that impacted right into his fellow guardian's face just as Wolf leaped into the air at the last second and shifted into his eagle form. He turned his head back as he soared higher through the mist and saw that the guardian that had suffered the blow had crumbled back to the earth, but his partner was pounding furiously along the path after Orion, racing on all fours like an enraged gorilla after him.

He beat his wings higher and the guardian pounded the earth with such force that it rumbled the land and air around him as he pushed off the ground and leaped straight for Orion. He extended his arm of rocks straight for him and swung a powerful blow that connected with the eagle mid-flight. Orion felt his side almost cave in with the impact of the blow, pain blasting from his torso. But as he fell from the sky, barely able to beat his wings now, he saw the guardian fall below him and smash into the end of the valley's trail, just before the meadow. It crumbled back into a thousand tiny pieces as it landed just outside of its territory.

Orion was barely able to glide to a safe landing in the meadow and shifted seconds before impact, tucking his wings – now arms – into himself as he crashed into the sweet grasses and wildflowers. His body smashed into the earth upon impact and rolled along the ground. He grimaced in pain, a groan scraping out as he tried catch his breath, winded. After a few minutes lying there, he realised he was not just winded; his ribs were broken, most likely crushed into his body. This was not going to be good.

The shifter dragged his pummelled body the best he could, wincing in agony every metre. After an indeterminate amount of time, all he was focused on now was getting to the lake of life. It could heal him. He would find Zee later, as he couldn't find her now if he let himself bleed to death. Or if his lungs were pierced and he passed out before he got the chance to heal as then it would all be over for *good* this time. Dirt forced its way into his fingernails as he dragged his body closer to the lake, unable to even crawl now. Dizzying sparks of light filled his vision.

No!

He was losing consciousness, but he was in the forest on the track to the temple, so the lake couldn't be far. Orion focused on the light before his eyes as it was now all he could see. They weren't just sparks of pain, of light – they were *millowisps*. They became brighter and brighter, and coloured light engulfed his whole body. He started floating, *Oh Gods, this was it.* He'd failed, he was dying... he'd failed her again.

Orion crushed his face in a grimace as the pain became unbearable and the light became too bright. He could feel he was going to lose consciousness any moment... but then he felt as if he were actually floating. *No.* He *was* actually floating, and he was *wet.* Millowisps surrounded him. They had carried his body to the lake, and water now flooded his face, his eyes and his mouth as he was pushed under the water. Coloured lights blurred through the liquid now over his face, and his body went still and numb as he hovered just under the lake's surface.

Next thing Orion knew, he awoke with his palms resting in soft sand with swarms of millowisps hovering around him. One came close, opening his eyelid like it was lifting a leaf on the forest floor to inspect underneath it. Orion sat up, scaring them, and they all flittered further away. His head was light, the pain was gone, and his side was healed.

'Thank you,' he called out to them in awe, now able to nod his head in respect. They zipped around him to their lily blooms on the water. As Orion's head hung down and he took in what had just transpired, he saw the ground beside him was darkened. He looked around further and realised there was a large patch of stained sand next to him. A deep reddish brown stained the grains of sand. *Blood.* He shifted into Wolf, his keen sense of smell taking in the dried, crusted smell of blood. Familiar blood. *Zee's* blood.

He didn't stop to think... he just *ran.*

Valley of Rivers

Ravaryn's heart threatened to smash through his chest. He was clenching his teeth so hard that they were aching. All he could do was sit there. Sit there and hold Zee's head in his hands and wait. Sahara had taken an unknown potion as well shortly after Zee had. She had not fallen but instead still sat cross-legged and motionless in front of them, her old eyes glazing over in a cloud of white, making her look even more otherworldly.

*

Zee felt like she had been sitting alone in front of the lake of life for hours. Just thinking, digesting what Gaia had told her. This was all real then: this place, the Mother. It was mindboggling to think that this really existed, and Zee had only dreamt about a life like this a few years ago. Now it was all rushing in towards her, filling her faster than a tsunami engulfing a small island, and she was struggling to hold her head above the water. Struggling to hold it all together. After a long while of watching the magical little millowisps flit from bloom to bloom, sometimes stopping to harass one another, Zee decided it was time to get up. Time to figure out what in the underworld she was supposed to be doing, and how she was going to heal her missing limb. She had never actually taken in the temple that stood behind her in any great detail as she had only been here two times. On both of those occasions, there had been much more pressing issues at hand.

She wandered past the elegant sandstone throne, and it pulsed out towards her with a strong energy. The small fungi and vines leaned in towards her as she passed, the little mushrooms glowing a bit brighter. Zee shrugged away an uneasy shiver and proceeded to venture further into the temple. The open verandas were full of plants, vines and small scuttling lizards, while a calm breeze wound through the intricately carved pillars. At the far back of the structure, she came to a stop. A large door was all that stood in the carved rock wall. Ancient languages that Zee didn't recognise filled every inch of the wall, which seemed to be the actual side of a mountain. Zee felt that it towered past the ceiling even though she couldn't see it there.

The door had a protruding stone handle right in the centre, carved in the shape of a crescent moon. Zee grabbed either side of it and tried to twist it one way then the other, using all her force. The moon finally shifted with a grinding, eye-squinting sound coming from it. Nothing happened. Zee stood back, disappointed. She lifted her left hand, the one that had been amputated, and placed it against the stone door, trying to feel the energy beyond it. A blast of light spewed forth, and a rumble shook the door, making the ground underneath her feet vibrate like an earthquake. The door shifted and creaked open. Beyond was a dark tunnel.

Great. My favourite thing: dark, dank tunnels. She hesitated, but as her eyes adjusted, light seemed to be coming from the distance. Zee took a deep breath and entered the tunnel, her hand igniting with a glowing green flame. *Mother, it felt good to use her magic again.* Before she knew it, the light had come closer, and Zee found herself standing upon the precipice of a mountain. A waterfall to her right cascaded powerfully down the side into a valley that stretched far beyond where the eye could see. An entire city stood up out of the rivers that surrounded beautiful stone structures. They glinted as though made of gold in the sunlight that shone down through the clouded sky. Zee's eyes widened, her whole body stilling as she took in the scenery before her.

'Breathtaking, isn't it?'

Zee yelped and jumped away from the voice that sounded behind her, coming dangerously close to the edge of the cliff.

Sahara stood there behind her, her sharp-toothed smile reaching her glossy eyes.

'Dear Mother's Earth! You scared the life out of me!'

Sahara barked with laughter. 'Someone ought to once in a while, don't you think?'

Zee burst into spontaneous laughter along with her.

'It's beautiful, isn't it?' Sahara said, taking in the city in the valley.

'It's-it's...' Zee was short for words. Nothing could explain how beautiful this place was. One word came to the tip of her tongue. '...incredible.' Her skin rippled with a powerful tingle.

'Sahara was this...? Was this your home?'

'Yes.' She closed her eyes and basked in the sunlight next to Zee. 'This is the city in the valley of rivers. The city of Tangaroa, and the true home Maya Village's people.

'Will you return now that the queen is gone?'

'We will return when the rightful queen and guardian sits on the throne. Now come, young one. Do you want to heal that arm or not? The people will be waiting for you to celebrate the Moon Festival. We don't have all night.' She walked back through the tunnel.

Zee almost couldn't pull herself away from the valley; it was like a powerful magnet begging her to stay, to explore. The rivers twisted in and around the little islands, sparkling like turquoise silk in the gentle sunlight. But she turned and hurried after Sahara through the tunnel, not bothering with a flame this time as she could see the light at the end. Next thing she knew, Zee was entering the centre of Maya Village. She turned to look back and saw she was passing through Sahara's door and out of the tree trunk back into the central building. Her stomach fluttered and she felt a hot wave come over her.

Curiously, no one looked her way... so she walked over to the middle of the gathering and past the wall of young men that had been lined up either side of Sahara when she'd taken the thick brew. There was Ravaryn kneeling down, his eyebrows drawn together, his jaw clenched as he stared down at her own lifeless body in his hands. Sahara was sitting adjacent, cross-legged and motionless.

Zee took a step back, and her eyes blinked rapidly at the image before her. Two hands poked her from behind in the ribs at the same moment the gravelly voice boomed, 'BOO!'

Zee's heart leaped in her chest once again. 'Woman, are you mad!'

Sahara barked with laughter so hard it ended in a coughing fit.

'What's going on? What's happening? Am I- am I dead?'

'Oh Mother, I hope not. Wouldn't that put a downer on the celebrations,' she replied, staring straight ahead at Zee in Ravaryn's grasp, her face deadpan. 'Now, all you have to do is gather the energy around you. Can you feel it? Can you feel the warmth and hope the people hold for you? Take every last grain as if it were sand, and use it with everything you have. Look down at your arm and imagine yourself back in your body, whole, safe and healed.'

Zee swallowed, her throat dry. 'What if can't do it?'

'Hmm, then you'll definitely have to get new boots. Too many laces on those ones to manage with one hand.' Sahara eyed Zee's boots.

Zee rolled her eyes. 'Well, when you put it that way.' Sarcasm coated her tongue.

She walked over to her unmoving body in Ravaryn's arms and kneeled beside herself, feeling so strange. Pulses of energy rushed around her veins, putting her even more on edge. Zee shut her eyes and concentrated. She felt the energy from the people, like a strong rumbling hive of bees, vibrating all at once. Glowing with hope - *for her*. She gathered all the energy from the room, and it came to swirl in a mass contained within her palms, like a ball of golden light, a sphere of hope and energy in the palms of her hands.

Lastly, she gathered the strong outpouring of dark energy from Ravaryn. It was so peculiar that no one saw her there, like she and Sahara were indeed in another realm, or even spirits, detached from their bodily vessels. Zee gathered his deep metal-like energy, not understanding why his was different to everyone else's, but it was powerful. She could feel the force of his energy and added it to the ball of light.

Next, the teeth, seeds, Diwa's necklace and Ravaryn's hair all rose in the air. She spun them around and around in the mix, life and death in her hands, and focused all her will, her concentration and power on her physical form before her. In the fortification of her mind, she saw herself whole, her arm back. *Healed.*

Zee had this image firmly cemented in her mind, believing with every ounce of her core that it would be true as she moulded the energy ball against her body. It twirled through the air like a ribbon in the wind, starting from the forearm and weaving in and out of itself, weaving her arm into existence. Like a small vine, the last layer grew. It glowed with brilliant green life as the small vines reformed her left arm, hand and fingers. The vines twisted, tattoo-like, encasing her new arm. They were vines of blood blooms, their velvety leaves black against the dull bronze of her skin. The vines stayed green like they were alive, glowing with life, and her new fingernails shone with a dark onyx, like the velvet of the blood bloom petals.

Zee shook as the energy left her control in front of the space before her. She felt woozy, and her body was shaking like she had run all day and night, 'Oh, my stars. I did it.' Tears of relief pricked her eyes as she looked down at the newly formed arm on her body resting in Ravaryn's hands. His eyes grew huge.

'Yes you did, my dear.' Sahara smiled gently this time, her hands pressed together with palms flat in front of her chest.

Zee looked away from her healed self to grin proudly at the amazing woman who had helped heal her, helped achieve the unbelievable. Sahara beamed back at Zee, and then clapped her hands loudly out in front of her.

Zee was catapulted into darkness, and she felt light. Her eyes flickered heavily like she was just waking up from a deep sleep...

'Zee. Zemira, wake up.' A gentle hand caressed her cheek, coaxing her to wake. 'That's it, come back to me.'

Her eyes opened to the midnight sky contained in Ravaryn's gaze.

'Look,' he prompted, helping her to sit up.

Zee stared down at the hand – the *hands* that gently rested in her lap. Her eyes glossed over as she stared down at the miracle before her; the work of art that adorned her new arm. *Her arm.* It sparkled light green with vines and deep black with velvet blooms. They twisted down her fingers and finished in dark shiny nails. She looked up at Sahara sitting still before her. The healer's eyes were cloudy but in a blink they switched to rich mahogany once more, and she grinned proudly back at Zee. 'Well done, Rim Walker.'

Dance of the Luna Moths

Maya Village, Lamiria

The villagers cheered and shouted their approval as Zee stood and Sahara showed off her healed arm. The moon was emerging from beyond the horizon as the sun set and the festivities began. Drums sounded from all around the perimeter and fires were lit.

Mirabel dragged Zee to the edge of the clearing where all the villagers were making their way. She felt giddy with anticipation. After profusely praising Zemira for her amazing feat, and confirming that the ceremony was the most amazing thing she had ever witnessed, Mirabel had calmed down. *Slightly.*

'Where are we going? What is happening?' Zee questioned, still digesting the feeling of being whole. She was ridiculously happy and calm all at once, and hadn't felt this way for so long she'd forgotten what it actually felt like. Her head was light and floaty, her body weightless. Zee was afraid to truly embrace it in case it were, in actual fact, just a dream.

'The dance of the Luna moths, of course! Don't you have Luna moths inside the Rim world?' Mirabel questioned.

'No, I don't think so,' Zee replied, puzzled. Why was the girl so excited about moths?

The drums started their deep, pounding tempo, and Ravaryn appeared at her side. 'I lost you after the gathering dispersed, but I see you're in good hands.' His smile was warm as he slid his smooth hand around Zee's new one, making her heart flutter. Her stomach threatened to float away like a bubble. The energy and excitement all around her was infectious.

'Here they come!' Mirabel pointed to the edge of the forest at the start of the clearing. The sun had now completely set, and the moon's glow was so bright it was lighting the whole clearing in a magical glow. Zee guessed she expected to see large numbers of small moths come out of slumber and wake for the night. The crowd became quiet, and all that filled Zee's ears was a steady rising beat of drums. She searched for any sign of the moths as everyone patiently waited. Then a gust of air and a sweep of wings beat from the forest canopy where everyone's eyes were directed. An enormous creature appeared, emerging from within the trees.

The moth was twice as large as a fully grown duellerat, its brown and tawny wings looking almost fluffy with fur. A rider clung to its back, tucked in snuggly while the moth glided over the crowd. Its long back wings stretched out in a beautiful teardrop shape, just like the Hercules moths from Aylenta. More and more of them poured from the forest and hovered over the crowd in a circle above. Zee squeezed Ravaryn's hand, unable to pull her eyes from the majestic creatures.

Ravaryn leaned close to Zee's ear, his voice like silk against the beat of the drums. 'That's not even the best part.'

Weightlessness filled her insides as the last of the Luna moths joined the large circle hovering above, varying in different shades of earthen amber, deep mahogany and light tawny. The drums picked up tempo, and the riders ushered their moths faster and faster above the crowd, their wings flurrying with their efforts, the moon glinting off the velvet extensions. Then the most amazing thing happened, as if the moths were transforming. They started to shed the furry coats encasing their powerful wings, and sparkling pieces of wing dust glittered down over the crowd like the sky was raining miniscule stars.

Zee's lips parted in awe as the moths sped round and round, their wings becoming silvery and silken in iridescent purples, blues and greens. She raised her hands up in a joyful V to catch the sparkles falling down onto her, relishing the feel of the dust in her fingers, on *both* her hands. She rubbed the shimmering powder together in them, euphoria filling her body like a rising tide.

Ravaryn watched her bathe in the magic; she caught his eye and smiled like a giddy child, wild and without any restraint. He smiled that handsome half smile as she reached out and traced the lines of his decorative Luna paint with the shimmering powder. She traced gently over his muscled arms, his neck, his forehead, and bravely close to his dark eyes. Zee didn't even realise other villagers were indulging in the same act, but in her core she instinctively knew this was just what you were supposed to do.

Ravaryn, without a word, reached his hand up and collected some of the sparkling dust, rubbed his palms together and started to trace over the lines of Zee's body, over the yellow and green patterns decorating her skin. He gently traced every line with tender fingers, Zee's skin warming and tingling from every point of contact. His fingers reached her face, and her eyes glowed brightly in the moon's soft light, turquoise sparkles in seas of forest green.

His fingers traced her cheeks, her forehead and very tenderly ran over her parted lips. Ravaryn leaned closer as the drums' tempo beat steadily, matching Zee's heart fluttering rapidly in her chest. She looked deep into his ebony eyes and realised she was utterly, wholly, deeply in love with this strange soul. As if Ravaryn somehow heard her heart's confession, he pulled her closely to him, his hands strong and firm around her waist, and kissed Zee deeply under the glittering night sky.

Her body filled with shockwaves that raced like maddened glow beetles in her veins. She kissed him back as her hands threaded through his silky dark curls, the feel accentuated tenfold in her left hand, her new, oversensitive fingers fresh to every new feel, every new sensation. Zee finally pulled away to take a breath, Ravaryn's grip around her waist warming her skin and making her body stir with want. She felt his need for her press warm and hard against her stomach.

'I have something for you,' he whispered in her ear, his warm breath so inviting against her skin. He removed his hands from her waist, her skin instantly crying out for the warmth of him in the night's cool wind as he pulled something from his pant pocket. Something that glinted on a string in the moonlight. Zee examined it further and realised it was her ring from him. The dark swirling gem moved in gentle swirls of silver and ebony on a thin woven band of soft leather.

Ravaryn moved closer to reach around Zee and secure it around her neck. 'May I?' He hesitated mid-way.

'Yes,' Zee replied, slightly breathless. 'Yes, of course.'

Ravaryn engulfed her lithe frame, and holding her against his firm body, he tied the woven band behind her neck. Bending down, he placed a kiss at the base of her neck, then righted himself and gazed down at her.

Zee grabbed the ring-turned-necklace in her hand and spun it around to look at it once more, the molten liquid inside somehow moving serenely in the stone.

'Happy birthday, Zemira.' His lips rose in a full smile this time. 'It's all I could muster on such short notice. You deserve so much more, but I thought it would do as a replacement for a while seeing as you had to sacrifice Diwa's necklace for the spell.'

'Thank you, it's beautiful.' Zee placed the necklace back down against her sparkling chest.

'You're welcome, but I think there are much more beautiful things to be had in this world.'

Zee blushed even through the sparkling dust still glittering down through the night sky as the Luna moths pounded their wings in the air above. The whole village glowed with luminescent colours and patterns, exuding a vibe of happiness, rejoicing and excitement. The moths finished their magnificent display, sweeping gently away on shimmering silky wings. The drums began to be accompanied by strings and wind instruments as the villagers returned to the centre of the celebrations and began to dance around the fires.

'Come on.' Zee pulled Ravaryn along with her, following Mirabel and her friends. 'Let's dance.' Her smile was warm and inviting, as if she were asking him much more than to just dance.

Ravaryn's face was glowing not just with the dust shimmer, but deep from within, and Zee could see it, she could *feel* it. She could see beneath his mask, beneath all of it now. And she decided that she liked very much what she saw. She had never felt happier in her entire life than she did in this moment. Ravaryn followed her, his hand still wrapped firmly around hers, smooth and warm.

'Anything for you,' was his reply.

They reached the centre of the festivities, and he spun her around in the growing group of dancers in front of the heat-giving fires. Her skirts and long dark braids spun out from her as sparkling dust floated around her body, shimmering in the firelight, encompassing her like a precious jewel.

A jewel that was now firmly imbedded into Ravaryn's heart.

Part III

Travelling East

Zee was wrapped in strong arms still covered in shimmery Luna moth dust. A soft pillow felt heavenly under her head and a small yellow and silver finch chirped in the dappled morning sunlight. She and Ravaryn had danced for hours at the Moon Festival. The people here celebrated the Mother in a different way but for still all the same reasons as those back home inside the old Rim world.

Last night had made her somehow connect to the Maya villagers on a deeper level. She felt accepted, more than she ever had back home. Zee had never imagined more beautiful creatures than the Luna moths, glittering dust down on the crowd. She'd had a little too much of the lily-pily wine, and had indulged in the many different foods that had been on offer. Her head swam a little, still fluffy and light, and her feet were sore from all the dancing. But her heart was warm and happy and full of promise. She was healed, wrapped in the safety of Ravaryn's arms, and she'd never felt as light as her heart was making her feel now. A deep pull within her being told her that this was *right*. She felt *balanced*. Like a missing part of her had finally been found.

Ravaryn made a deep sound behind her and squeezed her against him a little tighter as he started to awaken, his body solid and warm at her back. Just as they bathed in the quiet cocoon of their togetherness in the morning's promise of a fresh day, the door to their room rapped with a heavy knock.

'Ignore it,' Ravaryn groaned. 'I want you all to myself a little bit longer.'

The door shook again with a loud knock. Zee tried to get up out of bed, but Ravaryn held her to him. 'Stop that, it might be important.' She pried his hands away from her and dug him in the ribs with her finger, a large smile on her face.

Ravaryn's face shone back with a similar mischievous light.

Zee stumbled to the door and opened it to reveal Aytac standing with three packs on the small veranda. 'Morning, Zemira.' He dipped his head a little. 'As soon as you're ready, I'd like to get moving. The whole village is flowing with excitement at the news you are going to rescue Kyeitha's prisoners.' His smile was warm and hopeful.

Zee's head throbbed and she wanted to dive right back into that bed and sleep the day away in Ravaryn's arms. Instead, she said, 'Yes, of course, Aytac. A promise is a promise.'

'I'll have breakfast sent up to you and a bath prepared.' He eyed the festival's glitter still adorning her skin and her colourful outfit from the previous night.

'Thank you, that's very thoughtful. I'll be ready as soon as I can.'

With that, Aytac nodded and proceeded hastily to retrieve some food and someone to fill the bath.

Zee shut the door and groaned. 'I wish I had one day, just one day to myself to enjoy not being cursed.' She flopped back on the bed wearily.

'Being in high demand can become exhausting, can it not?' Ravaryn squeezed her tightly.

'How did you do it? Being king all those years?'

'I whinged *a lot*, mostly to Caden. Why do you think he was so quiet?' he chuckled. 'Come on, Rim Walker, time to get up. You have people to save.'

Zee groaned her reply and buried her head under her pillow. 'Five more minutes...'

*

A very enthusiastic Aytac, a weary Zee and an annoyed Ravaryn left later that morning and headed east to find the mysterious Dark Rim that Aytac had been told about by none other than Diwa herself.

'So how do you know that they're in there if Kyeitha had never told you where she had taken them?' Zee had enquired upon their departure from Maya Village.

'The seer told me.'

'What exactly did she tell you?' Ravaryn asked, his annoyance at having to travel with the watcher momentarily overtaken by his curiosity. 'She can be... misguiding with her words sometimes.'

'The old seer said that the Rim Walker would be the only one who could pass in and out of the Dark Rim wall. That it was similar to the Rim world the humans had lived in, but worked the opposite way, containing the forest folk instead of the humans.'

Zee felt an ominous sharp prickle in her hand. She clenched her fist to brush away the foreboding sensation. Experience should have taught her not to ignore such sensations, especially after what she had been through when she ignored the pain signalling there was something wrong with her arm after ending Kyeitha. But this seemed different, so she brushed it away for now as she had more important things to focus on.

'Is that all she said?' Ravaryn pried Aytac in a disgruntled tone. He didn't appreciate his early morning wake-up call nor their hasty departure so soon after Zee had recovered from such a massive ordeal. She had insisted that she was fine, but he could see the exhaustion still lingering there.

'She also said,' Aytac explained in an irritable tone at Ravaryn's untrusting presence, 'that there was a great danger, great darkness held within, and to be careful to avoid it at all costs.'

'That sounds like Diwa,' Zee added sarcastically. 'Always so precise on the important details.'

The trio carried on, treading through wild parts of the lush green forest and crossing over a few small creek beds with clear, cool water until they reached what must have been the beginning of the deadlands. Zee had seen them once before when she'd been with Gaia, who had explained that the ancient humans had destroyed and poisoned so much of her, causing much destruction. How could Gaia have any love left for them after what they had done? Zee couldn't understand how the Mother could be so powerful, so caring and still so trusting of her children. The more she thought about Gaia, the more she wished she herself were just as forgiving.

It was said that humans had been at the peak of their civilisation, with all the tools at their disposal to have or create anything they wanted, but instead they chose their own demise. Zee was baffled about the past, even with what little she had learned. She couldn't fathom their greed or why had they done it. It was all so foreign to her.

'Zemira.' Aytac's tone was respectful as he cut away a path to the opening of a sparsely grassed cliff. He extended a hand out to help her step over the last of the brush and followed her out, letting go of the branches he held to fling back into Ravaryn's face. Ravaryn just clenched his fist with restraint as he came to stand on the opposite side of Zemira and watched her face aghast with emotion as she took in the expanse of the deadened land.

In the distance before them was the Dark Rim. It looked so much smaller than the Rim world that had contained and protected the humans since the war of 2032, and nearly the whole half of its circumference was visible from their elevated position. They could almost see the prison from end to end, or it seemed that way from their vantage point.

Dense energy seeped into Zee from the earth she now stood on. This Rim *contained* the roiling black clouds and blue lightning streaking around within it instead of keeping it out, like her Rim world had. Black-burned trees scattered the desolate rocky land of the Dark Rim. Lifeless tree-like sentinels imbedded in the forsaken earth were cemented like the soldiers of a forgotten war, and mist twisted in and around them, covering most of the land beyond.

'We're nearly there.' Aytac's strong voice held hope.

Zee inwardly cringed. This land felt poisoned, wrong - but she wouldn't back down on her promise. She rubbed her newly healed and vine-patterned left hand, as if soothing its concern.

'It should take less than an hour to cross these deadlands and reach the Dark Rim's walls from here,' Ravaryn supplied, uneasy as the rest of them, it seemed. 'Let's break now, rest and eat, then head on to the wall.'

Aytac nodded with agreement. At least they could agree on one thing,

Zee slumped her pack off and searched for her water and something to eat. She was famished yet her headache was finally starting to ease off from the morning. She sat up against a large boulder and chewed away at a dried piece of spiced meat, knees up in front of her as she stared out at the mysterious Dark Rim. Ravaryn came to sit beside her, his hands clasping in front of his own raised knees.

'I can't believe that there's another Rim world,' Zee said, awestruck. 'Why would Diwa have never told us about it? Why only tell Aytac when he knew to specifically ask where the prisoners were being held? It just doesn't make sense why Diwa would want to hide this. To let those poor people suffer?'

Zee was upset with the realisation that her old friend must have known of this Rim's existence for a very long time. It just didn't make sense to her.

'There are a great many things that woman knows, Zee, and she has to choose what to say and when to say it. I'm sure she has her reasons, and I'm sure that they are very good ones for her to choose secrecy over telling us. For her to be burdened with the knowledge that her secrecy has kept those prisoners in there for all this time, she wouldn't have made the decision lightly.' Ravaryn said, defending his mother's decision even though he was just as perplexed as Zee. 'But they'll be free soon, all thanks to you.' He nudged her shoulder. 'You should be proud that you have changed the world so much already. This entire realm is lucky to have you, Zemira Creedence, hero of both worlds.'

Zee's smile was small. 'I *have* changed the world...' she agreed. She just wasn't sure whether that had actually been a good thing though. Had she done more good than bad? Or had her actions actually caused more damage? A dark, foreboding feeling was growing within her, and she sensed something coming. She felt the ominous, pulsing energy ahead, contained inside the expanse that was the Dark Rim, waiting for its chance to somehow emerge.

An Unexpected Attraction

Zenya, Kymera

Paxton had left the Bramble's warm house full of love and light early that morning. He'd met a tired George Bramble just beforehand, his bear-like form barely squeezing into the narrow blue front door, his strong hand-shake nearly crushing all the bones in Paxton's right hand. George's smile was broad and huge, exactly like Tye's, and he had light earthen eyes and dusty brown hair sprinkled with just a few greys that made him look as kind and inviting as the rest of the Bramble family, even considering his size.

Pax had promised to visit again soon after finding Zee and making sure she was alright. How he envied Tye for the family life he possessed, and he felt a spark of luck that they'd met, despite the horrible circum-stances. He now had a friend he knew he could count on if he ever needed anything. Tye had apologised profusely for not coming with him, even though he didn't need to. Pax completely understood his hesitancy to enter the castle again after what had happened to him. He also understood that if he were in Tye's shoes, he would have chosen to stay and look after his family rather than seeking out the king who had caused them both so much harm.

Tye's place was at home with his family. Paxton wanted Diwa's medicine to be real, and he also wanted to see Kyra Bramble cured of the horrible snow lung affliction. He didn't know much about it, but after seeing her rattled breaths sucking into her sunken chest, as if she were drowning somehow in her own body, a shiver went down his spine. He definitely prayed to the Mother that the cure was real.

When George had sat down at the kitchen table, he produced a letter from inside his shirt. The envelope had a small seal of black wings encased in a serpent laced with gold trim, and he hesitantly offered it to his son, bracing for his reaction. 'It's for you, Tye. It was delivered to my work this morning, and it's a letter from the king.'

*

Paxton stood in front of the ice-coated steel gates with Kymera's signature snowflake-tipped spears at the entrance to the castle in the heart of Zenya. His legs felt liquid-like at the thought of what he would have to confront inside, but the burning warmth in his gut at the thought of seeing Zee again spurred him on. Two guards stood at the closed metal gates, still in their thick black and gold moscows, the king's insignia of a gold serpent surrounding a pair of wings stitched into their heavy uniforms. They both had swords at their sides, and Paxton guessed they were probably made from the Borztan metal that he'd had to suffer and slave for to procure for the king. His fists clenched at his sides the same time as his jaw. Pax approached one of the guards, the shorter, less-intimidating one, he had thought.

'I wish to gain entrance to the castle. I wish to see the king. He has a... a visitor that I need to visit with.' Pax's voice sounded confident but he felt angry at having to see the king again.

'And who do we say is requesting to be seen?' the guard asked in turn. His face barely made any expression, and his hands did not move from their position crossed over his sword.

'Paxton. Paxton Raker. I'm here to see Zemira Creedence. I've been told that she's here, with the king.'

The guard turned his head to look at his fellow guard. They exchanged looks then he turned to open the gates before Pax. 'Follow me.'

The closer they got to the castle's large stone entrance the more it seemed to tower menacingly over Paxton. He hoped he'd never have to relive anything to do with the castle, the king or the mines ever again. He still battled with his mental and physical scars almost every night.

Without speaking, the guard led Paxton up a staircase and through two large doors frosted over by metal ice crystals. Once they entered the actual castle, the temperature warmed slightly, and Pax could once again feel his toes and his face. How did people live like this? In such freezing temperatures? He was led through corridors and large, open rooms but spotted no people. He thought it odd to be so deserted, but it made him a fraction more comfortable. They reached another guard in a room with soft cream carpet and the nicest furniture Pax had ever seen. Light illuminated the icy walls, and the ceiling sparkled like the Milky Way on a clear night. The first guard conveyed Paxton's request with the one who was dressed in the familiar metallic-armoured fabric laced with Borztan, then took his leave.

'Paxton, I'm Barrack, head guard of the royal house. Follow me.' He said this almost respectfully, there was no order in the statement. He didn't just turn on his heel and expect Paxton to follow either, but extended an arm and gestured to the hallway behind him, waiting for Pax to proceed.

Paxton though of Zee and forced his legs forward.

'So you wish to see the king. Why, may I ask?' Barrack's voice was steady, and Pax sensed there was no malice behind his words but he was still on edge. He didn't trust any soul who resided in this castle.

'I'm here to see my friend Zemira.'

'Ahh, the Rim Walker,' Barrack replied. 'I cannot unfortunately take you to see her as she's not here, lad,' Barrack explained, his tone neutral. 'But I can take you to someone who might be able to help you.'

'What do you mean she's not here?' Pax's voice came out an octave higher than he was comfortable with.

'I'm sorry, lad, that's all I know. I'm head guard now but I'm not as privy as Commander Caden once was.' Barrack stopped at the base of a winding stone staircase that disappeared in an upward trajectory. He nodded towards the staircase. 'There'll be answers up there for you. If you need anything else, you find me, and don't hesitate to ask.' He bowed slightly and left Paxton standing there, dumbfounded. He had not been expecting this level of hospitality.

Pax followed the stone staircase upwards. A few of the star lights lit the way, but only marginally. He felt the temperature drop as he got higher and realised when he reached the top that the staircase had led him to a rooftop. A gentle icy wind swept by, and the sun almost poked out through the thick cloud cover that Kymera was accustomed to. Pax took the rooftop in, and there before him was a large snow-white creature that almost blended into its surroundings. A caw left its beak and its fox-like ears pricked up then flexed back. Just as he was about to retreat back down the staircase to find Barrack and demand some answers, a head popped out from behind the beast. Wild red curls framed one of the most beautiful faces he had ever seen. Her pale skin was dusted lightly with freckles and her sharp eyes reminded him of the summer skies back home.

'Are you going to stand there and gawk or are you going to come over here and introduce yourself?' Her voice was authoritative, but sweet.

Pax felt his palms sweat as he mustered the courage to approach the young woman and her beast. He edged closer but rounded the beast a safe distance away from its maw, circling around to the fiery-haired young woman.

Extending his hand, he said, 'I'm Paxton.' He didn't know why, but all his words seemed to evade him like water through a sieve as he stood there, staring at her bright blue eyes, the corners of them crinkling a little as she noted his gesture.

She stopped brushing the furry parts of the beast before her and extended her own hand towards him, a delicate sliver ring of small vines adorning her thumb. 'I'm Mazda.'

Pax suddenly wished his palms weren't so sweaty. 'Mazda, nice to meet you. Are you the ah... stable hand for that creature?'

Mazda laughed. 'I guess you could say that.' Her teeth were perfect, and her smile lit up her delicate face. 'How can I help you, Paxton?'

'I'm looking for the king. He has my friend Zemira with him but I've been told they're not here. Barrack, the guard, told me you could help.'

'Did he now?' Mazda replied curiously, a touch of something coating her words. 'Did he tell you anything else?' she pried.

'He said if I needed anything to not hesitate to ask. To be honest with you, I'd rather not be here any longer than I have to. I loathe the king and just want to see Zemira. I want to know whether or not she is safe, that's all. Can you help me or not?'

Mazda raised two perfect eyebrows at him, making him instantly regret his stern tone. She oozed authority over him for some strange reason.

'I could help you. I *do* know where we might find them. You're awfully brave to say such things about the king in his own castle, might I add.'

'I have my reasons.' Paxton felt his fists clenching against his sides again.

The creature spun its head out towards him, sensing Paxton's rising anger as a threat to his companion.

'Blaze, calm. He doesn't mean us any harm. Do you?' She eyed Paxton, asking the question with more than her words, while caressing the creature's giant head.

'No, I don't. I'm just worried about Zemira, with *him*. Can you help me?' Pax pressed.

'That depends.'

'On what?' Pax felt himself completely off balance around this young woman.

'Can you fly?' Her smile was teasing and laced with an excited sparkle in her eye.

'What? You don't mean... on one of those?' Pax stared at the creature's horrid eyes, all pinpointed still on him.

'Yes, I mean one of *these*. This is Blaze. He's a duellerat and can understand everything you're saying. He could also slice you in half if he chose too, so I suggest you be nice.'

Paxton gulped and felt his stomach liquefy. 'You've got to be kidding me.' His eyes were owl-like.

'Oh no...' Mazda's grin was pure mischief. 'I'm dead serious.'

*

Tye held the letter in his hands as if it were poison, disgust and fear pouring from him as his eyes traced the perfect swirls of handwritten lines.

Dear Master Tyson Bramble

I hope this letter finds you well and in the warmth and safety of your family's home. There are no words to explain how unfairly you were treated in the mine as a direct consequence of my actions. I can never ask your forgiveness for the hardships you've endured, so I won't. But please understand that I am truly sorry for the horror that befell you and your family, along with many others who became intertwined in my quest to end the Rim guardian's hold over this world.

As you have now met my mother, Diwa, you may understand that there is more to this world than just black and white, and that miracles are possible. I hope that by now you have started treating your mother for snow lung, and that in the following days to come she shows signs of a steadfast recovery.

I am not writing this letter to try and gain your trust, or forgiveness from you in any way as what I did was inexcusable. I am writing to offer you a position as head horticulturalist and healer in the newly built glass houses at the edge of Zenya city. Diwa and I have devised a way to grow all the ingredients that are needed to make the cure for snow lung, along with many other rare and important herbs and plants for healing, most of which cannot be as potent or powerful once harvested and imported from Aylenta.

There is much prosperity and healing in the future for Kymera and the whole of the old Rim world. Please consider this offer carefully as you could change and heal so many lives. It is a lot to ask, but please don't let the past or your feelings towards me hinder your decision.

If you decide that this is something you are interested in, please report to the glasshouses as soon as you are fit and able.

The King of Kymera
Ravaryn Bellford Black

Illusion Spores

The Dark Rim

After staring at the intimidating, swirling mass of energy inside the Dark Rim, Zee, Aytac and Ravaryn scaled the craggy dead cliff down to the flat blackened expanse of land between them and the wall of the Dark Rim. Twisted remnants of dead trees were the only objects scattering the land, their gnarled branches reaching out from their trunks, black like they'd been burned, but lifeless all the same.

Zee felt that they had reached their halfway point through the ominous terrain, much like the land she had seen with Gaia, the land that the Mother worked tirelessly to heal, when a thick mist started to creep in and around them from nowhere. No wind had brought it, and the way it twisted around them, it seemed that it had a life of its own. A cold tingle crept through Zee's left arm, spreading up her shoulder and down her spine, setting her on edge.

'Something's wrong,' she stated to the other two, clearly already assessing the situation for danger. 'Did Diwa mention anything about this, Aytac?'

'No. She was scarce on details and spoke with riddles,' he said, annoyance clear in his voice.

Zee rolled her eyes. That was exactly like Diwa then. *Right*. They would have to figure this out on their own.

'It doesn't seem to be doing anything other than lowering visibility at this stage,' Ravaryn said. 'I say we carry on and not linger to find out what it may be hiding.'

'Agreed,' Aytac and Zee replied simultaneously, Zee's voice a little more concerned than Aytac's sure reply.

They trekked on close together through the barren mist-covered land as visibility was now limited. Zee noted that there seemed to be more and more of the deadened trees almost clustering closer to them.

'Did any of you see these trees so closely clustered from the peak before?' Zee's arm tingled with what felt like warning, and she tried to swallow down her rising anxiety. She had sat while they rested, staring out at the tundra, and had noted that none of the trees had been so close together as they now seemed.

'No,' Ravaryn replied with an agreeable tone. 'They had all been perfectly spaced over the tundra. I recall because it seemed an odd formation for a forest, even a dead forest, to have grown in.'

The three came to a halt, Aytac at the lead stopping in his tracks. A perfect row of the blackened gnarled trees stood before them, their branches towering out over the trio's heads. The trees were *moving*. With groaning, crackling sounds, small black beetles poured away from their trunks and underneath their open root structures, scuttling away in black waves.

Zee stepped back closer to Ravaryn as the mist swept in around the trees. From the outstretched limbs, black fruit-like spheres started to swell into existence like large raindrops, growing to the size of dewfruit.

'Guys, I don't like this! I think we should run!'

'Follow me!' Aytac replied, voice urgent.

'Stay close! *Do not* lose sight of each other!' Ravaryn commanded.

The three raced forth zigzagging through the tight spaces as the tree continued to crowd them. The swelling black orbs began to burst, raining down black mist... no not mist... tiny spores.

'Cover your mouths!' Aytac roared.

But the air was so thick with them, and the spores hung like fog, the mist coaxing it thickly around them. Zee's throat burned, and she saw Aytac drop to the ground before her.

'*Aytac!*'

She spun to see Ravaryn at her back, clutching at his throat, his eyes wide as he dropped to his knees and leaned forward. Zee felt dizzy and her vision clouded as she reached out to Ravaryn and clasped his hand tightly in her own. Then she too dropped to her knees as they clutched at their throats and succumbed to the poison of the strange spores.

*

Zee awoke all alone in the dead forest, the mist so thick she could barely see her hands and her onyx fingernails right in front of face.

'Ravaryn? Aytac? Where are you?' she called through the mist.

No replies came, but as though she were hallucinating, out from the mist stepped Paxton.

Mother's Earth. 'Pax, is that you?'

He didn't answer, and his eyes and face had an expression that looked wrong. Zee had never seen him this way before.

'How could you?' he seethed. 'How could you choose *him?*' The mist spiralled madly around his form.

'Pax, please let me explain,' Zee stuttered, then Paxton disappeared into the mist and Orion replaced him where he stood. Zee was lying rigid on the ground, her body now frozen.

'Zemira, I'm so disappointed in you. *How... could... you?* After what he's done to this family. I can't bear it. You're no longer my little wolf... you're a disappointment, a mistake.'

'No, Dad, please...' Zee reached for him, tears now streaking down her face, her heart clenching painfully like the life was being squeezed from it.

'Dad, I can explain...'

Orion turned away from her, his face filled with disgust. Then he swirled and there before her stood her mother, her face full of hate, actual hate, towards her. 'After everything I did for you, after everything I sacrificed to keep you hidden, to keep him away from you! I gave up half my life!' she spat. 'And this is how you repay me!'

'Mum, no. I didn't mean to. I...' Sobs wracked Zee's body. *What have I done? How could I have let this happen? How could I have been so selfish?*

The mist spun once again before her, and there with her sinister mulberry smile and hateful eyes stood Kyeitha in all her finery. Ravaryn kneeled before her, his hands bound and his hair grasped in her hand as she held his head back, neck exposed, to Zee.

NO. You're dead.

This wasn't real... couldn't be real...

'Rim Walker, pfft,' she crooned. 'Destroyer of worlds more like it... the almighty powerful Zemira. But you couldn't help yourself when it came to Ravaryn, could you? Do you know what you have done?' She pulled Ravaryn's head back painfully. He grit his teeth but still said nothing.

Not real.

Not real.

Not real.

'Do you even know what you've fallen for?' She cackled and raked her free hand down Ravaryn's throat. 'Feast your eyes on your love.'

'NO!' Zee screamed and reached out, her body like stone where she sat.

His skin peeled back in Kyeitha's grasp and fell away, revealing a creature before her, sharp teeth glistening. Ravaryn's wings protruded from its scaly, muscled back, and clawed hands with dark talons appeared as Ravaryn transformed before her eyes.

Wake up... wake up...

'STOP!' Zee screamed and forced her eyes shut.

Not real... It's... not ...real! Tears streamed down her face, clouding her vision.

*

Aytac moved through the thick fog and dead trees. 'Zemira? Ravaryn?' He called out in search of them but only the spinning fog surrounded him.

'Aytac...' a strangled voice whispered in his ear. He turned around and there she stood. His twin, his sister, but she wasn't her... this woman was sucked of all life, grey skin stretched over bones, her eyes leaking black blood down her face, her hair barely clinging to her scalp in thin patches. The scent of carrion filled his nose. 'How could you have left me? You *let* her do this to me. You said you'd come for me... you said you'd save me...'

Aytac's not-sister reached out a rotting finger towards him, pointing accusatorily. Black beetles scurried over her decayed skin, and she opened her mouth wide as if to speak... but instead she coughed, and maggots sprayed out from within her rotting vessel.

Aytac backed away from the creature.

'You promised... you promised... you promised,' it wept, 'to protect me... big brother...'

Aytac's heart smashed in his chest.

Tricks.

He spun on his heel and fled from the corpse portraying his twin sister. *No. She's not dead, she can't be... I would feel it... I would know.*

He shifted into his black wolf form and raced away with all his might through the trees, only to see her ghostly form following him through the mist. He turned his head back to tear his view away from her again and again. The mist thickened, and as he raced, he smashed his head into the trunk of a blackened tree.

*

Ravaryn was startled awake, his hand still clasped in Zee's. She was slumped forward on the ground, reaching towards him.

249

'Zemira!' Panic coated his voice. His body was heavy, like his limbs were full of lead. He forced himself forward and slid her into his lap, cradling her head. 'Zee, wake up!' He swept a delicate finger over her cheek.

A movement before him caught his eye in the mist. 'Aytac! Is that you?' Ravaryn called out.

The figure moved slowly, coming forward without answering him, and then materialised from the mist in front of him.

Ravaryn felt fire quicken through his veins, and his very core turned ablaze with fury as he clutched Zee's lifeless form to him.

There before him stood Kyeitha, inspecting a fingernail as if he were the least interesting thing in the world.

Her face finally looked at his with a sinister smirk. 'You can't save her this time, Rav,' she sing-songed.

A cough came from Zee. She opened her eyes and then there in his arms, her black braided hair turned lighter, streaked with earthen browns, and Zee's turquoise-specked emerald eyes became deeper, richer, and her similar face structure shifted slightly.

'Liara,' Ravaryn breathed, tears of shock seeping down his face.

Liara just stared back from his hold as a baby's cry echoed from beyond in the mist.

'It's our Aida.' Liara's elegant hand swept at his tears. 'Go. Save her,' Liara whispered. 'You said you would protect us... you said that... that...' she stuttered on the words. 'That you loved us.' Tears poured from her accusing eyes.

Kyeitha stood over them, 'It's your fault, you know. Your *love* killed them both,' she hissed down at him. 'If you had just obeyed like the creature that you are, they would still be here.'

Ravaryn seethed with anger, his heart fracturing into a million pieces like a shattered mirror. 'You're an aberration!'

'Look again,' she crooned. 'Someone else is just waiting for you to let them down.'

Kyeitha raised her perfect eyebrows, her eyes empty of emotion, and stared at the face in Ravaryn's grasp.

Ravaryn looked down at Liara and before his eyes, she transformed. The hair became midnight black and twisted into braids, her eyes became a lighter shade of forest green with small speckles of turquoise within, and her features changed slightly, her full mouth and lips reforming back into Zee's. She reached up with her adorned hand, the black blooms shifting around like the mist, and rested her palm on his face, wet with tears of pain.

'I'm sorry. I'm so sorry,' he choked out.

'Shhh.' Zee swept his tears away. 'Come closer...'

Ravaryn bent his head closer to hear her strained voice.

'W...'

'Wake...' Zee whispered into his ear.

'What?' he strained to hear her, leaning in further.

Her voice became louder, stronger, more urgent, laced with concern. '*Ravaryn... wake... up! WAKE...UP!*'

Burrownut Biscuits & Tea

Black Forest, Aylenta

'Motherwort, chickweed, meadowsweet and lavender,' Diwa sang to herself in her garden grove in the morning's first sunrays as she collected herbs and shook away the morning dew. Her old knees protested only slightly and held her weight while she foraged through the garden like a small fiddle deer.

'Echinacea and arnica, maybe some yarrow too! Hawthorn and celery seed, it's not enough yet. What more do I need? Skullcap, witch hazel and dandelion puffs. Surely that sounds right, surely that's enough!'

She cradled her woven basket in her gnarled hand, full of nature's magical ingredients, and made her way through the garden patch and down the winding track that led to her cottage door. She smiled at the huge fig tree protruding from the roof, its roots encapsulating the home in its strong grasp.

'Good morning,' she addressed the fig as she entered the dwelling, her basket full to the brim of goods. 'Time for a brew! A concoction will do! I think yes... that's what I'll do, I'll make a new brew!' She cackled away to herself, happy as a child with cake.

After crafting away in her colourful kitchen, Diwa sat at the table with a cup of newly brewed tea and some elderflower and burrownut biscuits she'd made the previous day. She blew at the hot tea and took a small sip, her smile content as she stared at the wooden box before her in the centre of the table. As always in times of worry, when knowing the future's path weighed on her more than usual, she dug out this wooden box and the object it contained: a round almost-translucent crystal, an orb that was the failsafe to calm her jittery heart.

'How is she doing?' Diwa asked aloud to her fig tree as she took another sip of her newest tea creation. 'Little bit too much celery seed, I think. ' She clucked her tongue. 'She did it! Oh, I knew she would. She's so strong. Such a fighter. And my son, Ravaryn, did he help her?'

She chatted away to the tree. 'Oh my heart, I'm so glad they're okay. Yes, I had a visit from Aytac, such a strong will that one, such a burdened heart though. He's been through a lot. He is wary, untrusting. He misses his sister.'

Diwa felt saddened by the guilt and turmoil she had felt from Aytac upon his visit. She hung her head slightly, examining the spinning fragments in her deep moss-coloured tea.

'Alright, my dear.' She popped her head up again. 'Talk soon.'

Diwa finished her tea and burrownut biscuits in silence, staring out the window opposite her over her hollow of flowers. A cool chill swept through the grove in the mid-morning dappled sunlight.

'Yes, I might light the fire. That sounds like a grand idea,' she said now to herself.

Diwa left the teacup, adorned with little beetles and snails trailing silver tracks all over the delicate porcelain, on the table. The tea leaves slowly shifted and settled into a formation, an image, while she started a fire in her old fireplace in the lounge room. After a few minutes, the image became clearer in the remnants of the tea, and a set of bat-like wings, edges sharp, and a sharp-toothed maw appeared in the bottom of the dainty cup.

*

Sayde, sat on the ground of the cold cave at the edge of the blackened sea inside the Dark Rim and stared into the fire's flickering flames. She let them mesmerise her in the cold night, as she couldn't sleep, she could barely eat. Sorrow was eating her alive from the inside out. She missed Noah, she missed his light, his smile, his voice, his touch. Tears cascaded from her puffy, sunken eyes. The rest of the cave's inhabitants, the other prisoners, were all asleep. If she had to guess, it must be nearing midnight. This place was always dark, so how could anyone really know? Her body ached from the cold, and she was so lonely that she wished she could lie down and the earth would cave in around her and swallow her whole.

A hobbling form appeared next to her at the fire and sat down. Flinnigan stared at the flames with Sayde, not speaking for a long while, just being there next to her and sharing in her loss and grief. After a long while, he cleared his old throat and spoke softly to her. 'It only hurts so much, my dear, because your love for him was so strong. You may not ever rid yourself of this pain but you will learn to live with it. Over time, I cannot promise you it will disappear, but I *can* promise that it will fade, and there will be more room for other things. Light will return to you one day, Sayde, I know it.'

More tears streaked down her lost and empty face, reflecting the light in the fire's dim flames.

'I miss my wife, daughters and granddaughter with all my heart, and I have to believe I will see them again one day. I will feel their joy and warmth again.' Tears of his own shone in his cloudy ocean-blue eyes fixed on the flames.

'Tell me about them.' Sayde's voice was weak with underuse, and the words scratched their way to the surface.

Flinnigan stilled at the sound; he hadn't heard her speak since the day Noah was taken. He quickly recovered from his surprise and proceeded to tell Sayde about his family, his own grief on hold for the moment with the greater need to share with Sayde and ease her suffering in any way he could.

After a while of reminiscing about his wife, her smile, her talent in the kitchen and her warm, sweet glow she always saved especially for him, and his daughters - all so different but all so strong-willed in their own way - he spoke of his granddaughter.

'You know you remind me of her, my Mirabel. She is tough just like you and has an inner glow that shines no matter how she tries to hide it. She was ten when I last saw her. Oh my stars, how she must have grown. I think she'd like you, Sayde. You two would be thick as thieves in a different world.' His gentle smile came to light his face as his eyes shone.

He got unsteadily to his feet and grasped the old stick he used to aid his balance. Placing a hand on Sayde's shoulder, he left the fireplace to try and ease his aching body and find some solace in sleep. 'Hang in there, love. You'll get through this.' His hand squeezed a small amount of warmth into her shoulder and then he released it.

Sayde felt hollowed out, the slight reprieve of listening to him talk of his family was just that, a small life-float in the wild sea of pain she was drowning in. She leaned to the side and tucked her knees to her chest, dropping onto the hard ground next to the fire and crying silent tears into the floor until exhaustion took her away from the pain. Until the morning would let it all rapidly flow back in again.

Breaking Through

The Dark Rim

Aytac awoke from the spore poison first, for he knew deep in his heart that his sister must still be alive. At least his hope was strong enough that it had broken the illusion's grip over him. He found Zemira slumped forward on the ground, her hand over Ravaryn's, and pulled her to him, coaxing her from her own nightmare that she must have been enduring. Zee woke with a gasp, her face laced with pain. The pair then tried to rouse Ravaryn from his poisonous coma. Minutes passed with no luck, and the pair became more and more nervous that the tree sentinels protecting the border around the Dark Rim's wall would sense their presence once again and return.

'We have to move,' Zee told Aytac.

'We have to get out of here before they come back. Can you carry him?'

Aytac was just as large as Ravaryn, and nearly as tall. 'I'll try.' He hoisted Ravaryn's heavy, limp form and wrapped his arm around his neck then began to drag him away from the deadly forest spores.

'They must be some kind of safeguard system to stop anyone from reaching the Rim,' Zee said, her mind trying to figure out what had just happened to the three of them.

As they trudged ahead, the mist dispersed, opening up to a flat stretch of land just before a rockier formation, beyond which was the Dark Rim wall.

Aytac's brow sweated with the strain of carrying Ravaryn's extra weight, but he still didn't stir.

What nightmares must he be reliving? Zee's mouth was dry. *Why wasn't he waking?*

They reached the rockier outcrop and settled near a large overhang. Aytac slumped Ravaryn's body down from him and sat to recuperate.

'What did you see?' Zee asked him.

Aytac's eyes looked haunted. He had been strangely quiet; more so than usual. 'My sister,' he said gruffly. 'She was, she was a corpse, and she blamed me for her death.'

Zee gasped. 'How horrible, but none of it was real, Aytac. We'll find them. We'll free them soon, I promise.'

She placed a strong hand laced with vines over Ravaryn's shoulder as she yelled, 'Wake up! Wings, wake up!' Frustration was setting in.

'Why don't you try slapping him,' Aytac volunteered with a small smirk, some of the colour finally coming back into his face.

Zee just shot him an unimpressed glare.

Actually...

She raised her palm at the same time she shouted, 'WAKE UP!'

Ravaryn gasped air, his hands shooting to clasp at his throat. 'Zee.' His eyes were wide, frantic.

What horrors had he just been stuck in? And for much longer than she and Aytac had had to endure? 'I'm here. I'm here, Ravaryn. She cradled his head against her chest, squeezing him tightly.

His grip on her was vice-like. 'I thought... I thought, you were gone.'

'It wasn't real. You're here, and I'm here. None of it was real, whatever they made you see.'

His rapid breaths eased, and he roughly wiped at his wet face. Grasping Zee's face in his hands, he looked into her eyes then kissed her roughly. 'I thought I'd lost you.'

Zee felt his fear. 'You're not getting rid of me that easily, Wings.' She hugged him close.

Aytac took the pair in. How he envied them. He didn't hate Ravaryn as much now, after seeing his reaction to whatever he must have seen, his own horrors still rolling around in his head.

The trio made camp under the safety of the rock overhang and rested a while, their final destination within their grasp. What other surprises were in stall for them? Zemira didn't want to know, but she knew there was no way any of them were crossing the dead forest again. The return trip home would be a much longer one as they would have to circle the edges and travel around the expanse of poisoned trees. What would have happened if none of them had awoken? What would happen to someone who couldn't overcome their worst fears? Zee didn't want to think about the answers to that. They rested, ate and recuperated what energy they could. Then readied themselves to approach the Dark Rim wall.

*

The ominous ripple of the Dark Rim wall now towered up over them.

'Okay, Rim Walker. Do your thing.' Aytac bowed slightly, giving Zee what he thought was his most encouraging smile.

It just made her more nervous as the look was wrong on his stoic face, like he was more nervous than confident.

Ravaryn looked paler than usual at her other side. 'You've got this, Zee. We'll see you soon.' His smile was even worse; it was forced and laced with false bravado.

A deep breath expelled itself from her chest as she lifted her left palm, the blood blooms on her skin shimmering like velvet in the strange energy contained within the wall. Her hand zinged, and a cold chill swept through her body as she passed through the translucent wall of magic before her. With one step, she was on the other side. It was that easy. She was after all, a being of both human and forest folk. Zee turned to look at the slightly blurry pair on the other side of the rippling wall opposite her.

Ravaryn gave her a nod, as did Aytac.

Zemira turned around and headed into the unknown on her own to try and find any survivors that may be living inside this dark world. Feeling more alone than ever, a swift wind blew her hair across the vision of the grim trip ahead, and then a thought came to her mind. *Why should I have to do this alone? Why shouldn't they come with me? I've destroyed one Rim wall... or at least blasted a hole in it. Maybe I can do it again? Wouldn't the world be better off without such a place? Better off without this cage, this prison for forest folk?*

Zee backtracked and stepped through the threshold to a waiting Aytac and Ravaryn.

'What's wrong? Are you okay?' Ravaryn's tone was stressed.

'Everything's all good. I just had a thought though.' Zee dropped her pack to her side. She hadn't really used much of her powers since her arm had been healed, and the pain was finally gone. Kneeling down, she extended both hands and held them on the Rim wall's rippling surface.

Zee closed her eyes and focused. She tried to remember the feeling, the *power* that the vile Greymouth had evoked from her upon forcing her to blast a hole in her own world's wall. She mustered all her will and magic to the surface; it vibrated and sped through her veins, gathering around her. Green flames burst out from her palms, and her eyes, upon opening again, were ignited from within, power flickering in their depths.

The power blasted out from her and connected with the wall's magic, sizzling and fizzing and throwing out lashings of spent magic back at her. She gritted her teeth and forced on, blasting with all her might and using the thought of the prisoners, of how unjust their punishment had been. Zee channelled all her energy within, determination forcing strength into her veins. A scream of frustration tore from her as her last attempt ended in a massive blast. It left her empty, and panting. She lowered her hands and looked at the wall to see if her efforts had made any effect at all.

A small part of the wall shimmered in front of her where her hands had been. It rippled like a stone had been dropped in a body of water then it dissipated away, leaving a circular hole the size of a small fire pit in its wake. Zee eyes widened like a leamura's and a stunned laugh left her.

Aytac and Ravaryn just stared back at Zee, shock all over their features.

She rubbed her hands together and stood, grabbing her pack. 'Now I don't have to go by myself.' Zee smiled back at them. 'Come on,' she prompted, stepping once again through the Rim wall.

A dazed Aytac still stood in shock but Ravaryn had seen her do amazing things before. He snapped from his stupor quicker than Aytac, his ease immense at knowing he could go with Zee instead of waiting and worrying about her proceeding on alone. He squeezed his body awkwardly through the knee-high hole in the wall.

Zee held in her laughter at the ridiculous way Ravaryn had to morph his body to fit through. Her facial expression showed her amusement, no words needed.

Aytac followed after him, struggling just as much if not more so. Zee scoffed under her breath but tried not to let it come out louder.

'Right,' she smiled, pleased with herself. 'Now there's a chance we'll succeed with three of us. If one gets eaten by something horrid, at least the other two can still find the survivors.'

'Not the best time for your sarcasm, Zee,' Ravaryn confirmed.

'I was being serious. Come on, the hard part's over. Besides, what's the worst that could happen?' Her smile crept higher, and her confidence returned a little.

Behind them, the Rim wall shimmered and fractured into tiny shards, disappearing into thin air. Then the wall started to melt away, the hole becoming larger and larger, the entire wall disappearing, piece by piece.

*

Sayde stood on the top of the grey cliff outside the entrance to the clan's cave, staring out at the sparse mist covering the dark waters of the sea.

She was hollow inside, the pain there had nearly consumed every inch of her. She couldn't survive much longer like this. *Noah...* her heart begged. Her chest ached as did her ribs from the racking sobs that overtook her core every day. When she was empty and completely expelled of all her minimal energy reserves, she had just laid there in the bed they had shared in the cave's deep recesses, smelling the lingering scent of him. She took a step closer to the cliff's edge, a few small stones crumbling away at her feet. It wouldn't hurt... not for long. Then all the pain would be gone, it would be over, and she would be at peace.

Would she see him again? In the afterlife? Wind whipped at her messy hair, flicking it to and fro in front of her face. *Noah...* her heart pleaded again. 'Give me a sign!' she screamed out into the emptiness of the ocean before her, her throat stinging with the effort.

'Anything!' she wept. 'Please.' Her face cascaded again with fresh tears, blurring her vision. She inched closer to the edge and took a deep breath.

The mist cleared before her as a single-stranded ray of light tried to force its way through the thick layer of cloud that always covered the Dark Rim's sky. Sayde noted the change in light, being so sensitive to any slight change. She always hoped that the sun would somehow miraculously shine through. Wiping her wet eyes, she looked out over the churning water and there before her was a large pod of sea shinners. They leaped in and out of the ocean before her, not far out from the coastline, their joyful display visible to her. Noah had always joked that they might see them from this peak, their long white pectoral fins streaking out from the water like knives through butter.

Sayde dropped to her knees, laughing through her tears. 'That's not fair, Noah,' she said as she wept, his voice echoing in her head... *Never forget...You make your own light.*

She stared at the rare sight, at the beauty of the majestic creatures in the first weak light she had seen break through the Rim's dark cocoon in years, remembering how Noah had always found the positive in everything. A voice slid past her, rippling in the strong wind, *Hold on,* it begged. *Hold on...hold...on...hold....on...*

The Rescue

Inside the Dark Rim

The air felt thick, and the landscape was barren, sucked of life. The earth was grey and cracked, and there was no sunlight able to push its way through the charcoal cloud cover above them. The three walked into the unknown, all their senses on high alert. They moved through the dead sparse grass and over the craggy mountain outcrop, eyes peeled and heartrates elevated.

The mountainous cliff came to a sharp halt, and an expanse of rough dark ocean greeted them with vicious winds. The wind lashed at them while the waves pounded the black sands of the shore far below. They stood together and absorbed the landscape.

Zee's arm felt the wind's caress, then she felt an infinitesimal pull. A pull to the right of her, an energy reaching out, one of pain and desperation, but one that still held life within it.

'I think we should head right...' her voice petered off as she followed the energy calling to her, mesmerised. 'I just have a feeling...'

Aytac eyed Ravaryn, and he just gave a sure nod. The men followed behind Zee, staying away from the crumbling rocky edge of the cliff, the mist becoming thicker still. It flowed around them and in front of their path.

Zee forged ahead, and as if out of nowhere in the fog before her, a figure appeared. She nearly ran straight into the being, his grey-covered skin smeared with clay, making him almost blend into the mists around him like a spirit. The startle caused Zee's palms to ignite with green flames. The mist hissed and cleared around her magic as if it were toxic, and within moments it cleared into a large enough bubble around the four figures for them all to get a good look at the stranger. His eyes widened at the sight of Zee's magic, and she feared she had scared the frail-looking elderly man so extinguished her flames immediately.

'How is it possible? Your magic? No one in this Rim world can conjure their gifts...' His voice came like a croak lingering in the depths of his throat.

'We've come to free you, you and any other survivors. The queen is dead,' Zee explained awkwardly. She hadn't thought about how the people imprisoned here wouldn't have known about Kyeitha's demise, or of the human Rim world.

The man just stood there, clutching to his stick for balance. 'Dead?' he whispered, his eyes widening even more.

He was in shock, Zee realised. 'Let me help you.' She came towards the man to maybe help him sit or to support him. He looked as though a strong wind might knock him over any moment.

'No!' he found his words. 'We must get out of the open. You're not covered! It'll scent you!' He came back to reality, realising the newcomers were all out in the open. In danger.

'What will scent us?' Aytac spoke up.

'The dark one, the beast! Follow me!' The stranger turned and teetered back, a little shocked, but he quickly regained his composure before leading them down the path he'd come from before they intercepted him.

Zee shrugged her shoulders as if to say, *Oh well, let's see where this leads us*...but felt her heartrate rise at what the old man had said.

264

The dark one...

This must have been what Diwa had tried to warn Aytac about. They followed the man who was stumbling along as fast as his legs could take him. Gods, he was so thin. After a while, the mist became thinner and the narrow track opened up to a wider flat area that looked out to the sea on one side and opened into a cave system on the other. The man came to a halt, panting wearily, and stared out at a bent-over figure on the cliff's edge opposite the cave's entrance. It was hard to make out whether the figure was male or female, young or old from this distance, but Zee could tell that they were defeated... broken. She could see from the shaking movements that the figure was weeping.

The old man's eyes shined over at noticing the same thing. 'Oh, Sayde.' His voice cracked with concern.

'What did you say?' Aytac pushed past Ravaryn to come up beside the man. 'What did you say?' he pressed.

The old man lifted his head, his eyes clouded over. 'She lost her partner, her *balance*, to the creature not too long ago, and she's been suffering ever since.'

'No, what is her name?' Aytac demanded.

His rheumy eyes connected with Aytac's yellow ones. 'Sayde.'

Aytac's body stilled, his limbs ceasing to move for a moment as time slowed down. *She made it...she's alive...*

His senses snapped back to him and he ran for the cliff, for Sayde, his heart clenching with pain for her. With the pain he felt as he approached her.

'*Sayde.*' Her name barely scraped from his throat as he fell to his knees beside her. Hollow eyes looked up and met his own, sitting deep in the tear-stained skin of her face.

'Aytac?' she breathed, not believing the vision before her. She stared at him for a long moment then a manic laugh bubbled from her as more tears spilled. 'About time.'

The shifter embraced his twin, pulling her up into his strong arms and holding her to him. He held on tight, afraid to let go of her, afraid that he would lose her again if he so much as loosened his grip on her.

Sayde drank in the comfort of her twin brother, her longest and dearest friend in this world, fresh sobs now leaving her. These ones still of sadness but laced with relief.

Zee watched the pair embrace from afar, her own eyes swimming with tears. What must it have been like to have been trapped in here for so long? To never know if you'd see your loved ones again?

'Come,' the old man spoke softly. 'We will inform the others of your arrival. Come in out of the mist.'

'Of course,' Zee replied. 'Sorry, I didn't get your name. I'm Zemira and this is Ravaryn.'

'I'm Flinnigan, Flinder for short, and I am ecstatic to meet you both, as everyone else will be. Please, follow me.'

The entire clan resided deeper within the cavern, grey mud covering a few of them. Their eyes looked saddened at the sight of the two newcomers until Flinder informed them that Kyeitha was dead.

'They've come!' Flinder shook with joy as he announced their freedom to the rest of the clan. He grasped Zee's adorned hand and held it high for them to see. 'We will see our families again!'

Shocked gasps and tears spread through the crowd, along with laughs and some shouts of joy.

Zee's cheeks heated for these poor people. If she had known...if only she had known, she would have ended their suffering so much sooner. She eyed Ravaryn guiltily, and he shook his head, his eyes reassuring. She felt him, his warmth and comfort, in the blood blooms adorning her arm as they opened wider and shimmered.

'Gather yourselves! We leave at once!' Zee commanded.

The starving people sprang to life before Zee, gathering their meagre items and wrapping themselves with ragged coats and scraps of animal hide.

The hell they must have endured for all these years broke her heart. She turned and took Ravaryn's hand then proceeded to the mouth of the cave. And there was Aytac, still embracing his sister.

'I think I despise him a little less now,' Ravaryn admitted.

'Aww, look at you making a friend,' Zee teased.

He just smirked and raised one brow at her.

'How he must have missed her all those years that he was forced to be Kyeitha's right hand,' she said.

A shudder then ran through her like the wind was picking up. The rumble of clouds indicated that rain must be close, or at least that's what she could gather from this odd climate inside the Dark Rim world. A bolt of lightning cracked overhead, and Flinder gathered the jittery group of weary people to the mouth of the cavern while Aytac helped Sayde up and away from the open.

Zee and Ravaryn walked over to meet them half way between the cave mouth and the cliff edge. Another rumble, this time deafeningly close, and the clouds out from the ledge started to glow orange behind Aytac and Sayde. Sayde's eyes bulged at the sound and she spun around to see the orange glow. Knowing that sound all too well, her face contorted into a look of pure terror.

'RUN!' she screamed, spinning back and dragging Aytac past the pair coming to meet them.

Zee was not sure what they were running from but heeded Sayde's warning cry all the same. Before she turned, panic ignited in her veins as a winged creature with onyx scales and huge talons materialised from the clouds, its menacing eyes glowing straight at her. Zee caught a glimpse of shining silver teeth as a deafening roar split her ear drums.

They bolted to mouth of the cave, her heart beating wildly, Ravaryn almost dragging her along with him as she tried to match his long strides. Just as they reached the cave entrance, the creature took aim. Its talons shot forth and clasped powerfully into Ravaryn's shoulders, ripping him away from Zee, a deep cry of pain escaping him.

'NO!' Zee screamed, as the winged beast tore him out of her grasp and into the spinning vortex of mist it had come from. Her legs ignited with energy and she tore off down the track they had come, the wind behind her forcing her momentum on. She could see the mist thickening in front of her as the onyx dragon cut a path ahead of her. Fire burned in her throat and she ran harder and faster, compelling herself to keep sight of Ravaryn.

No... no... no!

She lost sight of the dragon tail ahead of her, but still let the power in her veins move her forward with a speed like nothing she'd ever imagined she contained. Her heart hammered in her chest like a raspors's wings as she sprinted towards the Dark Rim wall where the three had entered not too long ago. She pulled up to the hole in the wall's magic that *she* had created, yet she now saw *out*, out past where the wall had been. It was gone, destroyed, eaten up by the magic she had poured into it. Zee stared out into the open and saw a winged black figure disappearing further off into the distance, dragging a motionless body in its talons. The entire field of illusion trees glowed orange and burned in the wild fire that had poured from the dragon's mouth.

Oh Gods... what had she done? What had she released?

Zee fell to her knees in despair.

Salvador's Return

Black Forest, Aylenta

Diwa sat at her table sipping a cup of tea. As she went to fetch another biscuit from her stash in the kitchen, she clutched at her chest as an agonising pain ripped into her. Her skin felt as if it were clothed in garments five sizes to small, suffocating her in her own body. She fell to the ground and crawled forward, grasping for the trunk of the fig tree in the centre of her cottage.

'What's happening?' she demanded of the tree, her silver eyes cringing shut at the pain tearing through her.

'Oh dear,' a youthful voice sang in her head.

'Gaia, please!' Diwa insisted through her grimace. 'I didn't foresee this. What has happened?'

Magic ripped through the cottage like a strong wind, circling leaves and debris in through the open windows and door, whirling like a cyclone within the walls. Diwa's fuzzy grey hair straightened and smoothed, her legs grew longer, and her back rippled in pain as it straightened, causing her hunchback to disappear. The wrinkles covering her face and neck smoothed, leaving only smile lines around her sparkling silver eyes.

'I think you know,' Gaia's solemn voice explained to her through the fig tree. 'Your magic, the immense amount you expelled to create the Dark Rim, the prison for him, has been released.'

'But how?' Diwa choked out through her clenched jaw as her body continued its transformation.

Oh no. Zemira.

'She was only supposed to pass *through* the wall! Not destroy it!' Diwa panted then righted herself up against the tree's large trunk, coming to sit with her back leaning against it for support. She sucked in ragged breaths as her legs stretched out before her, magic still rippling into her and all about the cottage, the wind easing slightly. She held out her once-knobbly hands before her, and they were again youthful, spots faded, her fingers slimmed and straightened.

'Oh dear,' she breathed.

'Yes,' agreed Gaia through the tree. 'He is free, my old friend. Your cage has been broken. Salvador is free.'

*

Thaylon's travels finally brought him to his destination, the crumbling monument, the ancient ones' building that had once towered in the desolate expanse of the deadlands north of Lamiria. The place he and his master had first found upon entering this peculiar new world years previously.

The blackened skeleton of the once-great building brought a twitch to Thaylon's lip, a small smirk lingering there. His menacing smirk didn't reach his emotionless eyes though. *He* was finally out of that cage, and the waiting would be worth it. His lord would be here soon, and they would decimate and rule over these lower life forms very, very soon.

Thaylon would help his dark lord create a world of obedience, a world where the humans – the cattle – would be imprisoned appropriately, and his minions would reign over all the lands. There would be nothing Gaia could do, the weak being who currently ruled over this realm. When the earth had died, thanks to the ancient humans, it had created cracks and tears, doorways like small cuts in the fabric between the worlds. It had been heard even in his own realm, and had provided a rich opportunity. It was then that Thaylon had accompanied his lord willingly through the passageway, the strange fracture that had led them both to this vulnerable world, ripe for the picking. The humans would be the example they would use to create this world anew to their liking.

He approached the crumbling remains of the ancient building; a dark cave-like entrance was etched into the grounds beneath, and everything was still here. It stood waiting to welcome them back, just like the day they had arrived and started their reign. If it hadn't been for those conniving Rim guardians, those vile women imprisoning his lord and Thaylon all those years ago, they would have surely already ruled over these lands with no rivals.

Now she was gone, Kyeitha, his lover who would not consent, would not sacrifice her powers to the cause. He had found snippets of useful information from the humans, the little cockroaches along the way. The ones he had talked to during his travels mentioned a girl, a Rim Walker, who had killed the queen and destroyed the Rim wall, leaving the pathetic humans vulnerable. Oh, how they whined about her, the Rim Walker. His eyes almost rolled in his head at the thought of some of those humans. *If anything, she freed you from your cage, you morons.* All those moments he had endured, listening to their whingeing on the boat that crossed the Alvion Sea, ate at the thin sliver of patience he barely contained. But it was worth it for the precious information he had gleaned.

His smile now crept higher, and he would have been handsome if it weren't for the venom in his gaze. Kyeitha, the bitch, she had banished him, imprisoning him inside that festering Rim world with those human creatures she knew he hated. She could have joined him and his lord in their quest to conquer this world, she had had so much power, but she was afraid. She wouldn't let him rule over her and she wouldn't submit. The queen had been weak, she had been *a fool.*

And their son... his hands shook as rage ripped through him. He had never had a chance to meet his son, his blood, his only heir. He clenched his fists, igniting a violent burst of dark red flames, the colour of fresh blood, for the first time since his banishment. He breathed in the poisoned earth scent and relished in it. Oh, Kyeitha had been weak alright, and she should have killed him when she had the chance.

But it seemed he had another descendent, another heir, a granddaughter who carried both his powers and that of the Rim guardians. His tongue slid over his smooth teeth. And to think that she'd killed her own grandmother. Thaylon chuckled, the sound deep and menacing. The power she must contain. And his lord would soon be free, he felt it. Together they would find her, unite with her, his granddaughter. Zemira they had said was her name.

Zemira, what a fitting name for such a powerful being. Thaylon continued on into the familiar den of crumbled stone, concrete and twisted, rusted metal. At least the ancients had done something right. This building, although dilapidated and crumbling with time, still held true. It was the perfect place, the old stronghold, the old-world prison that had lines and lines of free cells ready to go, ready to be filled with pets. Thaylon walked through the silent dark building and began to prepare for Salvador's return.

*

Ravaryn tried to blink one eye, the other swollen to the point it would no longer open. He could feel the throbbing there as his black eye swelled larger with each pulse of pain. His one good eye tried to adjust to the dark surroundings in attempt to gauge where he might be. A cold breeze swept past him. He followed its direction, turning his stiff neck. He was sitting up against the slick wet wall of a dim cave. The walls were shimmering like the stone had been drenched in metallic oil. Water dripped, making more sound in the distance, and even more water streaked down the wall in front of him into pools on the dirt floor of the cave. His eye focused on the space, then out to the opening of the cave where dull grey light filtered in, the rain spraying wildly outside.

He tried to move his stiff legs, but they felt numb with cold. They ached as though they were crushed. *Where in Mother's earth am I?* he thought with alarm.

He remembered talons puncturing his shoulder... mist... flying. His legs impacting then scraping along the ground as an enormous creature flew through the larger almost house-sized hole in the Dark Rim wall.

What had they done? What had they released?

Clasping his hands, bloody with scratches, against his chest for warmth, he then tucked them under his arms tightly as shivers started to rake through his body. His heart beat in a rhythm of panic, but not for himself.

Zemira.

Where was she? Was she okay? Oh Gods, did the creature get to her? He forced his legs to obey his mind's commands, but they remained stiff and numb.

He took in deep breaths, his body shaking with the cold, and not just from the wind. This place was wrong, and it was pulling on something deep within his core.

He didn't like this one bit.

Ravaryn tried to call upon his magic to conjure his wings. A deep roar rumbled at the cave's entrance, stopping him, and a whirling mass of fire blasted into the cave. It connected with a pile of something that looked like bleached driftwood, towards the back of the cave away from him. He could barely move let alone defend himself from the creature at this point. His best bet was to talk with it if he could. To try to strike a deal or bargain with it to see what it wanted.

The fire illuminated the dank cave cell, and to Ravaryn's horror he saw that the pile of wood now ignited was in fact bones. Large, pounding steps shook the cave foundations, making some small pieces of rubble fall from the ceiling. Metallic dust showered down, and Ravaryn could see the terrifying creature coming towards him through his one damaged eye. Black scales dripped with rain and eyes glowed from a menacing thorned head. Enormous wings shook away rain and tucked in alongside the beast's body as it entered further into the space, taking up the entire entrance of the cave. It dropped a large animal carcass dripping with rain and blood on the floor right before Ravaryn.

The intimidating creature stared into him; the *black dragon* stared at Ravaryn. A dark energy stirred within him, a familiar unwanted connection. A connection that was being uncovered like an ancient creature's bones being unearthed after centuries in the ground. The pulsing energy inside of him felt strangely familiar, and he noticed the dragon's scales matched the metallic sheen of the cave walls. In the fire's flickering flames, Ravaryn could see the shine flick off each individual scale.

A roar ripped from the dragon's maw and a ripple swept over its skin, making the scales lift in a wave over its head to its hide. Its eyes locked on Ravaryn's, and the creature started to transform before him, black swirling mists encompassing its shape until there before him stood a man. His tall frame towered over Ravaryn, and his dark hair was sprinkled with a bit of grey, matching a short beard. He took in the chiselled face, a face that was so familiar to Ravaryn, familiar in a way that made his throat tighten in the grip of dark intuition, like he'd swallowed a handful of sharp tacks. Gold rings encased the ebony hooded eyes that glowed in the firelight, making them intense and threatening. The man took a step closer to Ravaryn, still just staring down at him. His clothes were ragged like he'd worn them for years, but they still showed the finery that was once there, that had not been lost. A wicked grin lit up his dark features, his weathered but still-handsome face dripping with the frigid rain, eyes crinkling slightly at the corners. Gold-rimmed ebony eyes met Ravaryn's silver-dappled ones, and he spoke.

'Hello, son.' His voice was deep and velvety, and the rim of gold flickered in his obsidian eyes, making them luminous. 'So nice to finally meet you.'

Epilogue

Orion's heart beat furiously in his chest. He had raced the whole way here from the lake of life, following the scent until it faded. All he'd found was this village, and the healer. He left the den of the healer's room in the trunk of the ancient tree god of the forest. She had explained everything, and the days of turmoil thinking the worst about his daughter had finally started to ease. There was a commotion coming from the villagers below them. Orion's heart sped up for a split second, all his senses on edge in his human form. He couldn't tell whether or not the sound was distress or celebratory. No, they were sounds of happiness, of relief. Cries, but of joy.

They had returned with the prisoners! Zemira had done it; she'd freed them, and Orion was finally going to see his daughter again. He turned back to look at Sahara, a shining grin lighting up her face, those sharp-filed teeth making her look a little sinister.

'The choice is yours,' she gleamed, swinging her staff out in front of her and motioning towards the balcony that looked out over the villagers below, her many colourful bangles and ornaments jingling together pleasantly.

Orion gave her a gentle nod. He wasn't sure why he wasn't wary of the healer, but he somehow knew she was 'other'; she smelled otherworldly to him. He gave her a look that conveyed his thanks for the talk, having been brought up to speed with all that had transpired. Setting off to find his daughter, a sense of relief flittered in his chest, laced with anger at the thought of seeing Ravaryn. He wasn't sure what he would do, but as his clenched fists flexed, he knew he *wanted* to do. Gods, it would be nice to smash the king's handsome face into the back of his skull and get him as far away from his daughter as he could.

But if Sahara's warning was to be heeded, that would not be a wise action to take. It would also hurt Zee. Orion huffed out a tired breath that felt like it was dredged from the bottom of his chest as he made his way down the spiralling stairway, the noise of rejoicing growing louder.

Nobody ever tells you how hard it is to be a father. Thank the Mother she's okay. And I thought it was hard when she was little and all she wanted was to chase floxels through the forest every waking hour of the day. Orion rubbed a tattooed hand over his face as if trying to rub away the turmoil he felt within. *It doesn't matter.* All that mattered was that his daughter was safe. He reached the forest floor and looked around for the smiling face and sparkling emerald eyes that he thought Zee would be emitting at her success. Not spotting her in the crowd, something then caught his eye, a lone figure from afar ascending the timber stairs at the top of the walkway. She was alone. Zee's dark hair shone ebony in the sun, but her shoulders slumped as she dragged her feet and entered the bird nest-shaped room, a dwelling she'd stayed in, he guessed, high up in the village's first level. But why was she alone?

*

Diwa hastily packed a bag, stuffing it with everything she thought she would need. Her heart raced and her hands, her unfamiliar youthful hands, shook. She had not seen or felt this version of herself for a very long time. Diwa rushed, forcing her boots on and tightening the straps, strapping on her pack and braiding her now smooth light-silver hair away from her younger, more angular face. She took one look at her cottage and her fig tree at the heart of her home and left. Left her sanctuary, her safe haven that had housed and nourished her soul for many years.

'Talk soon!' she yelled out to Gaia through the fig tree.

'Safe travels, my friend,' Gaia's sweet voice sang out towards her, a little forlorn.

And just like that, Diwa Mumasumi left the old Rim world and headed for Lamiria, her body restored from the power she had spent years ago to contain a threat that was far greater than this world had ever seen. One she still didn't know how to destroy for good. A demon... a creature from another realm, the black dragon, and also Ravaryn's father.

*

Zemira had travelled back to Maya Village with the group they'd rescued from the Dark Rim, her heart heavy with the unknown. What was that monster? Was Ravaryn okay? Was he still alive? And how could Diwa have known that such a monstrous thing was inside the Dark Rim and not have told anyone of it?

She barely spoke, hardly any of them did, all eager to return to their families but all so weary and undernourished that their bodies held them back from returning sooner. Sayde hovered close to Aytac at all times. She also barely spoke, her haunted eyes emitting their sadness and grief without the need for more tears.

They had arrived days later to the celebratory cries of the villagers. Teary embraces and tears of joy echoed all around, but none of them had been enough to stop the swirl of sickening loneliness Zemira now felt without Ravaryn beside her. She longed for her hand to be tucked safely within his. Sneaking away from the happy reunions, Aytac had watched her go. She rubbed her left forearm with her right hand, the tattooed pattern of the blood blooms now shut tight. Zee slipped exhausted into the room she and Ravaryn had shared before they'd left to find the Dark

Rim, and there waiting, perched on the edge of their bed was a woman, her familiar sparkling silver eyes shining from a much more youthful face.

Diwa?

Zee dropped her pack in surprise, and just stared at the woman she now recognised as Diwa, but different. She had a youthfulness to her, a shine, a glow of power. Zee wanted so badly to run to her and let her friend hug away her pain, but she felt anger like it was Diwa's fault that Ravaryn was gone, even though she knew deep down it had been her own. She had broken yet another Rim wall. She had broken yet another *world*. Her guilt was vice-like. Zee had freed the darkness within the Dark Rim upon them all. She came to sit on the bed next to the beautiful younger-looking Diwa.

'What have I done?' she asked, her eyes wide.

'You haven't done anything, my dear. We will get him back. I-I'm so sorry, let me explain. Let me explain everything.' Diwa's silver eyes glistened with tears, a very rare emotion from her.

Zee relented and squeezed her in a tight hug.

Diwa's smoother, sweeter voice spoke in Zee's ear. '*We will get him back.*'

*

Salvador's hands clenched into fists at his sides as he strode through the dark halls of the ancient ones' crumbling building. This building he had found long ago when he and Thaylon had first come to this realm through the thin tear in the magic that separated all worlds, the very one the humans had unknowingly created when they destroyed themselves.

The dark concrete hall jutted in places with rusted metal from within the damaged structure, and black mould coated the walls like poison seeping up from the damaged soil here, decorating it nicely, and Salvador felt right at home. He felt he had returned to his castle, where he would again begin his rule. His faithful follower and devout servant Thaylon had done well so far.

Salvador flexed his shoulders in the new finely made attire he now wore. The long black coat was well made and the buttons shone golden in contrast. The rags of the Dark Rim were far behind him now, and his gold-rimmed ebony eyes shone like deep voids, just the surface of them reflected in the flames from the sconces that had lain barren and unlit for so long. Until now. They now flickered with a gentle light from sky-pine seeds and lit the way deeper into the building's maze of dungeons.

Salvador came to a halt before Thaylon, ever so patiently awaiting him. He was a good servant – true, loyal and full of venom for the parasites of this world: the humans.

Right on cue, he bowed reverently to Salvador. 'My lord.'

Salvador did not return the greeting. 'How many, Thaylon?' he questioned, his tone neutral and unimpressed.

'Six this time, my lord.'

'Six?' Salvador's brow quivered ever so slightly, revealing a tiny flicker of emotion that lay with in the darkened shell of the creature he truly was.

'Yes, my lord. They were *aware* of my presence this time. Somehow, the villagers were ready. It won't happen again, and I will return with many more once the first batch are fully recovered and ready to serve – after their transformations are complete.'

Salvador waved an unamused hand, silencing Thaylon's explanations. 'Show me them.'

'Yes, my lord. This way.'

Salvador followed Thaylon further into the concrete maze, the only sound being their footfalls and the drip, drip, drip of black liquid seeping through the building walls. It was long since waterproof but incredibly still standing after the havoc these pathetic life forms had wrecked on their own habitat.

Sounds echoed in the air around them as they approached the cells; whimpers, heavy breaths and sobs laced the cold air now. They all emitted from just one cell, and inside it were the six humans. The corridor ahead was lit, and tens upon tens of cells either side of the humans were full of creatures silently pacing back and forth, their footfalls barely creating a sound. The inhabitants of these cells were *very* far from being human.

279

Salvador crossed his gloved hands behind his back, his head raising slightly as he took in the scent of the humans. A scowl crossed his face as his nose scrunched at them, the golden rims of his eyes flickering in disgust. 'Transform them all at once. We need to grow our army as swiftly as possible. I will *not* fail this time.'

Thaylon nodded. 'Yes, my lord.'

One of the humans in the cell before them let out a cry of despair; they all huddled closer together in a group, terror leaching from their pores.

Thaylon sensed Salvador's disgust and suggested a distraction, one that he knew would lighten his lord's spirits and possibly sway his mood, hopefully masking his disappointment in him at only being able to procure six this time. 'Would you like to see the first group that have been transformed, my lord? They are progressing rather nicely.'

Salvador's lip curled ever so slightly as he pulled his menacing gaze away from the small group of humans that cowered before him, changing his expression from disdain to intrigue. 'Yes. Let's see how my army is growing, shall we?' His grin was terrifying.

Thaylon matched it, his grin just as sinister, the pair revelling in the pain and despair that they were cultivating. 'This way, my lord.'

Acknowledgements

Writing a book is something I've always wanted to do, but the challenging road life has taken me on hasn't afforded me the time until recently. After suffering a debilitating back injury and being bedridden for months, I lay there feeling very much like my own modern-day version of Frida Kahlo and thought the universe had given me a very back-handed gift, which I was determined not to waste! So I started to write and materialise this story.

A massive –massive thank you to my amazing editor and independent publisher Dr Juliette Lachemeier, you're an absolute legend. Thank you for believing in me and telling me you loved my story. There is no greater gift than someone lifting you up and telling you that something you created is worthy.

Thank you to Judith San Nicolas for the awesome book cover and map illustration.

Summer, my angel, my daughter, thank you for looking after me, putting on my socks, bringing me vegemite toast and watching movies with me while I was recovering. Thank you for your gorgeous, bright, happy light that you've brought into my world. I love you more than anything in this entire universe and I always will. This book is for you.

Thank you to Josh/George, my sturdy rock, for your unwavering love, and for your patience of a Jedi master.

For Sadie, my rescue greyhound, for your constant company and cuddles, sharing your retirement with us.

Katie, for putting up with me in this life and the next. There is nothing more amazing than having a sister, someone who knows you inside-out and has been with you through the rocky path that life has made us walk, and we can still laugh about it all.

Kaitlynd, a girl couldn't ask for a better friend. You're a gift that I will never let go of! You're stuck with me forever. I don't know how you create your amazing light but I'm glad you share it with me. I thank you and Davo for being my first readers. Your words of encouragement have helped me more than you'll ever know.

For Liv and Annie. Thank you for being the most loving and selfless mothers to me. Your belief in me and encouragement have changed my life, you were there when I didn't even know how much I needed you both.

Uncle David, for giving me a home and a sanctuary when I needed it most. I don't think you'll ever know how much you changed my life for the better.

Jess, your bright soul, and never fading confidence in me. Your light always fills me up whenever I see you. You make every room brighter just with your presence alone. I'm so lucky to have you in my life.

Ruby, for your brilliant aura, your ability to tell the best stories and to shine positivity on even the most horrific situations and turn them into a good laugh. Thank you for always having my back and your ruthless honesty.

My three awesome brothers, who all in their own way have taught me to be tough in this life. Growing up with brothers is a gift not everyone gets and I'm so lucky I have you all!

Kerry and Ben, for always being there and offering a helping hand without hesitation.

And thank you to the rest of my amazing women that I hold so dear to my heart and that lift me up and fill me with happiness and love. I don't know what I would do without you all: Kirsty, Edie, April, Laura, Myra, Jayme and Sofie. You are my secret weapons to tackle life, and I thank you with all my heart for accepting me just the way I am.

Mum, for letting the fairies live in the garden, I hope they are still out there with you.

And to everyone who reads this little piece of my heart that I have finally let free onto paper, thank you so much. This book is for you. I hope you get lost in it and forget real life... just for a moment.

ABOUT THE AUTHOR

Fantasy Weaver | Wordsmith | Dream Architect

Immerse yourself in worlds of magic and mystery with Publishers Weekly rising-star author Renee Hayes. As a true dream architect, Renee crafts captivating tales that transport readers to realms where the extraordinary becomes reality.

With a boundless imagination and a heart that beats for fantasy, Renee weaves enchanting stories that resonate with both young and new adults. From daring heroines to mythical creatures, her characters come alive on the pages, inviting you to journey alongside them.

Whether it's uncovering hidden secrets, battling ancient forces or embracing the power within, Renee's narratives explore the depths of courage and the wonders of the unknown. Her spellbinding prose and vivid worlds will sweep you off your feet and into a world of endless possibility.

Dive into the pages of her novels and embark on quests that challenge destiny, ignite magic and remind us all that even in the darkest of times, hope shines brightest. Join the legion of readers who have been captivated by Renee's tales and discover the magic that lies within her words.

Renee Hayes grew up in Tropical Far North Queensland. Reading fantasy was an invaluable tool of escapism from the troubles of real life. Her imagination and vivid dreams coated almost all of the memories that she has from her childhood.

Her own fantasy stories continue to come to life, and the magic is growing with them in her new stage of life, and she can't wait to see where it leads her...

Enjoyed the book? You can follow Renee Hayes at:

Facebook: www.facebook.com/profile.php?id=100086763157926 (Renee Hayes Author)

Instagram: https:/instagram.com/reneehayesauthor

TikTok: Renee Hayes Author

Email: rennnay@outlook.com

If you liked the book, please leave a review on Amazon, Goodreads or with the author directly. Reviews are invaluable in supporting an author's hard work and are greatly appreciated.

www.ingramcontent.com/pod-product-compliance
Lightning Source LLC
Chambersburg PA
CBHW030605120726
47904CB00006B/1773